FINAL FIX

CAROLYN RIDDER ASPENSON

SEVERN RIVER
PUBLISHING

Severn River Publishing
www.SevernRiverBooks.com

This is a work of fiction. Names, characters, businesses, places, events and incidents are either the products of the author's imagination or used in a fictitious manner. Any resemblance to actual persons, living or dead, or actual events is purely coincidental.

ISBN: 978-1-64875-510-1 (Paperback)

ALSO BY CAROLYN RIDDER ASPENSON

The Rachel Ryder Thriller Series

Damaging Secrets

Hunted Girl

Overkill

Countdown

Body Count

Fatal Silence

Deadly Means

Final Fix

Dark Intent

To find out more about Carolyn Ridder Aspenson and her books, visit severnriverbooks.com

PROLOGUE

The room was shrouded in darkness punctuated only by a faint ray of sunlight peeking through the closed blinds on the small windows. He knew where he was, yet it was earlier than normal and felt unfamiliar, even strange. He shouldn't have brought the baby, but his wife had needed rest, and she deserved it. His body tensed and his mind clouded with fear. "Please, I have a family. I won't say anything. Tell them I won't say anything."

Three figures emerged from the shadows, their faces obscured by sinister black masks of anonymity. The scrape of their shoes on the gritty floor reverberated through the room, a haunting rhythm that sent shivers down the man's spine. He tried to escape, but the muscular man blocking the exit pushed him into the back wall.

A chilling whisper pierced the silence. "Shut up!" The sound slithered through the air, two twisted words he knew might be the last things he'd hear. His stomach tightened as the other two men approached. "Please. I'm sorry! I have a daughter. I'll do whatever you ask, just don't hurt her." He held his hands to try to protect himself from the inevitable. "No!"

The two men held him there as the other man laughed. Gloved hands grasped his arms with deft, precise fingers like icy tendrils against his clammy skin. The metallic tang of fear assaulted his nostrils. His vision blurred and his cloudy gaze fixed on the needle gleaming dully in the slowly brightening light. "No, wait!" He struggled, begging his body to move under the men's grips, but it was impossible. They were too strong.

The sharp sting pierced his flesh. Then a rush of an odd feeling, bittersweet relief, perhaps, or a fleeting respite from the fear that consumed him, an ending to something he never should have started. The taste of bitterness lingered on his tongue, a cruel reminder that the momentary solace came at a grave cost.

He thought of his daughter. Her soft, chubby toes. How they wiggled when she smiled. He saw his wife's face. Her ocean blue eyes, the curve of her smile. "Please," he whispered, his breath slowing to nearly nothing.

A torrent of sensations assaulted him as the venomous concoction coursed through his veins. A surge of warmth spread like wildfire, melting away his pain.

His senses became a blurred tapestry of agony and euphoria. His sight distorted, morphing reality into a hallucinatory haze. Sounds echoed, harsh discordant whispers and inaudible words, each note a reminder of his fading connection to the world outside.

His existence grew more fragile as his body succumbed to the lethal cocktail injected into his veins. The room closed in on him, his breaths shallow and labored. He fought to hold on to the flickering embers of life, but he knew they were quickly dying.

The last thing he thought about was his wife and daughter, and then everything went black.

1

We stood at the beer booth of the Hamby spring festival. Lauren Levy, our newest detective, her partner Justin Michels, Rob Bishop, his lady friend Cathy, our police chief Jimmy, and his pregnant wife Savannah, Kyle, and, of course, me. We'd all planned a night out, and I'd lost the coin toss. I'd suggested beer and wings at Duke's, but instead, they dragged me kicking and screaming to the festival. I wasn't a beer fan, though I'd grown to tolerate it more than when I'd lived in Chicago, but I would have preferred having it with wings at Duke's and nowhere near carnival rides. I adjusted my weapon in its holster while nursing my Yuengling Light. None of us left the house without a weapon.

Lauren and Michels discussed their recent call. Her eyes sparkled with excitement as she described the grandeur of Haverty Ranch. She occasionally gestured with her hands as if trying to paint a vivid picture for everyone. "It's the mac-daddy of horse ranches." Her face lit up. "I've never seen anything like it."

Michels's voice held a hint of concern, and his brows furrowed slightly as he spoke about the recent horse deaths. He seemed genuinely worried about the situation. "If they'd keep their horses alive it'd be much better."

"Didn't we get a call from there last month, too?" Bishop asked, raising an eyebrow.

Michels nodded, his expression turning serious. "They've lost three horses in the last four months. All recent purchases from Texas," he added, his voice tinged with concern. "I was supposed to take my fiancé Ashley to dinner, but I ended up dealing with the horse deaths. I didn't have much of an appetite after that."

"His fiancé Ashley," Bishop said. "As if we didn't know her. I sensed a hint of sadness in Bishop's voice when he added, "That's awful about the horses."

"Sounds fishy," I said. "Or maybe horsey would be better?"

Kyle cleared his throat, his eyes gleaming with amusement. He couldn't suppress his small smile. "That was bad, Rach."

I shrugged nonchalantly. "Never claimed to be a comedian."

Levy's lips curled into a playful grin. The blinking lights of the tilt-a-whirl were giving me a headache. "Anyway, the vet came and took the horse. He said the previous autopsies showed heart issues, so he expects this breeder has a bad broodmare or stallion with some hereditary heart condition." She took a sip of her beer as she spoke.

"Always blaming the parents," Jimmy said. He winked at his wife. She laughed.

Jimmy's worst fear was not being present for his family, but from what I could tell, he'd been a raging success.

"You think it's worth looking into?" I asked.

Michels shook his head, his tone slightly dismissive. "He'd only had each horse for three or four days. If there's an issue, it's not on his end."

Bishop's voice held a tinge of curiosity as he asked, "Why were you called out then?"

"Suspicious circumstances," Levy said. "One of the ranch hands called it in."

"Bet he got fired," I said.

Levy rolled her eyes, her frustration evident. As she took a sip of her beer, her lips turned downward in annoyance. "Not sure. He wouldn't give his name on the call."

Kyle brought up the possibility of the cartel's involvement, showing how seriously he took his job as a DEA agent. "A shipment of injectable equine medication bottles imported from Mexico to Texas, Longview, I think, was actually liquid methamphetamine." His eyes darted around, almost as if he was assessing his surroundings for any signs of danger. "A vet in the area reported multiple equine deaths over a short period of time. He ran tests, saw what it was, and reported it. We were able to trace where the bottles came from and busted them with the next shipment."

Cathy's voice turned somber as she remembered the news about the equine medication incident. She sighed softly, her heart going out to the horses affected. "I think I read about that. It was so sad."

"You think someone gave these horses meth?" Bishop asked. "Wouldn't that show up in the autopsy?"

"It should," I said.

"Yes," Kyle said. "It should. It's just something to watch for. The cartel endangers animals in multiple ways. Telling you all of them would take hours."

Savannah smoothed her hand over her big baby bump. It was a gentle and tender movement, one that seemed involuntary. "I rode for years. Horses are stunning creatures who should be protected." Her eyes darkened with intensity as she added, "People who buy them for racing ought to have their balls cut off." Her voice carried a big dose of brewing anger.

"A lot of men ought to have their balls cut off. Present company excluded, of course."

Levy's playful remark made the men take a step back, even though her voice was laced with humor and sarcasm.

"I wouldn't go that far," Savannah said.

"Damn," Michels said. "Is it that time of the month for y'all or something?"

Bishop coughed and said, "Idiot," at the same time.

Kyle had been standing near Michels and moved away. "Nope. Not going to associate myself with that."

Levy pointed at Michels. "Dude. Uncool."

"Bless his heart." Savannah said. "He must have missed that week in middle school health class." She patted her baby bump. "FYI, Justin, I'm off that grid for a while. Though I am a hot mess of hormones on the regular." She sighed. "This baby is twice the size he should be right now." She grabbed hold of Jimmy's arm. "You're going to need a moving truck to haul me to the hospital when I'm in labor."

He knew better than to respond to that. "Not much we can do about the horses but notify Texas, which we have." He chugged the last of his beer and checked his watch. "Our free babysitter is leaving in an hour. Let's get the last bang for our buck at this thing."

Fall festivals weren't on any list of things I loved to do. I'd worked a lot of festivals as a slick sleeve in Chicago where I'd fought with and arrested more people than I could count. Festivals were breeding grounds for crime, germs, and accidents. I hadn't wanted to come to the one set up for Hamby's Festival, but peer pressure is no joke, and I knew if I didn't, I'd never hear the end of it. I had my limit, and Jimmy reached it when he stood in front of the ride I detested the most.

I held my palms out and shook my head at Kyle, my live-in partner, as I backed away from it. My hands trembled, my obvious fear frustrating me even more. "There is no way in hell you're getting me on that thing."

"Don't be afraid," Savannah said. "It's just a Ferris wheel."

I swallowed hard. My best friend had just betrayed me. I stared up at the monstrosity of rusted metal and tilted cages that had seen far better days. "Just a Ferris wheel? Are you serious right now? The thing is a piece of junk." If I believed in God, I would have thought he was on my side in that moment because the ride creaked and groaned as it spun slowly around, its rickety frame swaying in the breeze. "Did you hear that?" I stuffed my hands in my jean pockets. "You all dragged me here, and I'm here. Isn't that enough?" I hitched out my hip and gave my head a firm, quick shake. "It's not happening people, so give it up."

Holding Cathy's hand, Bishop applied more verbal pressure. "I'll do it if you do it."

If I didn't like the guy so much, I would have kneed him in the groin. "Nice try." I rolled my eyes. "That didn't work on me when I was ten, and it won't work on me now."

Michels said, "I'm not going on that thing either. It looks like it's going to break apart right now."

Finally, someone who understood the dangers of crappy carnival equipment. I pointed at him. "That's what I think!"

Kyle grabbed my hand and tugged me toward the line. "I'll keep you safe," he said while laughing.

Oh, no. He wasn't going to win that fight. I attempted to pull away, to yank my hand out of his, but Kyle's a hundred pounds of muscle heavier than me, and he wouldn't let go. Drastic measures were necessary. I used a common move most law enforcement learned the first week of training, the wrist twist. I twisted my hand in the opposite direction of the way he pulled me. The move was supposed to cause pain for the gripper and force them to let go. But nope. Not with Kyle. He was prepared for it and just tugged me closer toward him.

"Jerk," I mumbled under my breath. Even after being shot several times, the guy was as strong as a bull.

The corners of his mouth twitched. He wrapped his arms around me and kissed my forehead. "I'd never force you to do something that scares you, babe."

Bishop snorted. Michels cleared his throat, and Savannah burst into laughter. I dropped my head and shook it to hide my smile. Then, forcing a scowl on my face, I glared at Kyle, and I pulled out of his grip, annoyed but amused because he'd said that intentionally.

I pointed to the Ferris wheel for one more attempt to save face. "See that rust? The beams are so rotted you can't even call them metal anymore. You all go on it." I crossed my arms over my chest. "I'll watch you fall out and make sure to say I told you so." I took two big steps and stood at Michels's side. "We'll meet you back at the beer tent."

"I can't go on that thing," Savannah said. She stumbled over her words. "I'm pregnant and my baby's afraid of heights."

Jimmy shook his head. "Y'all are weak. I thought we'd hired better than that."

"Nope," Michels said.

"I second that," I added.

"So much for one last crazy night before the kid comes."

"Honey, our crazy nights were over the minute we found out I was pregnant the first time."

"The beer tent again, it is," he said. "Honestly, I don't think any of us want to risk our lives on that ride anyway."

"I don't want to risk my life on any of them." I laughed. "But y'all think I'm the weak one. Nice."

Savannah giggled. "Did you just hear yourself?"

"What?" I asked with a tilted head.

"You just said y'all."

I furrowed my brow. "No, I didn't."

Collectively, the group said, "Yes, you did."

I realized they were right, and I couldn't argue against that kind of offense. "Can we get another beer now?"

Savannah grabbed my free hand and pulled me away from Kyle and toward the tent. "Yes, because you love beer so much."

"It beats carnival rides any day of the week."

Ferris wheel aside, the festival wasn't too bad. The spring temperatures had set in with warmer days in the seventies and nights topping out in the low fifties. The air was crisp, and flowers and trees bloomed, creating a beautiful backdrop for the festivities.

The smell of funnel cakes and kettle corn wafted through the air, making my stomach rumble, though not for the same reason as the others. In fifth grade I'd snarfed down an entire stick of bubblegum cotton candy then proceeded to toss it up in front of a boy I liked. I'd had a lot of embarrassing moments in my time on the planet, but that was the first monumental one, and it had stuck. I've stayed away from festival food ever since.

Kyle begged me to try a fried Oreo, which I did out of guilt for not going on the death ride, though under complete duress. Fried chocolate and cream didn't sound appealing in the least, but the flavor was unexpected. I snatched the rest of the Oreo from his hand and stuffed it into my mouth.

"If I didn't know better," Savannah said, "I'd think you were pregnant."

I spit out fried Oreo crumbs. "Never in a million years." I forced a slightly panicked look from my face. The truth was, I'd never thought I wanted kids. My deceased husband Tommy and I had talked about it, but neither of us were ready at the time. Little did I know that fate would cruelly intervene and snatch away my husband along with any reluctant dreams of motherhood in the blink of an eye, as a crooked politician had had Tommy callously executed before my very eyes. That moment forever stole any chance of bearing his child and the happily ever after we'd been in the middle of living.

Since that fateful day, I had buried even the thought of motherhood deep within, locking it away in the recesses of my mind. But lately, when least expected, it emerged like an unwelcome visitor, tormenting my thoughts and stabbing my soul. I silently placed the blame on Savannah and her growing family, though I would never admit to that. The sight of her expanding belly stirred a whirlwind of emotions within me. If motherhood was a path I wanted to take, I needed to hurry. Time was slipping away, and Kyle and I had never even broached the subject.

"Hey pig!"

The familiar derogatory slang stopped us all in our tracks.

"And here we go," Bishop grumbled. "Never fails. Any time we go to a public event, some moron has to start something."

That was the other problem with festivals. Inevitably an officer butted heads with someone from their past, a previous arrest, convicted criminal, or one of their family members, and it rarely went well.

2

A hulking, thick man with a long, unkempt, graying beard and disheveled hair partially covered with a baseball cap approached us, his lumbering movements only accentuating his drunken stupor.

"Shit," Jimmy said. He eyes narrowed with recognition. He flicked his head to the side. "Get Savannah and Cathy out of here."

Kyle and Michels obliged, while Bishop, Levy, Jimmy, and I stood side by side, forming a line of defense behind Jimmy.

The man stopped in front of Jimmy, his hands at his side. I noticed the sidearm on his belt and placed my hand on mine. "Well, look here fellas," he said to the two beefy and equally drunk goons behind him. "It's Jimmy Abernathy. Our pathetic excuse for a police chief." He stepped closer to Jimmy. Levy, Bishop, and I took a step forward. He held his palms out in defense. "Now don't go getting all tough on me. I'm just having a conversation, is all."

"Back off, Bobby," Jimmy said. His calm voice surprised me.

Bobby spit out a clump of chew.

"Step back," Bishop said.

A small crowd had gathered around us. Great. Someone would inevitably video the situation and we'd be thrown to the media wolves whether deserved or not. I hated technology. Thankfully, three Hamby patrol officers manning the festival approached and pushed back the crowd. They caught Jimmy's eye and moved to step in, but he held up a finger, telling them to hold off.

Bobby stared at Bishop, his eyes traveling up and down my partner's newly trim and surprisingly fit body, looked into his eyes, and finally, took a step back. "I just want to talk to the chief, is all. Last I heard it's a free country, and I can still do that." His muscled sidekicks behind him moved to his sides.

"We have nothing to talk about, Bobby," Jimmy said. "Now get on out of here before we have a problem."

His head swiveled from one beefy buddy to the other. "You hear that?" He pointed at Jimmy. "This pig thinks we have nothing to talk about." He laughed. "Ain't that the funniest shit you've ever heard?" The other two men laughed. Bobby spit out some of the chew in his mouth, sized up Bishop again, then Levy, and me. He shared a big toothy smile with two bottom teeth missing then said to his friends, "You think I can take this old man and these two chicks all at once?" He eyed Levy and me again. "That one's kind of hot, but I don't need no old lady. Had me my fill of those."

Old lady? Was he talking about me or Levy? Either way, both of us would show him what an old lady could do, and we'd have fun doing it. Bobby's muscle men laughed. I clenched my fist and jiggled my gun in its holster. Bishop cleared his throat.

"I'm not going to say it again," Jimmy said. "Our business is done, and you're drunk. Go home Bobby before I toss your sorry ass in jail again."

Bobby's eyes darkened. His face switched from a pinkish glow to a burning red. He leaned toward Jimmy, who moved closer to him. The three of us followed suit.

He breathed liquor-scented breath at Jimmy, the smell so intense I smelled it as well. "I ain't breaking no laws. Pig." The two had a tense, ten second standoff before he added, "Time we settle the wrong you did on me, don't you think?" He took a step back, spit on the ground, and rubbed his palms together.

It all happened so quickly. Bobby, fueled by liquid courage and his inflated ego, swung his beefy fist through the air, its trajectory a crude arc of misplaced confidence. He'd missed his target by several inches and couldn't complete his swing. Jimmy's reaction was a blur of swift movement. His forearm rose to block the assault, catching Bobby off guard. The powerful force of Jimmy's forearm against Bobby's put the drunk off balance. He teetered to his left and grumbled out an f-bomb.

Jimmy took advantage of Bobby's shaky balance and delivered a calculated blow to his midsection.

The few people left watching gasped as the impact sent a shockwave through the festival's atmosphere. Gravity triumphed. Bobby crashed to the ground, his unsteady legs giving way to the unforgiving asphalt surface beneath him. His buddies moved back as he flailed his limbs in a desperate attempt to regain balance. For me, his fall only reinforced his image as a drunken idiot.

One punch. One punch was all it took to drop a 250-pound smartass drunk.

"Cuff him." Jimmy said to the festival officers. He wiped his mouth with the back of his hand. "He's under arrest for secondary assault against a police officer and public intoxication." He glared at each of Bobby's friends one at a time and laughed as they took off running.

"Got it," an officer said.

Levy offered to assist, but the officers said they'd take care of it.

"Impressive," Bishop said, smiling at our boss. "I haven't seen those kinds of moves from you in a while."

Jimmy rubbed his forearm. "I haven't done those kinds of moves in a while." He shook his fist lightly. "That hurt."

"I'll bring him in," one of the officers said. "The others will look for his cronies."

"Sounds like a plan," Jimmy said.

Michels and Kyle returned with Cathy and Savannah.

Savannah immediately rushed to Jimmy and pulled him into a tight hug. "Baby, that was hot."

Jimmy smiled at us. "I've still got it," he said as he wrapped his arms around his wife.

"There's always one of them in the crowd," Levy said.

"There's Ash," Michels said. Ashley, our former crime scene tech and Michels had begun dating a while back. It led to an engagement, and their wedding was just a few months away. He jogged to her and pulled her into an embrace.

Cathy elbowed Bishop. "How come everyone hugs but us?"

Levy raised her hand. "Uh, I don't have anyone to hug."

I raised my hand as well. "And I'm not a PDA person."

"But I am," Kyle said. He pulled me close and wrapped me in his arms. I wanted to act as though I didn't like it, but I did. Though I quickly withdrew from the embrace when I spotted a familiar face coming toward us.

Bishop caught my look and followed my eyes. He leaned toward me and whispered, "Is that Sean Higgins?"

"Yes," I said through gritted teeth. Sean and I had made eye contact, so running to hide wasn't an option. I groaned at the thought of facing my past and how it had ended a relationship that had barely even started.

"Haven't seen him in ages," Bishop said.

"Neither have I," I said.

"Well, this is awkward," he said. "When was the last time you spoke to him?"

"We haven't talked since the Petrowski situation."

"Really? I thought you'd seen him at least once since then."

"Nope."

"Who's the guy?" Kyle asked. "An old bust of yours?"

"No. It's Sean Higgins," I muttered.

The corners of his mouth twitched. "That's Higgins? He looks beat. You must have really crushed him."

"Kyle," I said in a terse tone. "It wasn't like that, and it was a long time ago."

He gave me a soft smile. "I was kidding."

"I know, but I'm uncomfortable."

Savannah gripped my arm. "That's a stroller. He's got a child? Is he married?"

I peeled her fingers off my arm one by one. "How should I know? Oh, God. He's coming over."

Sean and I had spent time together shortly after I'd moved to Hamby. It was too casual and early to call it anything by the time it ended. And the end was my fault.

Chris Petrowski was the crooked Chicago politician Tommy had built a case against who had him murdered to shut him up. After Tommy's murder, and once I was able to breathe again, I'd made it my life's goal to bring the bastard down, and I had. He was given a multi-year prison sentence only to be released a few years later. Crooked politicians have powerful friends in a dirty city.

After his release, he'd hunted me down in Hamby and sought revenge, only he didn't get it. He got killed instead. Unfortunately, in the process, the POS mistook a close friend of Bishop's who had been working in my home for Sean and killed him. Petrowski assumed Sean and I had fallen in love, and he wanted him dead so I'd suffer, and I had, but mainly at the loss of Bishop's friend who'd simply been in the wrong place at the wrong time.

Sean and I never spoke again. His decision made clear by ignoring me when I saw him at Duke's once, though I completely understood.

I'd run into him once since, but we hadn't talked. But even though I barely knew him, as he walked toward us, I knew something was off. Kyle had nailed it. He didn't look the same. Instead of fresh and happy, he appeared worn and tired. Either the child in the stroller was his and he was exhausted, or it was something else.

There was an unmistakable tension in his posture as he approached. His body leaned slightly forward as if expecting an imminent threat, and, only a few feet away from us, his eyes darted anxiously around, shifting from person to person. He scanned our surroundings with a hyper-vigilance. The furrowed lines on his forehead spoke volumes.

Our eyes briefly met, and in that fleeting connection, I sensed the vulnerability that lay beneath his guarded facade. They held a blend of fear and exhaustion, silently pleading for something I couldn't quite make out.

I swallowed the urge to apologize for our past and said hello.

3

"Rachel," he said. "Long time." He clenched and unclenched his hands, his fingers tightly gripping the handle of the baby stroller. An attractive woman stood beside him.

A balloon popped and he jerked, quickly studying the area around us again. Even the most minute sounds, a child yelling, someone laughing, triggered a heightened response from him, causing a ripple of tension to coat the air. He let out a slow breath of weariness evident in the lines of exhaustion etched upon his face.

"It's good to see you." I smiled at the woman and peeked into the stroller. Noting the pink outfit, I added, "What a beautiful girl."

Bishop, Levy, and the others gave us some distance. Kyle, however, stuck close to my side.

"Thank you," the woman said. "I'm Jessica. Sean's wife."

I offered her my hand. "Rachel Ryder. Nice to meet you." I glanced at Sean and then back to Kyle. "This is Kyle Olsen." I stumbled over my words when I tried to define our relationship. "He's my uh, partner."

Kyle shook Sean's hand, then smiled at Jessica. "Nice to meet you."

"Partner? So, you don't work with Rob Bishop anymore?" Sean asked.

His wife gave him a blatantly obvious side eye. "Sean. Seriously?" Ouch.

He didn't drop eye contact, though he rocked back and forth. I hadn't recalled Sean being fidgety. In fact, he'd always been calm and relaxed around me. I furrowed my brow and tilted my head to the side. He wasn't acting like himself. Not that I knew him all that well. Was I over-analyzing him because of our past? "Yes, I mean, no. I still work with Rob. Kyle is my significant other." God, I felt like an idiot. "So, you're married and have a baby. Congratulations."

"Thanks," he said. His eyes pivoted from side to side again. "Well, it was nice seeing you, but we have to get going."

"Sure, no problem. Great seeing you too." I smiled at his wife. "And nice meeting you, Jessica."

"You too," she said.

As I turned to walk back to Bishop and the others, Sean said, "Rachel?"

"Yes?" I said, pivoting back to him.

"Uh, have fun." His eyes told me he wanted to say more but something had stopped him.

I positioned myself beside Bishop and faced the direction Sean and his family had walked. I watched as Jessica strolled past the dunking machine, her walk confident and carefree, unlike Sean who continued to scan the area and walk as if he thought someone was watching him.

The bathroom was just across from them, and when they walked past it, Jessica turned around, took the stroller from Sean, and rolled to the family entrance. Sean stood close to the dunking tank, his back pressed against the side of the wood fence around the tank.

"I'll be right back," I said. I felt Kyle's eyes burning into my back. I stopped, turned toward him, and smiled. "Just give me a minute, okay?"

"Sure."

Sean's eyes darted around, scanning the crowd with an intensity that sent a chill down my spine. As I drew closer, I noticed sweat glistening on his forehead despite the cool spring air. Was he tripping on something? I couldn't imagine that was the case. He wasn't into drugs when I knew him, but people did change. Though I wouldn't expect that kind of change from him. He was straight as an arrow, as Lenny, my former Chicago PD boss and father figure, would say.

I watched as he headed toward me, each step quickening, while glancing over his shoulder. His jaw clenched, and his muscles were taut with tension. His paranoid behavior intensified with each urgent step in my direction. "Rachel?"

"Sean? Are you okay? You're acting weird."

He turned around and glanced at the bathroom. "Yeah, I'm fine." He rocked back on his heels again. "Is your number the same?"

I nodded. "Do you need to talk to me about something?"

His brow furrowed as he stared behind me. "Yeah. It's—" he stopped and looked around.

"Not here. I'll call you tomorrow."

"If it's something police related, we should talk now."

He examined the area again and shook his head. "No, it's all good." He lifted his head and smiled. "Nice to see you again," he said, then flipped around and jogged to the family restroom.

I walked back to Kyle. "Everything okay?" he asked.

"I'm not sure, but if I had to guess, I'd say no."

"I'll understand if you want to catch up with him."

"No, it's all right. He's got my number. He'll call if it's important."

An hour later we returned home. I fed my beta fish Louie, blew him a kiss goodnight, and headed toward the bedroom with Kyle a few steps behind. He set his shoes on our closet floor. After his undercover mission and subsequent recovery, which he was still in, we'd packed up his place in the city and he'd moved in with me. We'd picked what furniture of his to keep and sold the rest. Thankfully, our tastes were similar, and the place looked perfect with our joined belongings.

He finished undressing then checked his scar. "It's not as thick as a few weeks ago."

I ran my finger over the rough, bulging skin, a not-so-gentle-reminder of Kyle's experience. The panic and fear I'd felt when I heard he'd been shot had wrapped itself into a ball along with the trauma from Tommy's murder. Sometimes I'd think about one or the other and my stomach would tighten with a burst of anxiety racing through me.

He held my hand and kissed my fingers. "I'm fine."

"I know," I said. I undressed and stepped into a pair of his boxers and a tank top, and I was just getting into bed when my cell phone dinged with a text message. I saw the sender and clicked open the message. *It's Sean. I need to talk to you, but not on the phone. Can you come by the ranch in the morning?*

I typed back a quick response. *I have court at nine, but I can come before or after.*

I watched the three blue dots and waited for his reply. *After. I'll be alone then. Don't bring Bishop.*

Is everything okay?

The three dots appeared again. *CU tomorrow.*

"Everything okay?" Kyle asked.

"It was Sean. He wants me to come by tomorrow morning. Without Rob."

"Hmm. Sounds interesting. Maybe he wants to get back together."

I snuggled up against Kyle and pulled the blanket up to my shoulder. "Not with the way he was behaving. Let's just hope it's nothing to worry about."

4

I called Bishop on my way to Sean's ranch. "How was court?" he asked.

"Continued. Again."

"That's the third time. Surprised the judge isn't pushing back on that."

"It's Judge Reynolds. You know how soft he is."

He laughed. "Rarely puts anyone away."

"Exactly, which will be the case in this too, so I'm not sure why he doesn't just sentence him to his typical year of probation and get it over with."

"How far out are you?"

"Not far, but I need to make a quick stop first. Everything okay at the station?"

"Aside from the coffee, it's fine. Which reminds me, can you make a stop at Dunkin'?"

I glanced down at my empty Starbucks cup. I'd gone there because it was close, but I did prefer the less burnt taste of Dunkin' coffee. "You want your usual?"

"If you mean my new usual, yes."

Since Bishop had begun his new fit and healthy routine, he'd given up adding anything tasty to his coffee and drank it black. I'd done that many times, but every so often, the combination rush from caffeine and sugar was much needed. "Got it. See you in a bit."

I navigated my department-issued vehicle down the rural street where Sean's ranch was located. The drive was a stunning, picturesque road flanked by horse ranches and multi-million-dollar homes. I'd been in Hamby long enough to appreciate the tranquility of the countryside and enjoy the scent of freshly mown hay mingling with the earthy fragrance of horses. When I'd first moved to Georgia, I had trouble with how it smelled. I'd been so used to engine exhaust and garbage, I had no idea what the rest of the world might smell like.

I noticed something in the road rounding a bend just before the entrance to Sean's. I slowed as I drove closer. A pair of horses and an unbelievably enormous pig stood defiantly in the middle of the road.

"What the?" I eased my vehicle to a stop, my tires crunching on the gravel shoulder at the edge of Sean's ranch. As I stepped out of my vehicle, the faint jingle of the horses' harnesses and the grunting of the prodigious pig drowned out the highway sounds in the distance. "Great." My boots thudded against the ground, the cacophony adding to the mix. I patted the closest horse on the side, a black and white patterned appaloosa. "Where are your parents, pretty girl?"

The other horse eyed me curiously, her large expressive eyes seemingly amused by their predicament. A vehicle appeared from the opposite direction. I stood in front of the animals and waved it into the other lane.

The vehicle slowed, and the man driving rolled down his window. "Need some help?"

I showed him my badge clipped to my belt. "I'm okay, but thanks."

"Might want to keep your gate closed. Everyone speeds on this road and the cops don't give a damn."

I gave him a thumbs up. "Got it."

He rolled up the window. As he drove away, I said to one of the horses, "He's right even though he's a jerk for bad-mouthing me."

I had noticed the gate to Sean's ranch open, and I quickly escorted the first horse back to it, making sure to close the gate with her behind it. I guided the second horse, also an appaloosa, to the gate, opened it for her, and pulled it closed again. I typed a message to Sean.

On the road in front of the ranch. Gate was open and two horses and a pig were on the road. Got the horses in but need help with the pig.

I did make a valiant effort to move the pig, but my one-hundred-twenty-pound frame had nothing on its minimum four-hundred-pound one. I tried reasoning with it, my voice tinged with a trifecta of frustration, concern, and amusement. I gestured towards the open gate leading to the ranch, hoping to entice the monster bacon bit across the gate onto the ranch with the prospect of a tasty treat, a day-old donut from Dunkin' from breakfast the morning before.

But the pig remained unmoved. Literally and figuratively.

I scratched my head in disbelief, the absurdity of the situation sinking in. "You're a stubborn one, aren't you?" I muttered to myself, resigned to the fact that this was a task beyond my solo powers of persuasion.

I texted Sean again, not paying attention to the delivered message I'd sent a few minutes earlier. I should have realized then it hadn't been marked read.

I reached for my radio and called for backup, hoping Bishop and crew would find the hilarity and urgency in my plea. I didn't bother with ten-codes. The city had them for wildlife and farm animals, but the situation was too funny to bother with professionalism. "Dispatch, this is Detective Ryder requesting back up. I've got a situation here. Two horses and a colossal pig blocking the road. I repeat, a colossal pig." I gave her my location.

"Copy that, Detective. Wait. Did you say a pig in the road?" the dispatcher chuckled.

"You heard me right. I've contacted the owner but haven't received a response."

Her acknowledgement crackled through the radio, a mix of laughter and disbelief evident in her voice. "Copy that, Detective. Back up is enroute. Over."

"Copy that. Pig is likely four-hundred pounds," I said. "Please send the strongest patrol on duty." I'd dealt with many humans on the road, but the horses and pig were my first livestock.

"Can you repeat that?"

I took a breath and then exhaled my frustration at what I knew I'd hear back at the department. "Minimum four-hundred-pound pig. Very defiant and stubborn. It didn't move when I yelled at it."

"I'll get a vet out there as well," she said.

I checked my phone, but Sean still hadn't responded. I glanced up his drive and saw a pickup, and assuming it was his, I decided to head up his drive. If someone came speeding down the road, it wouldn't end well for the pig or the vehicle, but my being there wouldn't change that.

5

It had been a while since I last walked into the ranch's main office. It had changed some since then, a basic remodel, mostly fresh paint, and reorganization of the supply store area, and a new counter, but otherwise it was the same. Simple and without thrills. My footsteps echoed against the worn wooden floor, a sound I recalled instantly. The familiar scent of hay and leather blended with a faint aroma of damp earth and something else.

Vomit.

My entire body stiffened as my heart sank into the pit of my stomach. I stood in the middle of the small room and called out for Sean and his sister Connie. A baby wailed at the sound of my voice. My heart bottomed out, knowing what was coming, dropping even lower than my stomach. I ran toward the cry.

Sean's daughter was lying in a bassinet bawling her eyes out. Behind her, against the wall, Sean sat motionless and lifeless, his empty eyes staring past me. My breath caught in my chest. My eyes darted to the band wrapped around his arm and then to the needle lying on the floor beside him. Vomit covered his mouth and shirt. He was gone, I knew that, but logic lost as my emotions got the best of me. "Sean!" I rushed toward him, tripping over myself and nearly falling on top of him. I lightly patted his face, staring into his eyes frozen in his final moment. "Wake up!" I checked for a pulse. "Damn it, Sean! Wake up!" I held my ear close to his mouth, too focused on Sean to care about the vomit stench. No breath left his lips. His skin, clammy and warm, brought me out of shock. I moved him down with his back against the floor and began chest compressions. "One, two, three —come on, dammit! Breathe!"

Nothing.

I wiped his mouth with my jacket and blew into it then began compressions once again. "Come on Sean!" Sweat beaded my forehead and slid down into my eyes. I wiped my eyes with the back of my hand. "Dammit, Sean!"

Push. Push. Push. I'd lost count. I breathed into his mouth again. *Push. Push. Push.* "Come on!"

Still nothing.

His eyes didn't flicker. He didn't blink. He didn't move. He was gone.

The baby cried. I caught my breath, wiped the sweat off my cheeks, and rushed to her. I picked her up gently and said, "It's okay, little one. I've got you." I held her close with one arm while I called dispatch with the other. "This is Detective Rachel Ryder. I've got a possible drug overdose with a deceased victim."

"Copy that Detective, what's your twenty?"

I gave her the location for Sean's ranch.

"Ten-four, Detective. I've got assistance and fire on their way, and I just put in a notification to Dr. Barron."

The baby cried again. "Copy that," I said. I disconnected the call and patted her back. "Shh. It's okay." I checked around the bassinet and saw a diaper bag. Careful to retrace my steps as best I could, I grabbed the bag and turned back to Sean. I looked directly into his eyes and froze. Something didn't look right. What was I missing? After a quick glance down at the syringe, I rushed out of the building.

I stood outside on auto pilot, rubbing the baby's back, easing her cries with soft sounds, all while struggling to breathe. My body shook. Breathe, Rachel. Just breathe. I paced in a straight line rubbing her back and cooing on auto pilot. Sean didn't overdose. He couldn't. He had a family.

Panic enveloped me. I gasped for air, my breaths just wheezing efforts of failure. I felt the baby tense even more in my embrace. Calm the hell down,

I told myself. I inhaled deeply, finally able to force air into my lungs. "It's okay, sweetie. It's okay." I patted her back again and held her tight against my shoulder.

It hit me then. Where was the bottle that held the drugs obviously shot into Sean's arm? Or the spoon and aluminum foil? The lighter? Usually, drug deaths included some or all of the paraphernalia necessary to get high. But all I saw near Sean was the syringe. I walked back and forth in front of the office, cradling the baby, and trying without much success to relax both of us.

Two patrol officers finally rolled up the driveway.

"The pig," one said. "He or she won't budge."

"We have more officers and paramedics on the way, and dispatch is contacting a vet," the other officer said. "What do you need us to do?"

The baby cried in my arms. I handed the bag to the other officer. "Right now? Please check for a bottle. She's hungry." When had she eaten last? How long had they been there? What did this poor child see? I held her up and sniffed her bottom. The first officer grimaced.

"There's a body inside," I said to the second officer. "Start taping off the scene, please."

The first officer handed me a bottle. "Do you have kids?" I asked. I'd finally gathered control over my emotions and did what had become natural with Scarlet, Savannah's baby.

"No, ma'am." I shook the bottle, then dripped some onto my hand. It was lukewarm. "Thank God," I said as I stuffed it into her mouth. "Thank you." I looked at the officer and eyed his nametag. "John Smith?" Who named their kid John with a last name like Smith? It was so basic and an invitation to identity theft. Distracting myself meant I wasn't in control like I thought. It was a defense mechanism and what I needed to do to maintain calm sometimes. "Did you say a vet is on the way?"

"Yes, ma'am. Should be here right quick."

"Great. Please go direct traffic away from the pig. We don't need another death on scene."

He flicked his head toward the ranch office. "What about inside?"

"The other officer is securing the scene." I pointed toward the road. The sirens grew louder and closer. "Someone will be here in a minute. We need to get the pig off the road." I could tell by the look on his face he was more interested in Sean's death than a pig, but that wasn't my problem.

Bishop pulled up and around the two squad cars. Levy and Michels were right behind him, and Nikki, our crime scene tech, behind them.

"Is it Sean?" Bishop asked.

I nodded knowing I would break down if I said it out loud. Sean didn't need me doing that. He needed me to take care of his child.

"Damn."

Two other squads arrived. The officer in the first one jumped out and rushed over. "Deceased?"

I nodded.

"Did you secure the scene?" Bishop asked.

"There's an officer inside now." I couldn't speak as the lump in my throat pushed close to release.

"Go help him, officer," he said.

"Yes, sir," he said. He grabbed the other officer and ran toward the building.

Bishop eyed me cautiously. "Take a breath."

I panted out a rough, "I'm fine." I wasn't, but I needed to pretend I was. Seeing dead bodies was never easy, but seeing the dead body of someone I knew conjured emotions I'd worked hard to shut off.

"How?" he asked.

"Drugs, but there's only a syringe, Bishop."

"What?"

"Next to his body. There's no other drug paraphernalia. That doesn't make sense."

"We'll figure it out," he said. "Have you called his sister Connie?"

"I don't have Connie's number, and I can't even remember his wife's name. We need to send someone to both of them."

Levy approached. "I'll handle that. I'm sure there's a directory or something inside." She headed toward the office.

Bishop placed his hand on my shoulder. "You going to be okay?"

I bit my lip and shook my head. The baby had guzzled the whole bottle down in under five minutes. I held her over my shoulder and gently patted her back. After she burped, I felt the weight of her head as she fell asleep against my shoulder. "I don't want to go back in there with the baby."

"You shouldn't." He nodded toward Michels. "We've got this. You take care of her."

"I need a paramedic to take a look at her."

Bishop nodded and got right on his radio to make sure that happened.

Levy rushed out. "I got his sister first. She's going to pick up Jessica. She told me not to call her."

"Probably smart," Michels said.

"I took a quick look at him," Levy said. "Was he an addict?"

"No," I said.

Bishop said, "We don't—"

But I cut Bishop off. "He wasn't a user."

"Maybe not when you knew him, but it's been a while now, Rachel," Bishop said.

"People change."

Not Sean. I refused to believe that, no matter what I might have thought the night before. I didn't know him all that well, but I'd never once gotten the drug vibe from him. Sometimes my intuition could pinpoint a future addict. I didn't know why or how, but it hadn't been wrong. And it hadn't picked Sean. "You saw him last night. He acted strange, yeah, but then he texted me and said he wanted to talk to me in person. What if this has something to do with that?"

Bishop nodded. "We'll find out." The three of them headed into the building.

I kept the baby close to my chest and gave directions to everyone who approached until the paramedic arrived and carted her off to check her over. "I'd like her back when you're done with her, please."

"Of course," the female paramedic said.

"Thank you."

"We got the pig," Officer Smith said as he jogged over. "Vet almost had to knock her out with a shot." He turned toward the entrance. "He was able to corral her onto his truck bed, so he's bringing her in now. Her name's Bertha. She's deaf and has no sense of direction. Vet said Sean rescued her from an abusive situation near Chattanooga."

Of course, he did. That brought a small smile to my face. "Deaf? Probably why she ignored me then."

He laughed. "Vet said Sean rescued her about six months ago. She's escaped from her pen a few times. She likes to hang with the horses." The truck with the largest pig I'd ever seen pulled up and onto the grass next to the fence. "He's the ranch's vet. Said he'll stick around for a while. He wants to make sure Sean's sister Connie knows what happened."

Last I knew, Connie owned the ranch and Sean worked for her, so that made sense. We could do that, but if he had a good relationship with either Connie or Sean, it would be beneficial to have him there. "Thanks for the help," I said. "Oh, one more thing." I saw the paramedic walking over with the baby. "Don't leave," I said to Officer Smith.

The paramedic handed her to me. The baby cooed and smiled. "She appears fine, but the parents will want to take her to the doctor just in case."

"The parent," I said.

"I'm sorry?"

I shook my head. "Nothing. Thank you for checking her."

"My pleasure." She nodded and walked away.

I lightly patted the baby's back and made calming, shushing sounds. "The owner, Connie Higgins, and the deceased's wife, Jessica will be arriving soon," I said to Officer Smith. "Please wait at the end of the driveway and make sure they come straight to me." I glanced at the office and the crime scene tape Nikki had draped around it. "They can't go in there. Do you understand?"

"Yes, ma'am," he said.

"Officer, please call me Detective instead of ma'am."

"Sure thing, ma—detective."

I smiled. "Thank you."

I stood on the outskirts of the sprawling horse ranch, my gaze fixed on the scene, soaking in every detail and storing it in my photographic memory for later. It had been thirty minutes and Connie still hadn't arrived with Jessica, but I imagined it would take time to get her moving once she found out about Sean. The baby slept soundly on my shoulder. Baby shampoo and lotion filled my nostrils.

Bright lights from police cruisers and wailing ambulance sirens competed with the sun, and their combination cast an eerie glow over the normally serene surroundings as the clouds covered the sun. The air crackled with a mixture of tension and curiosity. Officers, firefighters, and paramedics spoke in hushed tones trying to decipher the tragedy that had unfolded inside.

In the distance, several uniformed Fulton County Sheriff deputies stood waiting to offer their assistance. Some were huddled in deep conversation, gesturing animatedly, and watching while our team meticulously marked evidence and took photographs of the outside area.

And I held onto Sean's baby for dear life.

6

The horses, sensing the unusual energy, whinnied and stamped their hooves in restless protest. Bertha the pig, the only thing to make me smile, slept on that truck bed like a college kid in the jail's drunk tank.

A cruiser drove up with a small SUV behind it. Connie and Jessica had arrived. My heart quickened, knowing the raw urgency that emanated from the vehicle. The passenger car door flung open, and Jessica, tears streaming down her face, stumbled out, her breaths coming in ragged gasps. With every ounce of desperation, she sprinted toward me, her eyes fixated on her sleeping baby nestled in my arms.

Her voice cracked as she called out, a mix of anguish and hope interwoven in her plea. "Please...please tell me my baby is okay!"

My heart broke for her. When the reality of Sean's death hit her, the fear and desperation in her soul would stay there forever. Mine had, and still, it haunted me during my weakest moments.

Without hesitation, I loosened my hold on the baby and held her out. "She's fine," I said. "The paramedics examined her, and she just had a bottle about thirty minutes ago." The calmness in my voice hid my true feelings, the angst and sadness burning through my veins.

Her trembling hands reached out to cradle her baby against her chest. A wave of relief washed over her tear-streaked face, her eyes locking onto her child's peaceful countenance and then onto mine. "Sean? Is he okay? I need to see him."

She didn't know? Did Connie? Had Levy not given her the news? Had she just asked them to come? Connie had parked the car and rushed over pulling a stroller behind her. "What's going on? All the officer said was something's happened to Sean, and we needed to get here right away."

Giving a death notice was never easy, but it was particularly hard when it was to a parent or a spouse of the deceased. Knowing Sean made it personal, and as much as I tried to maintain my professional demeanor, the cracking in my voice gave away my emotions. "I'm sorry."

Connie gasped. Her hand flung to her mouth as she said, "Oh, my God, Sean!"

Jessica's eyes popped open. She was speechless for a moment, and then reality struck like a bolt of lightning. "What? No!" She collapsed onto her knees, cradling the baby close to her, and sobbed. "No!"

Connie crouched down and held her sister-in-law and the baby close. "What's going on? We were robbed? Did Sean have to defend himself?"

I wouldn't say Sean overdosed, whether intentionally or accidentally, until the coroner arrived, or we had solid evidence of something. His death was suspicious, but we couldn't determine whether it was by his own hand or homicide. Not without more information. "We're still figuring out what happened."

Connie set up the stroller and carefully took the baby from Jessica, then placed her inside. Jessica stood and wiped her tears with her hands. "You know something you're not telling us. What happened? Why is Sean dead? Did someone kill him?"

"We don't know what happened," I said. "But we will figure it out."

She sucked in a hiccup of air. "I'm telling you right now, he didn't kill himself."

"Can you tell me why you would say that?" I asked. I tried to speak calmly without emotion, but it was hard.

"I know you think it." She was looking at Connie, not me, when she said that. "He's been different lately, but he wouldn't do that. He loves us. He loves our life, our family."

Connie and I made eye contact. She said, "He's been stressed. I've tried to talk to him about it several times, but he just closes up. Won't say anything."

"What kind of stress? Work?" I glanced at Jessica. "Or family?"

She touched the side of her face and wiped away a tear. Her hands trembled as she looked me straight in the eyes. "It's not us. We're fine. He's just been different."

"Different how?" I asked.

Her voice trembled as she worked to form her words. "He was, I don't know how to explain it. Worried?" She clutched her elbows and rubbed her upper arms. "Paranoid sometimes even, maybe? He texted you last night. I saw his phone. He wanted to talk to you. I asked him what it was about, but he wouldn't tell me." She buried her face in her hands. I gave her a minute knowing she hadn't finished that train of thought. "What did he want to talk to you about?"

"I'm not sure. I came here this morning to find out, and that's when I saw the horses and the pig on the road." I angled my body toward the pig standing on the truck bed.

Connie's eyes widened as she noticed the pig trapped on the truck bed. "Bertha! Is she—"

"She's fine. Sleeping like a baby. The vet handled her like a pro, and I think he stuck around to check on you."

The strained cords of her neck softened, and her voice lost some of its panicked tone. "Oh, thank God."

"What about Sean?" Jessica asked, her mind focused on only her husband, understandably so. "Please, I need to see him."

"You will. Just not yet." I pointed to Dr. Mike Barron's vehicle as he parked on the side of the gravel driveway. "The coroner just arrived. We'll know more about what happened when he's finished with his examination. He can arrange for you to see Sean then, okay?"

She swallowed hard and shook her head. "No. I don't want to wait."

Connie grabbed her arm as she turned to follow Barron. "Jess, no. You don't want to see Sean like this."

"But I need to know what happened."

I exhaled, preparing myself to tell her what I knew. "Jessica, let's talk about what you said. Sean was worried. Paranoid sometimes, right?"

She nodded. "More so lately, but he wouldn't tell me why."

I made eye contact with her but spoke directly to Connie. "Did he have a history of drug use?"

Jessica didn't give Connie a chance to respond. She flung her hand to her chest and gasped. "What? No! Sean never did drugs. Why would you— oh, my God! What's going on?"

Connie held her sister-in-law tight against her side. My eyes shifted to Connie's. She said, "No. Sean wasn't into that. He barely even drank alcohol, and to the best of my knowledge, he's never even smoked pot or had one of those gummy things. He thought it was all stupid."

"What happened to my husband?" Jessica yelled. Tears streamed down her cheeks. "I want to know! Now!"

The baby stirred in her stroller, a soft moan suddenly exploding into a loud wail. "I've got her," Connie said.

I pressed my lips together before finally speaking again. She wanted the truth, and I didn't think she'd pull it together if she didn't get it. I didn't think she'd pull it together knowing, but it might stop her from distracting the team from doing their job. "I found Sean against the wall with a band wrapped around his upper arm and a needle beside him."

Jessica shouted, "No!" She took two steps back and bolted toward the office. Thankfully, two uniformed officers saw her coming and stopped her.

That didn't go entirely as planned. Poor woman. I knew her pain well.

"I'll talk with her," Connie said. "Sean wouldn't do this. He loved his wife and his daughter. He was excited to be a dad. He wouldn't do this."

BARRON WALKED toward me and Bishop after he finished a quick conversation with the vet. His slightly overweight body balanced with his tall stature, and his confident, in control stride not only gave the appearance of a man who took his job seriously but was comfortable doing it. Those from town knew he was incredibly smart, but when I first met him, I mistakenly assumed he was a man of average intelligence. I'd been wrong. Knowledge with no bounds and an intense belief in good crushing evil simmered underneath his gentle demeanor, all things that had earned him the trust and respect of the community, and of course, me. I prepared for a sparring over what I knew was a complicated scene. Determining whether the death was intentional or accidental wasn't easy, and was always debatable.

"Detectives," he said without smiling. Keeping his eyes glued to mine, he said in a slightly exasperated tone, "I've missed my tee time already, and I know you're going to want to move quickly on this."

A smile cracked the corners of Bishop's mouth. He knew Barron would disagree with my theory without hearing it. "Mike, Sean was an upstanding citizen in the community. I don't ever recall him having any narcotic issues."

Score a point for my partner.

When Barron sighed, his entire chest heaved upward, and his small belly shook as he exhaled. He dropped his head and then looked up at me again. He didn't have to say anything. He knew what I'd say. "I'll get to the autopsy as soon as possible, but it's complicated."

"I know," I said. "But I've seen these things before, and you know it's possible someone could have jabbed him with the needle and put it in his hand, and the fact that the drug paraphernalia isn't on scene..." The implied theory on that obvious, I left the comment unfinished.

"Understood. There are no obvious signs of a struggle," he said. "But I'll see what I find." He jerked his head toward the office. "Nikki's in there now." He smiled. "I like that girl. Bring her to the autopsy this time. I doubt she'll throw up like Michels always does."

I breathed a sigh of relief. "Thanks, Mike. I appreciate it."

He looked me in the eyes again. "I seem to recall you having a history with Mr. Higgins."

"Barely, and it was a long time ago."

"Nonetheless, we can't make decisions based on an emotional attachment to the deceased, no matter how small or long ago that attachment might be." He gave me a nod and walked to his vehicle.

Bishop turned to me. "That was easier than I thought."

"I think he's afraid of me."

He smirked. "I don't doubt that one bit."

7

An officer met us at the back entrance to the department. "Chief wants to see you in his office."

"Got it," Bishop said. "Thanks." He paused inside and turned to me. "Try not to be emotional."

Steeling my spine and putting on my snarky face, I said, "What, me? I don't get emotional."

He failed at hiding his disbelief. "All right then, how about this? Try not to get pushy."

"I wouldn't call me pushy," I said. "Assertive, maybe." I swallowed. "And it's Sean."

"I know." He placed his hand on my shoulder and squeezed softly. "I'm sorry, Rachel."

If I tried to speak, the words would have come out in sobs. I needed to keep my emotions intact. Jimmy would shut me down and take me off the investigation if I showed any emotional connection. We walked to the kitchen first for a fresh cup of engine oil from the Keurig.

"And I was being nice, by the way," he said.

I wanted to thank him for the snark. It focused me. "Gee, feeling the love, partner."

Jimmy had splurged and ordered two additional Keurigs for the kitchen, so we made our coffee at the same time. "You're better than you were when you first started, but you're still rough around the edges. Sometimes it's better to gently nudge toward what you want than to shove someone into a pit of fire and wait for the screams for help." He turned toward me as he dumped three sugar packets into his coffee. "All I'm saying is you attract more flies with sugar."

"What's with the sugar? I thought you'd given it up with this new healthy lifestyle thing?"

"I did. I have. But I need it right now."

"By the way, that whole, *you attract more flies with sugar* thing sounds like my mother."

"Then I think I'd like her."

He wouldn't. I barely did. "It's Sean," I said, bringing us back to the important subject.

"I know, but—"

"Understood," I said holding up a hand. "I'll try to be less passionate."

"That's not what I'm saying."

"Maybe not, but that's how I define my behavior, and this is personal to me. You, of all people, know how that feels."

He did. When your best friend is mistaken for Sean and murdered in your partner's home because of her past, taking it personally was the only option. Sean and I weren't close, but Petrowski's assumption that there was more than a casual relationship between Sean and me shows he wanted to hurt me like he had when he murdered my husband.

"I know," I said.

Jimmy was head down into a file folder when we walked in. He looked up with an exasperated expression and heaved a heavy sigh as we sat. He focused on me. "I'm sorry about Sean."

The large lump in my throat prohibited me from speaking without choking on it. I simply nodded once.

"I spoke to Mike. He's leaning toward accidental overdose but knows how important this is to you."

"Yes," I said with a raspy voice. "I spoke to Sean's sister and wife. Neither of them believes he's had any drug related issues, past or present. His sister even said he's never smoked pot or had a gummy. Also, the drugs and para-phernalia associated with injections weren't anywhere near him."

"Understood."

We'd left the door to his office partially open. Nikki knocked on it. "Got a second?"

"Come on in," Jimmy said.

She gave me a soft, resigned smile. Word must have gotten out about my previous almost relationship with the victim because it happened before Nikki's time. "The victim's prints are on the needle."

I jumped to Sean's defense. "That's to be expected. If someone set it up to look like an overdose, they'd make sure of that."

Bishop cleared his throat. I narrowed my eyes at him and hoped he felt the imaginary daggers shooting from them and piercing his soul.

"I'll agree with that," Jimmy said. He looked back to Nikki. "Did you find any other prints on it or the band?"

"No, Chief." She eyed me. "Sorry."

"Don't be. You're doing your job." I stared at Bishop as if to ask, was that nice enough?

"Jimmy," I said. "Barron suggested Nikki come to the autopsy."

"I'm aware." He smiled at Nikki. "You good with that?"

"Absolutely," she said, her excitement evident from her squeaky response. "What time?"

"He'll need you there in two hours," Jimmy said. He glanced at Bishop. "Tell me what you know."

Nikki excused herself as Bishop detailed what we'd learned. The fact that Jimmy asked him and not me made his thoughts clear. He knew I'd be emotional, and he was right, but it was for good reason. If there was going to be an investigation, he wanted me involved. He knew riling me up would force him to keep me out of it.

"There was no evidence of a struggle on scene," Bishop said. "If I didn't know the victim, I would have called it an accidental overdose from the start but given the history and the fact that his baby was in the office leads me to a different conclusion."

"People get high with their kids around," Jimmy said.

I blurted out, "Not Sean, and let me repeat, the only sign of drug use near him was the syringe."

"No other drug paraphernalia?" he asked as if he hadn't heard it already.

I shook my head. "He didn't do this to himself."

"The victim has no known history of drug use," Bishop continued. "Which was confirmed by his sister and wife. Of course, there's always a first, but given his odd behavior and texts to Rachel last night, I'm inclined to believe something nefarious happened rather than a self-inflicted overdose."

Jimmy eyed me. "Texts?"

"Yes. After we ran into him at the festival, where, as Bishop pointed out, he acted strange, he texted me and asked to meet. I asked what it was about, but he wanted to discuss it in person. That's why I was at his place this morning. To talk to him."

"And you have no idea what he wanted to discuss?"

"No, but his wife and sister both said he'd been acting different recently. His wife described his behavior as paranoid."

"Paranoia is a sign of drug abuse, and happens easily with drugs like cocaine for example," Jimmy said.

"Come on." My voice rose. I swallowed and spoke softly. "He would have shown signs of being under the influence. Someone would have noticed."

He looked at Bishop. "You think his death is suspicious." It wasn't a question.

"As I said before, I do," Bishop said. "And I'd like an opportunity to dig deeper."

Jimmy placed his hands on his desk, then stood. "I'll give you twenty-four hours. If you find something, bring it to me. But if this goes against Barron's autopsy results, it's got to be something big enough for the district attorney to want to move forward." His eyes shifted to me. "Understand?"

I smiled as I jumped out of my seat. "Yes, sir. Can we have Michels and Levy as well?"

"For the twenty-four hours. We'll go from there."

"Perfect," I said and rushed out of his office. As we walked toward Levy's cubicle, I said, "We need to talk to the ranch employees."

Michels leaned on the outside of Levy's partitioned entrance. He turned toward us. "Jimmy cleared for an investigation?"

"We have twenty-four hours to find something, but it'll be weighed against the autopsy results," Bishop said. "Jimmy's approved the four of us looking into it."

"Great," Levy said. "What can we do?"

"Ranch employees might know something. Both Sean's wife and sister said he'd been acting strange lately, a little paranoid," I said. "See if you can get anything from the staff."

"What about finances?" Michels asked. "Are we looking into them?"

"Not yet, but we'll get on it," I said. I aimed my gaze toward my partner. "Can you connect with Connie while I'm at the autopsy?"

He nodded. "I spoke to Connie briefly about the ranch's finances," Bishop said. "Sean handled them, and she thinks things are good, but she wasn't too involved in the process. As for his personal finances, I'll have to speak to his wife." He dragged his hand down his five o'clock shadow. "I'll talk to Connie again, and I'll also see if we can get his wife's approval for their personal finances as well. I'll make sure Bubba's on it."

Michels gave me a sly smile. "You know a guy in Chicago. You could always give him a call."

He was talking about my computer tech genius and informant Joey. Joey was excellent at his job, but he focused on illegal means of acquiring information, so I used him sparingly and off the record. "Not for this. We need to be by the book for this one." The three of them looked at me with huge smiles covering their faces. "What?" I asked. "I can follow the rules."

"And I'm a virgin," Levy said as she laughed.

"We all know that's a crock," Michels said. She threw a pencil at him. It smacked him in the middle of his forehead. Perfect aim. He rubbed the spot. "Ouch."

I retrieved my phone from my pocket and checked traffic to downtown Atlanta on my Waze app. "Great. It's all red."

"It's Friday. They're the worst days for traffic," Bishop said.

"This is an Atlanta suburb and most of the town works in the city. Every day is the worst day for traffic," Levy said.

We confirmed next actions and agreed to meet back at the department by the end of the day. I headed to the forensic lab to grab Nikki but stopped on the way to take a call from Kyle.

"You okay?" he asked. The genuine concern in his voice was clear.

I took a deep breath, the faint sound of my exhale mixing with the hum of the department's ventilation system in the background. "You heard?"

"It's a small town."

I leaned against the wall outside of Nikki's lab. "Damn it. What are people saying?"

"According to Savannah, he overdosed."

"She told you that?"

A faint shuffling sound came from Kyle's side, maybe him adjusting the phone against his ear. "She told me she's heard that, not that she thinks it's true."

I bit my bottom lip in an effort to keep my emotions in check. "Sean didn't do drugs."

"I believe you," he said. His voice was the reassuring anchor I needed.

I tried not to cry. Nikki stepped out of the lab, saw me, and walked back in, closing the door behind her. "His daughter was in the office."

Kyle exhaled. "I'm sorry."

"Me, too. I'm heading to the autopsy. Is everything okay with you?"

"I'm good," he said. "You don't need to worry about me."

As if that was even possible. After almost losing him to an undercover assignment with the DEA, I lived with the unsettling fear that what happened to Tommy could happen to him. "I'll be home late. We only have twenty-four hours to show Jimmy this is a murder."

"Let me know if I can help."

"I will." I disconnected the call and walked into the lab.

8

Nikki grinned up at me though her eyes showed concern. "Are you okay?"

"I've been better. You ready?"

"Yep." She grabbed her purse from her desk and shut off the light as we walked out. She closed and locked the door. "I've got some interesting news."

I eyed her with a hint of hope. I didn't like wanting to think someone I had once cared for was murdered, but thinking he'd accidentally or even intentionally taken his own life was just as bad, if not worse. "Did you find something?"

"Maybe."

We walked to my department issued vehicle, a new Ford Explorer, while she filled me in. "Based on my findings, it's not looking like a straight-forward overdose anymore."

My eyes shifted to her as I backed out of the parking spot. "What'd you find?"

"First, here's my question. If the victim overdosed, where's the rest of his stuff? Where's the bottle of drugs or the spoon and lighter? Did he prepare it somewhere else or buy the needle filled? I checked the entire building and didn't find anything related to drug use."

I turned toward the highway. "I thought the same thing, but I don't have a clear answer to that. Did you check the stables?"

"No, but we closed them off. We had the staff move the horses and I've got my part-timers going through it now."

"You trust them?" I'd worked with one before, and he had a lot to learn.

"They've had a lot of training recently, so yes. I trust them."

"Then so do I. Anything else?"

"Dr. Barron will probably have a different opinion on this, but first thing that caught my attention was the needle prick in the victim's arm." She hesitated for a moment and then said, "It seemed a little too neat for a typical drug overdose. The placement suggests that it was deliberately administered, not just a random injection."

"Did you get photos?"

"Of course. I'll show them to you and Dr. Barron. I'm not an expert on injections, but it appears that the needle happened first."

"Meaning what? The band was an afterthought?"

"Possibly."

"Can you prove that?"

"I don't think I can, but Dr. Barron might be able to. And honestly, I'm not sure I'm right. I had to use a magnifying glass to find the prick. Oh, and I didn't see any others near it. If he did this to himself, it was either his first time, or he stuck himself in other places. I couldn't check, obviously."

"He didn't do it himself."

"I didn't know him, but I trust you." She opened a file folder and mumbled something I couldn't understand. "Okay, I found additional fingerprints on the nearby furniture. I'm running them through the database, but since the office has a small shopping area for horse riding and training equipment attached, it could lead to nothing."

"It would be a big leap if it did, given the fluctuation of people in the office."

"I know. There's this experiment these two scientists conducted to see if they could determine the age of a fingerprint based on the extent to which biomolecules, ones like fatty acids, present in the ridges of the fingerprint, have migrated downwards into the lower part. What's called the valleys of the prints."

Nikki's IQ topped mine by several points. I didn't expect her to stay in crime scene tech long. She'd probably end up a forensic specialist in some big city. I entered the highway and merged quickly into the busy traffic. "Can you dumb it down a little for me, please?"

She laughed. "Scientists did an experiment to figure out how old a fingerprint is by looking in the lines and bumps of the print. They checked how far the stuff in them had moved down into the lower part of the print. It's complicated, but they think they've got it."

"Can you do it?"

"Not yet. They're in the process of testing materials to measure the differences in ages of fingerprints, but the equipment they're using isn't available to law enforcement. If we worked for the military we'd have access."

"So, let me get this straight. There might be a way to determine age of a fingerprint, but it's nothing you can do."

"Yes, but a good district attorney could cite the study and show reasonable doubt about the age of the prints. It's just something to note if we need to tighten our case."

It was a long shot, but if we had to, we'd present it to the DA. "Anything else?"

"I also took fingerprints from the baby's bassinet. I'll run them and compare them to the others."

"Perfect."

It took over an hour to get to Barron's office, but I'd called him, and he'd waited.

He greeted us outside the exam room. "Nikki, I'm glad you could come. Have you ever observed an autopsy before?"

She bounced on her toes. I hadn't seen her that excited before. "I have not, sir."

She was going into a room where a body would be cut open and the insides removed in front of her. I found nothing exciting in that, especially considering I knew the victim.

Barron handed her a mask. "If you feel like you're going to be sick, please use the garbage can I'll set aside for you inside."

"I'll be fine," she said. "I've experienced every level of disgusting imaginable at crime scenes already."

"That's unlikely," I said. Most crime scenes in Hamby, Georgia, held nothing over the ones in Chicago, though our number murders were by far creepier than anything there.

"I have to agree with Detective Ryder," Barron said.

"It's okay," Nikki said. She patted her stomach. "Nothing gets to this thing."

"Then we'll proceed," Barron said. "I'll go ahead and explain to you what's going to happen. That way you won't have any surprises."

Normally I would have cracked a snarky joke at that point to ease the tension always associated with autopsies, but I couldn't do that with Sean on the table. Barron held the door open and let us in before him. Nikki let me go first.

As usual, the atmosphere of the autopsy room was filled with an eerie silence, one disrupted only by the hum of the fluorescent lights overhead. The room mimicked a surgical space equipped with stainless steel tables, cabinets filled with various instruments, and the distinctive scent of disinfectants lingering in the air. The difference? The room lacked machines to keep the victim alive because the person on the table was dead.

Barron handed us both protective gowns and gloves to go with our face masks. He'd done that before, though it wasn't standard procedure until after the pandemic. We'd always had to dress accordingly in Chicago, but in some ways, the South was loose on rules, though that had been changing.

He also wore a face shield and asked us to stand back from the table. He didn't have to say why. "First," he said, "I'll record what I see to describe the deceased." He held a small recorder in his hands. "The man is in his thirties or forties, appearing physically fit and well-maintained. His skin is lightly tanned and appears healthy. He is muscular, with visibly low body fat." He continued with his description and then looked at Nikki as he picked up his camera. "I'm documenting the external characteristics of the body, noting any visible injuries, tattoos, or identifying marks." The sound of a camera shutter clicked, capturing detailed photographs from different angles to create a visual record. "There are several locations on the body used to administer drugs." He pointed out each of the locations and checked them at the same time. "The inner elbow, in between the toes, the femoral artery, the inner thighs, the groin." He lifted each of Sean's feet. "The sole of a foot is a big indicator of long-term drug use." He laid Sean's left foot gently on the exam table. "I see no signs of pricks or marks in any of these locations." He ran his fingers down the insides of Sean's arms. "Collapsed veins and skin poppings are also common."

"Skin poppings?" Nikki asked.

"When a person injects a drug into the muscle instead of veins, lumps form beneath the tissue and become scar tissue, thus creating a bumpy texture on the outer layer of skin."

"Really?" Her eyes widened. "I had no idea."

"My cursory examination shows nothing to indicate a drug problem." He glanced at me. "Though that doesn't mean our victim didn't use drugs in another way." He dipped his head to Nikki. "Tell me what you see."

"Me?" she asked pointing to herself. "Okay. May I step forward?" She handled it like a pro. I was impressed.

"Of course," he said.

She approached Sean's remains and examined them closely, noting variations in skin color, moles, dry skin patches, and ultimately, the syringe mark. "Doctor, I noticed the needle mark appears to be at an angle. Can you see that? And I can't be sure, but could the cloth have been tied around his arm after the needle went in?"

He smiled at me and then at her. "Excellent observation, Nikki. It's uncommon for an untrained eye to see something so small, but you're correct. I may have to remove that section of skin to examine it more closely, but for now we'll see what we can find through the photos on the screen. As for the band, significant bruising and redness can appear before and after death, so there's no way of knowing when the band was tied around his biceps."

My jaw tensed. We needed something to show homicide or at least suspicious death to continue our investigation. Nikki finished her detailed examination and moved back to my side as Barron congratulated her on a job well done. I stood holding back tears knowing what was coming, and wishing I could have stopped it from having to happen.

"I won't complete the entire autopsy with you here. There are several elements I leave for when I'm without an audience, but you'll have the report."

"Yes," I said. "I understand."

"I expected you would. That was more for Nikki." He set the camera down and said, "Now I'll cut into the body." He dropped his head down and gazed at Nikki. "You ready for this?"

"Yes, sir."

I noted the sense of excitement in her tone. She really wanted to be there.

Gripping the scalpel tightly, with a swift, deliberate motion, Barron glided the blade through the flesh. I cringed as the serrated edge met resistance, which resulted in a chilling, high-pitched scrape that sent shivers down my spine. I must have gasped because Barron paused and asked if I was all right. When I said I was, he continued. Each incision brought forth unsettling whispers from Sean's remains, almost as if his body protested the intrusion. As it should have. Sean shouldn't have been dead, and his body knew that. The sound reverberated through the room, serving as a grim reminder of the fragility of life and the cold reality of death. A reminder none of us needed or wanted.

The sight of blood pooling in the incision and the familiar sound of squelching that accompanied each cut, accentuated by the release of a faint metallic smell penetrating from his remains, hit me like a brick. My stomach clenched.

"Now, I'm going to cut the ribs," Barron said. He nodded to Nikki. "How're you doing?"

"I'm fine, Doctor. Don't worry about me."

He carefully used a rib cutter to separate the ribs. The cutting created a visceral crack that echoed throughout the room. After he exposed the chest cavity, he placed his hands into Sean's remains and palpated the organs. The sound of squishing body parts and our muffled breathing filled the room.

My heart raced. I hated seeing Sean in that position. It wasn't the way

I wanted to remember him. I'd wanted the chance to apologize, but I'd always been too uncomfortable to make that move, to bother him when I knew he didn't want me around. Now, I'd never have that chance. It wasn't about me. I knew that, and I wasn't trying to make it that way. I just hated how things had ended and how they would stay that way forever.

"I'll remove the organs now," he said. He inspected each one meticulously for any signs of trauma or pathology. Sean's organs, slick with fluids, emitted a distinct odor I would never forget.

I swallowed back the bile racing up my throat. I'd always worked hard to block the emotional aspect associated with autopsies, knowing I had to be professional, and I'd succeeded many times. But it was impossible when the person on the table was someone I'd begun to care for at one time.

Barron took samples for toxicological analysis after examining the organs individually. He explained in detail every step for Nikki's benefit. "These samples will provide crucial information regarding the presence of drugs or other substances in the man's system."

"The organs look pretty healthy," she said.

"They do," he said.

I let out a breath. "What's your initial finding?" I asked.

He removed his gloves, threw them in a special garbage can, then pulled up the photos on the computer screen. "I'll say this. Based on my initial findings, Mr. Higgins shows no visible signs of drug abuse. His organs appear healthy, though that isn't always an indicator of drug use." He flipped to the photos of the needle mark and zoomed in on the first one as much as he could without the photo blurring. "This is hard to see, but yes, I do agree the needle likely entered the skin at an angle facing down. I'll have to try some things to determine if we're correct, however, that doesn't mean the deceased didn't do it himself." He peered in my direction. "I'm sorry."

"So, what are you saying? That he overdosed by his own hand?"

He sighed. "I'm saying I can't be sure. If the labs come back with any damage I can associate with previous drug use, I would consider it an overdose. However, even if we're right about the angle of the needle, I can't determine if it was accidental or intentional. If there's no signs of drug abuse, I also can't rule out the possibility that our gentleman here didn't overdose his first time using."

"Mike," I said. "Can you please tag it as a suspicious death for now?"

He cast a glance at Sean's body and then back to me. "You feel strongly he didn't do this himself?"

"Yes. According to his sister he had no history of drug use and was very happy to be a father. We've got Bubba looking into the financials so that can tell us more, but I can say with ninety-nine percent confidence Sean wouldn't do this." As someone who'd seen every level of drug abuse, I felt I had an expert opinion on the subject.

"As I said, it could have been accidental," Barron said.

"We have twenty-four hours to come up with evidence, and we will. Please. I need your support on this."

"Okay. For now, I'll mark it as suspicious, but I can't guarantee that won't change."

"Can you put a rush on the labs?" I asked. I rocked from my heels to my toes and back. "Please?"

He sighed. "You're digging me an early grave, Detective."

"I'd do the same thing if that was you on the table."

"I have no doubt."

I wrapped him into a bear hug. "Thanks, Doc! You're the best."

9

The team met in the investigation room back at the department.

Bishop had had an officer put together a file on Sean's death, including photographs, notes, and other necessary information. He handed them to each of us. "Our reports are almost complete," he said, "but since this investigation is on a clock, I suggest we take notes."

I sat beside him and snatched a bottle of water from a dozen someone had placed in the middle of the table. I guzzled it down, not realizing I was so thirsty. Bishop eyed me with a tug of humor pulling on the corners of his mouth. "What?" I asked. "I was thirsty."

"I can tell," he said.

"Is Nikki coming?" Levy asked.

"She's making copies of information from Sean's autopsy. Like Bishop said, we're on a clock here, so let's get started. I have some good news. Barron is ruling the death as suspicious, with the caveat that it may change."

Nikki walked in and sat on my other side. She handed papers to everyone. She gave me a head tilt. "Nothing comes up from the prints on the bassinet."

"Thanks," I said.

"What's Barron's decision based on?" Michels asked.

"A few factors," Nikki said. She turned toward me. "May I?"

I smiled. "Please."

She reiterated what Barron had said and ended with, "There's no way to determine if the victim injected the drugs into himself or if someone else did. His organs show no signs of visible drug use, but the labs will tell us more, and he's put a rush on them. We all know I couldn't find any prints other than on the syringe, and there was no other drug paraphernalia, so that doesn't work to our benefit." She exhaled. "I'm sorry."

"Don't be sorry," Bishop said. "You have no control over what the evidence says."

"It's just frustrating," she said.

"Understood," Levy said. "We talked to one employee, Billy Pruitt, who said he was with the victim at Rucker's last week and saw him arguing separately with two other ranch owners from town."

Michels added, "But he doesn't know their names. He hasn't worked for the ranch long."

"What were they arguing about?" I asked.

"He claims he wasn't close enough to hear them. He just saw how they acted toward each other."

"Do you believe him?" Bishop asked.

Levy interjected with a, "No," and Michels agreed.

"What about other employees?" Bishop asked.

"They're not talking," Levy said.

"No one is talking," Michels said. "Which means someone knows something."

"We'll hit them up again if we need to," Bishop said.

Bubba entered. He gave Bishop a nod. "I've got the ranch's financials. Based on a quick review, they're making bank." He handed out his information to each of us.

"Making bank?" Bishop asked.

Levy chuckled. Poor Bishop. He'd never speak young and hip speak. Every investigation increased his modern-day slang.

"It's making a lot of money," Bubba said.

"And you couldn't just say that?"

"I did," Bubba said. "The ranch is making bank."

"Okay," I said. "We'll have this English lesson later." I angled my body toward Bishop. "How are Connie and Jessica?"

"Connie's in shock. She reiterated that Sean didn't do drugs. She knew he was stressed about something, but he wouldn't tell her what."

"Did she have any thoughts on what it might be?" Levy asked.

"None," Bishop said.

"Great," I said. "What about Jessica?"

"According to Connie, her parents are with her. She said to give it a few hours and then go by."

"Okay," I said. "I'd like to go back to the ranch and talk with this Pruitt guy, see if we can get the truth out of him, then give the other employees another shot."

Michels jotted something down on his file folder. "I think we need to check out the other ranches. The equestrian community is small, and most of the employees have worked at each of them at one time or another. They might know something."

"Good idea," Bishop said. "Levy? You good to go?"

"Yep."

"Wait," I said. "Not Haverty Ranch. Given what's happened there recently, I'd like to be there when we hit them."

"Sure thing," Levy said.

"I'll do some digging on them," Bubba said. "Sometimes I hit the jackpot when I'm not looking for something in particular."

"I understand that phrase," Bishop said.

Bubba laughed. "I thought you would. It's one my parents use."

Michels and Levy burst into laughter. Nikki kept her head down in her folder, but the way it bobbed up and down gave her away.

"Ouch," I said. "That was painful."

Bishop held up his palms. "I can't win."

~

CONNIE HAD RETURNED to the ranch when we arrived. Her eyes were red and puffy, and she sniffled often, but she said there was work to be done, and she had to do it. "It's what Sean would do. I just wish I didn't have to do it in the place where he died."

My heart ached for her. Even though I wasn't close to my siblings, I knew it would hurt to lose one tragically. It wasn't that we didn't get along. We just didn't talk a whole lot. I envied siblings who were close. "Yes, he would have, but he would want to make sure you're okay."

"I'm fine," she said. "As fine as I can be. Have you found out anything?"

I glanced at the ceiling. There was evidence of a security or camera system, but no cameras. "Did you have surveillance cameras in here?"

"We did. Sean was in the middle of replacing them. He said the system we had was old. He wanted something that he could see live. He bought a new one, and had taken the old cameras down, but I guess he hadn't gotten around to putting the new ones up."

"Were they just in the buildings or in the barns too?"

"They're in everything with a roof and then some."

"Outside?"

"Along some of the fences, but like I said, he took them all down."

"Connie," Bishop said in a soft tone. "Your employee Billy Pruitt mentioned Sean having confrontations with two other ranch owners at Rucker's. Did he talk to you about that?"

She stared over my shoulder at the spot where her brother had died. "Not specifically, no, but of the three other ranches in town, he only liked one owner."

"Which one?" I asked.

"The new ones. I can't recall their names at the moment."

"Who are the other two?" Bishop asked.

"Mason Baxter and Bennett Cooper."

I didn't know them, but their names weren't normal small-town names, so I assumed they were transplants. I instantly pictured men in seersucker shorts, pastel polo shirts with the collars flipped, and sweaters tied around their shoulders. "Why didn't he like them?"

"Sean has problems with snobs."

"Don't we all," I muttered under my breath.

"We'd like to talk to Mr. Pruitt," Bishop said. "Is he still here?"

"He should be," she said. She unclipped a radio from her belt and spoke into it. "Billy, can you come to the office, please?"

A few seconds later, Billy replied. "On my way."

Billy Pruitt walked over a few minutes later wearing a pair of faded jeans that hung low on his hips that fit like a potato sack and revealed his tighty-whities. The way he wore his jeans was a disservice to the brand.

His jaw stiffened when he saw us.

Bishop pulled his blazer to the side and showed Pruitt his badge. Mine was attached to my belt next to my holster. I pointed at it as Bishop said, "We've got some more questions for you."

"You can go into the empty office on the right," Connie said.

"Thank you," I said.

After introducing ourselves, Bishop said, "Mr. Pruitt, you told Detectives' Levy and Michels you saw Mr. Higgins arguing with two other ranch owners at Rucker's, correct?"

"Yes, sir."

"Do you happen to know their names?"

"No, sir."

"Then how do you know they're ranch owners?" Bishop asked.

Pruitt's face reddened. "I've seen them around is all."

Bishop jotted notes into his small spiral pad. "How long have you worked here?"

"About a year."

"Is this your first ranch job?"

"No, sir. I—" he stopped.

Bishop didn't give him time to figure out the rest of that sentence. "You've worked for the other ranches, but you don't know the owner's names?"

He bit his bottom lip. "I don't want no trouble. I just want to do my job."

"We're not here to make trouble," I said. "We're here investigating the death of Sean Higgins."

"Yes, ma'am, but he overdosed on drugs. Why would the arguments matter?"

"Mr. Higgins's death has been ruled suspicious, so everything matters," Bishop said.

I almost saw the gears in Pruitt's head turning. "I got a good reputation with the ranches. I can't lose that."

"Understood," Bishop said.

He exhaled. "It's Mr. Baxter and Mr. Cooper."

"And what were they arguing about?" I asked.

"I can't say for sure. Mr. Higgins asked me to give them some room when they came over. You know, like he wanted to keep things private."

"So, you heard nothing?" Bishop asked.

"Bits and pieces, but nothing that made sense." He stared at Bishop. "You're going to make me tell you, aren't you?"

Bishop said, "Yes," in a firm tone.

"All I heard was Mr. Baxter say Mr. Higgins needed to mind his own business. Mr. Cooper talked too soft for me to hear, and I don't think he said a whole lot anyway."

"You said their body language appeared angry," Bishop said. "Can you give us some examples?"

"You know, Mr. Baxter getting in Mr. Higgins's face, jabbing him in the chest with his finger. Stuff like that."

"And Mr. Cooper?" I asked.

He shifted his weight from his left leg to his right. "He just kind of stood there with his arms across his chest. Come to think of it, he wasn't right up in it. He said something at first, and Mr. Baxter jabbed his finger at him. Then he stepped back like he was waiting for them to throw fists or something. He's the biggest of them all, so he probably could have handled them both, but he walked away too. Looked like he didn't want to be involved after all."

"Did Mr. Higgins say anything to you afterward?"

"No, ma'am, and I didn't let him know I was watching."

"Did you work for Mr. Baxter?"

"A few years ago, but not for long. I ended up at Mr. Cooper's right quick because he paid more."

"How was Mr. Baxter toward you when you worked for him?"

"Mr. Baxter doesn't talk to the ranch hands. He talks to the supervisor."

"Was Mr. Higgins that way as well?" I asked.

"No, ma'am. He doesn't have a supervisor. He's the boss. He and Miss Connie, I mean."

"And Mr. Cooper?" I asked.

"Don't really know him. I didn't work there long. Came here a few months after I started there."

"Why?" I asked.

"Better pay, and I liked Sean. He was good people."

"Did you see anything nefarious at either ranch while employed there?" Bishop asked.

Mr. Pruitt rubbed his chin. "Not at the ranches, but there's been rumors about the horses."

"What kind of rumors?" I asked.

"About horses being drugged for better performance and stuff."

"Stuff?" I asked. "What kind of stuff?"

"Can't say for sure. It was all kind of on the downlow, you know what I mean? I'd hear bits and pieces, but nothing clear enough to make whole."

"At which ranch was this supposedly happening?" I asked.

"I'm not sure, but Mr. Higgins is the only one that doesn't buy and sell horses anymore, so it wouldn't be this one."

"Do you know why he stopped?" Bishop asked.

"Buying and selling?" He shrugged. "Money, if I had to guess. Can't say for sure."

"What about Haverty Ranch?" I asked.

He glanced at the ground. "Not much to say. 'Round here the ranches are all the same. That one's a lot fancier than the rest, but that don't mean much to me."

"Did you ever notice anything with the horses?" Bishop asked. "Maybe something to indicate they were drugged as the rumors suggest?"

"Here? No, sir. Mr. Higgins would never do anything like that, but if I'm being honest, I wasn't exactly paying attention. My job isn't with the horses. Wasn't at the other ranches either. I handle repairs and stuff like that."

"Like security systems?" I asked.

"Yes, ma'am if they want it, I can do it."

"Have you done any for any of the ranches?"

"No, ma'am."

We thanked him for his time and answers and talked with Connie again.

"Can we talk to the other employees?" I asked.

"I sent them home for the day. Billy stayed because he didn't want me here alone. They'll all be back tomorrow."

That explained why the ranch seemed abandoned.

"We'd like to go through Sean's office then," Bishop said.

"I thought that young lady did that already?"

"She only checked for things that could be directly related to the crime scene." I didn't want to say other drug paraphernalia. "We'd like to look for items that might be related to his death."

"Oh, then yes, of course. You can go through the front counter too, but we don't keep anything important there."

"What about a safe or locked filing cabinets?" Bishop asked. "Do you have any of those on the property?"

"Sean's got a filing cabinet in his office, and we have a gun safe." She angled toward the back office. "Would you like me to show you?"

"Please," I said.

She pulled a drawer on the counter open and removed a small key taped to the bottom of it. "Sean keeps a key here for me just in case."

She led us into the back office. It wasn't much of an office but more of a break room. The space was small, but functional. Other than the refrigerator, the gun safe was the biggest thing in there.

Inside, taped and hanging from the top shelf, was a picture of the safe. "Is that an inventory of what's inside?" I asked.

"Yes. No one has access but Sean and I, but he thinks we should keep a record."

"Are they all registered?" Bishop asked.

"I'm not sure. Sean handles that kind of thing."

I hated for her that she still spoke of her brother in the present tense. It meant she'd not yet come to terms with her loss. Then again, did anyone ever really come to terms with the loss of a loved one?

Bishop ran through a quick check of the safe's inventory, then stepped aside while I snapped photos with my cell phone. Connie locked it back up and returned the key to the bottom side of the drawer. Afterward, she led us to Sean's office.

"Take whatever you need," she said. She looked at me, her eyes pleading desperately for something. Maybe understanding? "Sean doesn't do drugs. He doesn't do this to himself. Neither accidentally nor on purpose. Please, find his killer."

10

Sean's small, dimly lit office carried the faint scents of leather and wood. The combined scent mingled with the unmistakable aura of fear I felt always hung around after a crime. I stood in the doorway and studied the space.

"Are you going in?" Bishop asked.

I moved to the side. "Sorry." The word caught in my throat. "It's just weird being back here."

"We'll figure out what happened. Let's just work this like we have our other investigations. We'll get answers to the questions swirling around in that brain of yours right now."

"I know." I placed my hand gently on his shoulder. I wanted to thank him for being on my side, for believing Sean hadn't taken his own life on purpose or accidentally, but I couldn't get the words out without breaking down, and I couldn't break down. Not until we found his killer.

He gave me a slight nod and walked into the office.

I followed after, ignoring the unsteadiness in my gait and the lump in my throat. Photographs of Sean with horses and various people I didn't recognize hung in groupings on his walls. A series of images capturing him with horses in both posed and action shots caught my eye. The trophies and awards were a testament to his dedication and skill, symbols of the passion that had filled his life. Dressage, show jumping, endurance riding, passions I'd known so little about. I didn't recall the trophies from the few times I'd been in his office, but that didn't mean they hadn't been there.

Sean's wooden desk stood against the far wall. Though basic and dated, from the looks of its smooth and unblemished surface, it had been well cared for. Neatly stacked piles of papers with the occasional file folder scattered amidst them anchored the left side. Framed photos of his wife and baby, a stapler, and a cup holding pens and pencils sat on the right.

My eyes drifted to the filing cabinet standing sentry by the desk's side. Its drawers were meticulously labeled with the small labels from an old-fashioned label maker. Lenny, my former supervisor in Chicago and father figure, still had his label maker. I smiled as I pictured Sean rotating the letters on the circular tool to the ones he needed, then squeezing the handle. I found comfort in the tidiness of my home, and I wondered if he had found it in his office.

Bishop studied the shelf filled with trophies, awards, and medallions. "Did you know he competed in rodeos?"

It saddened me that I really didn't know much about him. "No."

"He was good." He examined each of the several trophies and then slipped a latex glove over his hand and removed one from the shelf. "All first place going back to when he was in junior high."

My lack of that knowledge hit like a punch to my chest. I kept my head focused on the task at hand, not the things I didn't know about him. I couldn't change that, and feeling guilty over something that wasn't meant to be would get me nowhere.

While Bishop took photos, I slipped on my own gloves and went to work on the papers on his desk. The piles contained a variety of documents: financial records, correspondence, and contracts related to the ranch, and information on horses for sale in various states, and articles printed off the internet. "Hey. Come look at these." I studied a grouping of papers held together with a paperclip. "They're all articles about horses for sale in Texas."

Bishop scanned the articles. "He was probably looking to buy from one of the ranches there."

I snapped photos of the articles. Bishop knew our task at hand, but I couldn't help reiterating it. "We need to find something. Any clue, any shred of evidence that could have led to his murder."

"I'll take the filing cabinet."

Halfway into the search I stepped out and asked Connie for a few empty boxes. "It will be easier to take his papers back to the department to have our team go through them." I noticed the hesitation wash over her face. "We'll record everything and make copies. We won't keep any of the originals without letting you know."

"Thank you. I don't know what he's got that I might need."

"I know. If you realize you need something, I'll make sure you get it."

"I don't even know what's there," she said and then left to gather boxes.

"How's she doing?" Bishop asked.

"Outside of her grief? She seems worried about the ranch. Sean managed more of it than I realized. Connie owned the place on her own when we first met."

"What changed?"

"I don't know, but I'm going to ask." And I did when she returned with the boxes.

"I found four," she said. "Will that be enough?"

"We'll make it work," Bishop said. He retrieved a box, and after photographing the interior of the filing cabinet drawers, began emptying its contents.

"Connie, when I first met Sean, he said you owned the ranch. When did that change?"

"About four years ago. I was struggling with the business side of it, and Sean offered to buy in and take it over. He ended up taking over most everything, but I didn't mind."

"Were you considering retiring?"

"I'm a long way from that, but I don't think I'll ever officially retire. We grew up around horses. As a kid, I competed in dressage, barrel racing, jumping, you name it. I love the ranch, but the business side of things has always been a struggle for me. I wanted to focus on training others and on riding in general. Sean has a master's in business from Georgia Tech. His knowledge turned the ranch around. We made more profit in the last four years than I ever did on my own or even when our parents owned it." She glanced at Bishop. "I've already told Detective Bishop how well I thought the ranch has been doing."

"We just need to understand how things work." I brought up the other ranch owners again as if I didn't know them. "What are the other ranch names?"

"The Haverty Ranch, Sweetwater Ranch, and Cooper Creek Stables."

"The two owners he didn't like, which ranches do they own?"

"Mason Baxter owns Haverty. Bennett Cooper owns Cooper Creek." She rubbed her forearms. "It's not that he didn't like Bennett Cooper. I don't think he knew him very well." She angled her body slightly away from me and touched her face. "There's a lot of competition between the ranches. Mason Baxter plays dirty. He has since he moved here a while back. Bennett Cooper has undercut boarding rates and dropped training prices to gain business. Sean said it's all cut-throat, which is why he handled it."

I removed my cell phone from my pocket and typed a text message to Levy and Michels reiterating what Connie said.

"Mason Baxter has been in town for about six years. Cooper Creek used to be Castleberry Ranch when it was owned by John Castleberry. His daughter Julia married Ben, and when John died, he gave the ranch to her husband who quickly changed the name. It was a big deal because it should have gone to Julia, but John didn't think women had the business sense to run a ranch."

I rolled my eyes. "Sounds like a winner."

"Just your typical old-fashioned Southern man. He's not from here. I think they met in college?"

· I glanced at Bishop. "And Sweetwater?" I asked.

"It was sold recently. A couple from Peachtree City bought it." She pressed her lips together as if that helped her think. "I never can remember their names. Ray and Rebecca, maybe? The last name is Grant, but I'm not sure about their first names. I haven't met them yet, but Sean said they were pleasant."

"What's your thoughts on Haverty Ranch?" I asked.

"You mean the ranch itself or the elitist snob that owns it?"

My lips curved into a grin. "Both."

"Mason Baxter is a piece of work. He's friends with the mayor and everyone on city council. Ran the rotary club for a year and plays golf with the governor. The guy's got influence and he knows it."

"Hence the elitist snob comment?" I asked.

"Exactly. He likes to toss it around whenever he can. I'm surprised you haven't run into him in some capacity."

"We may have and just didn't know," I said. "Did Sean ever mention any concerns about their horses or in general?"

"Not theirs, no, but he stopped buying and selling. He thought the quality of horses had decreased."

"Do you know where he bought horses from?" I asked.

"I don't. He switched states periodically, so I can't say where he was talking about."

"What about the other two ranches?"

"I have no idea," she said.

"About the Grants," I asked. "You said they moved here recently. Do you recall when?"

"A few months ago, I think." She sighed. "I'm not really sure. Like I said, I focus mostly on training and try not to pay attention to the other ranches." Her upper lip twitched. "I don't know what I'm going to do now."

"You'll figure it out," I said. It was the only thing to say even though it could end up untrue. "Have you heard anything about Haverty's horses dying from performance drugs?"

"I've heard of them dying, but not performance drugs. That's a common rumor that always circulates around ranches. One day it might be Haverty that's accused, and the next, ours. I don't think anything's ever come from those kinds of rumors, and I've learned to ignore them. Though the horse deaths do concern me."

"Did Sean ever mention a new rumor going around?"

She thought about it for a moment. "Not that I recall, but he might have heard something and just didn't tell me."

Bishop stood beside me. "Everything's boxed up." He raised his eyes to Connie. "We're doing everything we can to find out what happened to your brother. At this time, the coroner has only temporarily marked Sean's death as suspicious. That could change, so if you hear or learn anything, you need to tell us right away."

She wrapped her arms across her chest and rubbed her shoulders. "What does that mean? Suspicious?"

"Drug overdoses are complicated," he said. "It's almost impossible to tell if the drug was self-administered. The scene of death normally tells the story, but Sean's was unique."

"Why?"

"We can't share that with you just yet. It could create problems for us to continue investigating," he said.

"Sean's death appears self-inflicted," I said. "But the medical examiner said his organs show no signs of drug use. The problem with that is someone can take a drug once, accidentally overdose, and die."

She narrowed her eyes and stared out the office door. "But it wasn't that. I told you. Sean didn't do drugs."

"And that's what we're banking on," I said. "But we have to look at a combination of things. Interviews with people who knew Sean, the business and financial records, cell phone records, things that could point to Sean not doing this himself. Do you understand?"

She nodded. "What can I do?"

"Tell us anything that comes to mind. Even the smallest things can make a difference."

"Okay."

"And we need to talk to Jessica. Do you think she's capable now?"

"Her parents are very protective, but I'll call them and let them know you're coming."

"Please," I said.

Bishop said, "Get us a list of people who knew Sean well. Customers, friends, family members. Anyone who can vouch for his character."

"Whatever happened to innocent before proven guilty?" she asked.

"That's only for the suspect, not the victim," I said.

"That's pathetic. We have to prove my brother wasn't a drug user so you can prove he was murdered." She scrubbed her already red eyes. "I can't believe this is happening."

"I know," I said. "I can't either."

She looked at me and her face softened. "He always liked you. He just couldn't—"

I stopped her. "I know. I understood." I held her hand in mine. "Connie, I don't believe Sean did this, and I promise you, Bishop and I will do everything we can to find his killer."

She squeezed my hand. "I know. Let me call Jessica for you."

11

We called Levy and Michels on speaker phone on our way to Sean and Jessica's house. "Anything?" Bishop asked.

"We hit Sweetwater first," Michels said. "Owners are new. Ray and Rebecca Grant. Only been in town a few months. They'd heard about Sean. Said they were shocked it was an overdose."

I drummed my fingers on Bishop's window while staring at the scenery passing by. "Amazing how that's already making the rounds."

"Hamby's still a small town when it comes to gossip," Michels said. "But they also said they saw no signs of drug abuse from him in the few interactions they had."

"They weren't looking for them," I said. "Most people aren't."

"Right," Levy said. "But Ray's brother was an addict. Overdosed last year. He said nothing about Sean resembled his brother."

"Good to know," Bishop said.

"We'll hit the other ranch now," Levy said. "You still want us to wait on Haverty?"

"Yes, please," I said.

Bishop glanced over at me. "You think the horse deaths are connected?"

"Let's call it a hunch."

"Your hunches are a tough gamble. Fifty-fifty at best," he said.

"I wouldn't bet against her," Levy said.

Bishop explained what we'd learned about the two other ranches, which wasn't much, then said, "We're on our way to interview Jessica Higgins. We'll meet you back at the station."

"Sure thing," Levy said, and disconnected the call.

I stared out the window watching the trees zip by in a blur of varying shades of green. "He rescued a deaf pig named Bertha."

"Sean was a good man."

An invisible knot formed in my throat making it practically impossible to speak. I kept my eyes focused out the window, still trying to process what had happened, and why Sean hadn't come to me sooner.

"I know this must be hard for you."

I didn't need sympathy. I needed answers. Bishop was trying to console me, and I did appreciate it. I swiped my hand over my eyes. "It's fine. I don't know why I'm so emotional about this. I barely knew him. It shouldn't bother me this much."

"Why not?" He turned into Sean's community. "You were beginning to care for him when the shit hit the fan. It's okay to mourn someone regardless of how long or how well you knew them."

He was right, but investigations had no room for emotional drama. Anger, frustration, even fear, sure, but sadness and regret? No.

Sean's house surprised me. The three-story home, made of a blend of brick and stone, stood proudly on a spacious plot, showcasing a well-manicured front lawn that stretched out from the curb to a grand entrance flanked by decorative columns on the porch. The home's combination of classic and contemporary architectural style wasn't at all what I would have imagined for Sean, and it reinforced the fact that I didn't really know him. I expected rustic and classic, but instead was met with a well-maintained home with fresh paint and clean lines. Large, symmetrical windows adorned the front of the house. Even though partially covered with plantation shutters, I could tell they allowed ample natural light to filter into the interior. The lawn itself was lush and green and filled with meticulously maintained hedges and vibrant flower beds. Had he maintained the yard himself, or had he hired a landscaping company?

"Wow," Bishop said pulling into the driveway. "Not at all what I expected."

"Me neither."

A tall man dressed in black dress pants and a button-down shirt answered the door. "May I help you?"

Bishop and I showed him our badges at the same time, but he spoke first. "I'm Detective Bishop, and this is my partner, Detective Ryder. We're here to talk with Mrs. Higgins."

He scanned us from bottom to top as if to determine if we were a threat or to analyze the level of damage we could do if he let us in. "She's not ready to talk to anyone just yet."

"Sir, we're investigating the murder of her husband, and we have questions only she can answer," Bishop said. "Questions that could help us find his killer."

"Killer?" His face paled. "He overdosed on drugs."

"Mr. Higgins's death has been ruled suspicious," I said. "And our odds of finding the killer are greatly reduced the longer it takes to gather information."

"I'm her father. I can answer any questions you have."

"Great." We'd need to speak to him anyway. "How about you start with your name?"

"Roger Doyle. Now," he said after clearing his throat. "What do you need to know?"

Jessica appeared beside him. Her long hair was clipped into a bun at the top of her head though small wisps of it fell around her face. Dark circles framed her red, swollen eyes. She adjusted her oversized University of Georgia sweatshirt when she saw us. "Daddy, it's okay. I need to talk to them. I want to."

He studied her. "Are you sure you're up for it?"

The baby cried from inside. A woman said, "I've got her."

"Yes, I'm fine, or as fine as can be expected," Jessica said. "Please," she looked at us. "Come on in."

Like the outside, the interior of the home wasn't what I'd imagined for Sean. He was a combination of rugged and retro, often wearing collared, button-down shirts with cowboy boots. The house's interior, at least the first floor, was a massive open space, and room separation was more implied than real. The home had a minimalist, mid-century modern flair. The two styles felt miles apart to me.

My footsteps echoed on the hardwood floor then bounced off the walls. I took a moment to survey the space more closely, my gaze sweeping over the carefully curated artwork on the walls and the spotless surfaces of the furniture. It was a stark contrast to the vibrant chaos that had once surrounded Sean. A pang of discomfort rushed through my chest.

We followed Jessica into the kitchen area. Word did get out fast in a small town. Bouquets of flowers crowded a small table. Several had been left still in their protective plastic wrapping on the large bench seat near the kitchen table. The smell of freshly brewed coffee mingled with the subtle notes of wood polish. Vacuum lines in the floor rug looked fresh. Other than the flowers, the home was immaculate. Someone had recently cleaned. Whether they did it on some sort of schedule or to keep their mind busy, I wasn't sure. The place felt unfamiliar, almost sterile, like stepping into a different world.

"Would you like some coffee?" Jessica asked. "My mother just made a fresh pot."

"That would be great," I said. Her calm demeanor surprised me.

"Yes, please," Bishop said.

"Have a seat at the counter," she said. "I'm sorry about the flowers. They're everywhere. My brother is taking them to an assisted living center in Alpharetta today." She rubbed her nose with a tissue. "I'm not normally allergic, but with this many, I think anyone would be."

My nose itched at the mention of allergies. "I can imagine," I said. Truthfully, I could more than imagine. When Tommy was murdered, half of Chicago sent flowers. We lived on the second floor of a three story walk up, and our place was too small for all the bouquets. Also, I couldn't stand seeing them. Flowers couldn't make up for the loss of a loved one, and no matter how much sympathy they intended to convey, they only served as a reminder of death. I should have donated them, but without a clear head, and angry beyond scale, I'd chosen to smash them and their vases into tiny pieces in our back alley. No one could park back there for weeks. I still felt no remorse for that. It was the only way to manage my pain in those first moments after he'd died.

Jessica handed us coffees, her eyes becoming clouded with grief. That controlled emotion, the façade she'd created to pretend she was okay, had begun to slip away. She sat next to her father across from us at her breakfast bar.

"Mrs. Higgins, thank you for allowing us to speak with you," Bishop said, his voice steady and composed. "We understand that this is an incredibly difficult time for you, but we hope you can help shed some light on your husband's recent activities."

"Please call me Jessica."

"Jessica," I said. "I'm so sorry for your loss."

She sniffled. "I know you've been through this. Does it get any easier?"

"Losing someone?"

"Yes," she said, her voice suddenly raspy.

"Living without the person you love is never easy, but eventually you find a way to breathe again."

"Sean told me your history. How you two were dating."

"It wasn't anything official."

She smiled. "That's what he said. He respected you. He said he never wanted to lose me the way you lost your husband, and now here I am, figuratively speaking, on your side of the table." A tear ran down her cheek.

Those raw, familiar emotions welled up within me, threatening to spill over like a dam on the brink of collapse. My breath caught in my chest, a silent plea for control. I swallowed hard, and the lump in my throat grew more pronounced, as if it was a physical manifestation of the anguish I was attempting to contain.

She must have noticed me fighting to maintain my composure. "I'm sorry. I didn't mean to—"

"It's okay. Like I said, it's never easy."

Bishop took over while I let my heartbeat drop into the normal range again. "I know you said Sean seemed anxious and worried recently. Can you elaborate on that?"

Jessica's composure finally shattered. Her eyes brimmed with tears as she shook her head. She excused herself for a moment and returned with a box of tissue. "Like I said at the ranch, he had been worried about something, I could tell, but he tried to hide it around me. I only noticed because I know my husband. I know his moods, his facial expressions. I know it all." Tears streamed down her face, but she continued. "We talked about our plans for the future, and he seemed excited about them."

Mr. Doyle cleared his throat and interjected his thoughts with a touch of bitterness. "He had been stressed about his industry for the past few months. The horse selling world has become more corrupt over the years. Sean often talked about his concerns regarding the quality of horses being sold from other states. He couldn't stand to see the industry go down that path. He also wasn't happy with local ranches buying those horses. He felt it impacted the reputation of all the ranches in the area."

I took notes of Mr. Doyle's thoughts, but it wasn't enough to point to a specific suspect. "Did he say which ranch in particular he was talking about?"

Mr. Doyle's eyes shifted toward his daughter. When they returned back to mine, he glanced at the counter and just said, "I don't remember."

"Did Sean change his routine recently?" Bishop asked, his voice gentle yet persistent. "Did he go out more often, or alter his pattern in any way?"

"No. Sean had his routine, his work at the ranch, and time with our baby. He didn't deviate from it," she said. "He was very devoted to us. We were his priority, and I knew that. That's why he took the baby with him. I was tired, and he wanted to give me extra time to sleep."

The cries of her baby echoed from upstairs. "I've got her again," a woman yelled from upstairs as well.

"Thanks, Mom," Jessica replied. She exhaled. "Daddy's right. Sean was worried about the quality of horses coming into the state. He said a few had died recently, and he thought they might have been given performance drugs or something to make them sell for more at auction."

"Did he say he was worried about horses at his ranch?" Bishop asked.

"No. He hasn't bought any in a few years."

"Did he say which ranch?"

"No. He didn't really want to talk about it." She dabbed her nose with a tissue. "I'm sorry."

"Did he have good relationships with the other ranch owners?" I asked.

Even though Connie had told us her thoughts, it was important to ask again. Sean may have portrayed his relationships differently to each of them.

"They were friendly, but not friends." She twisted her head toward the countertop then raised it again. "You know, I actually don't know if that's the case. He never said he didn't like any of them, but when we'd run into them, he treated them more like acquaintances than anything. He didn't invite any of them to our wedding." She paused then said, "Oh, he did invite someone who works at one of them. Maybe Haverty Ranch? I can't remember. His name is Damian Sayers. They went to college together."

"He told me Damian was a good guy," Mr. Doyle said.

I jotted that down and asked, "Has he mentioned Damian lately?"

Jessica pressed her lips together, and finally said, "I don't think so, but I'm so busy with the baby, I don't know what day it is half the time."

She would know from that point on. She'd count them. I counted until day 792 and only stopped after Lenny said Tommy would be disappointed if I'd kept going. He'd been right about that, too. "Did Sean keep a journal or a datebook, or anything like that?"

"He has a calendar in his office. It's upstairs."

"I'll get it," her mother said. She stood at the landing holding the baby and listening. "Where in his office?"

"I'm not sure if he put it away. If it's not on his desk, just check the drawers."

"Would it be okay if we looked in his office?" I asked.

"I'm not sure that's a good idea," Mr. Doyle said.

"Daddy, Sean and I have nothing to hide."

He grumbled something inaudible then crossed his arms. "I'd like to be there while you do."

"Not a problem," Bishop said.

Mr. Doyle showed us to Sean's office. An hour later we'd gone through everything and found nothing we could even remotely link to Sean's murder. Including his calendar.

"Can't you just focus on finding Sean's killer and leave us alone?" Mr. Doyle asked quietly.

"We are focusing on finding his killer," Bishop said. "Part of that focus requires us to look into his recent past and, most importantly, the last few days of his life. Usually, there's something there that can point us in the right direction."

"Clearly, it's not here. I wish you'd just leave us alone."

"Mr. Doyle, don't you think your daughter wants us to do everything possible to find her husband's killer?" Bishop asked.

His nostrils flared. "It's not about what she wants. It's about what she needs."

"In my experience finding the killer and getting justice is exactly what someone in her position needs," I said. "It's the only way they can move on."

"She can move on without knowing. She has to. What if whoever did this comes after her? What if they kill my girl or my granddaughter?"

Bishop placed his small spiral notebook in his blazer's pocket. "Is there something you're not telling us? Something that makes you think your daughter is in danger?"

His eyes shifted between us. "I already told you all I know. I just want my family safe. My granddaughter can't lose both parents."

"Then let us do our job so we can make sure that doesn't happen," Bishop said.

"You can't prove Sean didn't overdose himself," he whispered.

"Not at this time," I said.

"What if he did? What if you're dragging all this out, upsetting my family, and forcing my daughter to hold onto some hope she may never get? Is that really the right thing to do? He died from a drug overdose. What does it matter how he got it?"

"Ask your daughter that," I said. Frustration seeped from my pores. "Ask her what matters most, finding the truth and possibly a killer, or moving on. If you don't know the answer to that, then I suspect you don't know your daughter very well at all."

Bishop sensed I was close to exploding and got us out of there with a quick goodbye.

"He knows something," I said.

"I agree," Bishops said. "I think we should try to talk to him on his own.

He might not want to say anything in front of his daughter." He pulled out of Sean's driveway.

"He's pushing us to drop this. He's worried for his family. He definitely knows something. I'll call him."

"Jessica seems to be holding it together better than I expected."

"It's shock and adrenaline. The reality will hit once those wear off. That's usually the day after the funeral."

"How are you doing with this?"

How many times was he going to ask me that? I appreciated his concern, but I needed to separate my personal emotions from the investigation, and I couldn't if he continued to harp on me. I drummed my fingers on my jeans. "I'm fine."

"You sure?"

I exhaled. "I'm sure. Is it sad? Of course. Do I have regrets about Sean? From a while back, sure. Though I do wish I could have gotten to the ranch earlier. I might have been able to save him."

"Don't go down that road. You'll only crash and burn."

"I live on that road."

"There's a lot of truth in that statement."

"Bishop, I need a favor."

"Sure."

"Stop asking me if I'm okay. I know you mean well, but I need to focus on a professional level, not a personal one, and each time you ask, it drops me back into the personal zone."

"Noted." He turned toward the department. "I need a coffee. We're going to have to update Jimmy, and we don't have much."

"If all else fails, I'll call Savannah. She'll find a way to keep the investigation going."

He cleared his throat. "I don't even want to know what that might be."

"No, you don't," I said smiling.

12

We headed into the conference room. The details of the dingy room around me burst from fuzzy gray to sharp, technicolor clarity. My mind raced. I couldn't explain it, but I knew it in my gut. Sean's murder was somehow connected to the dead horses. I jotted dead horses on my note pad and drew a circle around it. "I really think there's a connection between Sean and the dead horses at Haverty Ranch."

"I know," Bishop said. "And the possibility of performance drugs."

"It's the only thing that makes sense. Why else would he have information on ranches in Texas?"

"We have to consider the fact that he could have been doing it for other reasons. Maybe he was going to buy horses again? Maybe he was looking at moving? There could be a dozen or more reasons. That's not enough to claim he was investigating ranches, or anything related to performance drugs."

I chewed on my nail. "What if he was looking into where Baxter bought the horses that died?"

"Again, possible, but we need more than that."

"Then we'll find it."

Bubba walked in carrying one opened laptop on top of another closed one, his head down and fingers clicking at a miraculous speed on the opened one. "I've been doing research on the ranches in town."

"Great," I said as Nikki, Michels, Levy, and Jimmy all arrived together.

"What do we have?" Jimmy asked.

"Nothing from Cooper Ranch," Levy said. "The owner wasn't there, and they've blocked us from talking to anyone until he returns." She sat at the table.

"You'd think they'd see a badge and act accordingly," Bishop said.

"That was probably them acting according to their boss's demands," I said.

"I think so," Michels said. "They were pretty nice about it. Just said they needed their boss there."

Bishop gave everyone a coffee. "We're developing a concept."

"Oh, thanks," Nikki said as she took a Styrofoam cup from Bishop. "I need the late day jolt."

Michels held up his cup. "I'll drink to that."

"Sean's father-in-law doesn't want us looking into this," I said. "He's worried someone's going to come after his daughter."

"Did he say who?" Michels asked.

"Nope," Bishop said. "But he was intense. We think he knows more than he's saying."

I added, "Jessica said Sean had expressed concern about performance drugs, that maybe that was why the horses had died recently, but that's it."

"If that's the case," Bishop said. "Sean could have called out one of the owners, and that's what got him killed."

"Mason Baxter," I said. "He argued with him at the feed store."

"Cooper was there as well," Bishop said.

"Yes, but according to Billy Pruitt, he wasn't really a part of the argument," I said.

Bubba, pounding his fingers quickly onto one of his laptop keyboards, said, "I've found Haverty Ranch's online presence. From what I can see, their Facebook mainly showcases horses and their achievements. Oh, and a few horses for sale, but each is marked sold." He rotated his laptop for the rest of us to see. "I've gone through their posts, comments, and interactions, but there's nothing unusual or suspicious. It's all standard ranch-related content. Whoever runs the page seems genuinely passionate about the ranch and the horses."

"Who's the admin?" Nikki asked. "The admin manages the page and posts content," she said to Bishop.

I pressed my lips together to hide my smile. Bishop was ancient to people Nikki's age, and he solidified that thought in her with his lack of modern technical knowledge, especially when it came to social media platforms.

"I know what an administrator is," Bishop said.

"It's admin," I said as I smiled.

"Whatever. They're the ones who put pictures and news up. Cathy's got one of those page thingies for her book club. She's the person who does all that."

Nikki giggled and smiled at Bubba. "Who's the *administrator* of the page?"

Bubba grinned. "Emma Baxter. I checked her page as well. She's seventeen, so I'm assuming she's the owner's kid."

"What about Sean's ranch? Do they have a page too?" I asked.

He spun the laptop back toward him, tapped at a rapid speed and turned it back to us. "It's not too current. Looks like the last post was about six months ago."

"Who's their admin?" Nikki asked.

"Jessica Higgins."

"Their baby is about six months old," I said. "She probably stopped updating the page once she was born."

"Check out Cooper Creek Ranch, and Sweetwater Ranch on that thingamajig," Bishop said to Bubba.

"Thingamajig?" Bubba asked.

Bishop pointed to the laptop. "The Facebook thing."

"Oh, right. Let me pull up their pages." He scooted his chair an inch or two in front of the second laptop. His fingers danced over the keys until he said, "Cooper Creek Ranch and Sweetwater Ranch have quite active social media presences. Their pages are filled with pictures of their horses, competitions they've participated in, and some horses for sale as well. So, yeah. The same as Haverty Ranch."

"Is there any mention of interactions or competitions between Sean's ranch and the other three?" I asked.

Bubba scrolled through their pages. "I don't see any direct interactions between the ranches. Wait. I forgot about this. I did find a few posts where some individuals have mentioned visiting multiple ranches, including Sean's, for different events or competitions. It seems like horse enthusiasts go to multiple ranches in the area."

"That makes sense," I said.

Bishop asked, "Did anyone mention horses dying?"

His eyes traveled over the screen as fast as he typed. "Not that I see."

I hated to think it, but mentioning a horse's death would help us get approval for the investigation. I eyed Jimmy, trying to read his micro expressions, but his face lacked any emotion. "Jimmy, we need to move forward without the worry of whether we'll have an investigation or not."

He dragged his hand down his face. "I've already spoken to the assistant district attorney. His first question was if we thought Sean's murder involved horse racing. He believes it's a hot ticket, so let's roll with it. But follow up with the father-in-law. If he knows something, we need to know what it is."

Nikki, Bubba, and Jimmy left, but the other four of us spent three hours going through Sean's financial records, work files, and what we knew, which wasn't much.

"There's nothing in any of this," I said. "If he knew something, he didn't write it down." I closed the last box. "I'll have an officer drop them back at the ranch and Sean's home."

"It's got to be a drugging thing," Levy said. "When does the blood test come back from the autopsy?"

I tapped my pencil on the desk. "Barron's got a rush on it. That's all I know."

"That Damian Sayers. I'll run the name," she said. "See if I can get an address."

"Please do," I said. I checked my watch. "It's late. Let's get a fresh start first thing in the morning."

"Sounds good," Michels said.

"You call Mr. Doyle tonight?" Bishop asked.

"I'll get his cell from Connie on my way home."

Levy stood and stretched. "I'm going for a run. I need blood flowing to my legs again."

"Not me," Michels said. "Ashley's forcing me to help her pick out a China pattern."

Levy busted out laughing. "People still do that?"

Michels and Ashley were in the middle of planning their shebang. I felt for him. And her.

"Southern weddings are very traditional," Michels said. "Ashley's born and raised in the South. Her mother is driving me crazy with this wedding stuff."

"Watch how you refer to it," Levy said.

I chuckled. "She's right. The wrath of the mother-in-law is real, and calling it wedding stuff in front of Ashley is a road you don't want to drive."

Michels looked to Bishop for support. Bishop held up his hands. "They're right. As for the China, I picked out ours. I picked out the ugliest pattern I could find. The ex got it in the divorce."

13

I gave Connie what little update I could. It wasn't much, but she wrapped it back to questions I'd previously asked her. "You think this has to do with the horses that died recently? The ones at Haverty Ranch?"

"We're still looking into it," I said. "Do you have Jessica's father's cell phone number by any chance?"

"Actually, I do. I'll text it to you."

"Great," I said. "Thanks."

I received it immediately and called him but had to leave a voicemail. "Mr. Doyle, this is Detective Rachel Ryder with the Hamby PD. I've got some additional questions for you. Could you please call me back?" I left my number and then called Kyle. "You hungry?"

"I've got Vietnamese from Pho and Go waiting."

My mouth watered. "You're incredible."

"I know," he said laughing. "Women tell me that daily. Mostly when I'm at the grocery store."

"I'm sure the ones in the produce aisle swoon over you."

"It's embarrassing."

I laughed. I didn't doubt they were swooning over him, but I doubted Kyle noticed. The man was clueless. He was always alert and aware, but to possible threats, not attractive women nearly fainting in his presence. "I'll be there in ten."

My cell phone rang about five minutes from home. I checked the caller ID. It was Tony Garcia, my former partner in Chicago. We hadn't talked in ages, so I happily answered the call. "Hey Tony G. What's up?" I smiled at the memory of hearing that greeting from just about every gang member in our district. They loved Anthony. Having come from the streets, he knew how to relate to them, and he always gave them a second chance. Most didn't deserve it, but the few who did were worth the effort on his part. His reputation worked to endear the community to me as well. Those gang members had saved my butt more than once.

"Hadn't talked in a while, thought I'd catch up."

"I'm working a murder. It's a tough one."

"A kid?" Garcia asked.

I climbed out of my Jeep. "Someone I used to know."

"Damn, that sucks."

"Yep. What's up at the department? The guys still miss me?"

"I wouldn't know," he said. "I quit about a month ago."

I closed the garage door as Kyle opened the door into our place. I smiled and held up a finger. "You're kidding, right?"

"Nope."

"Wait a minute. There's no way you quit. You got canned. Admit it."

"Talk to Lenny. He'll tell you. I'm tired of the BS. Everyone in the damn city is a crook, including two thirds of the department, at least on the management side."

"That's nothing new."

"I guess I got tired of it."

"What're you going to do now?"

"I just got my private investigator's license. Work is slow, but it'll pick up. Mostly insurance claims. Catching fakers pretending they're injured. That kind of thing."

"So, basically, you're bored to death."

"Out of my mind."

I laughed. "That's bad. Maybe you should work for the state or something?"

He groaned. "Not going to happen. I'm over working for the man. It's time I do my own thing. I'll figure it out. Just need to find my niche."

"Let me know when you do," I said.

"Sure thing. I got to run. Keep in touch, you hear?"

"Yes, sir," I said. I walked inside reeling from the fact that my previous partner had walked away from a solid pension and years' worth of training and experience just to hunt down insurance fraud cases.

Kyle had set our dinner up on the trunk we used as a coffee table. I quickly checked on Louie, my beta fish. He cared nothing about my big face stuck against his glass house, but I was ecstatic to see him swimming around as always. "Did you feed him?" I asked Kyle.

"Always do. Now, come eat. You look hangry."

"Borderline," I said. "Bishop's given up everything good because of this stupid health kick. Yesterday he brought tuna salad for lunch, and it didn't have any mustard or mayo in it."

Kyle gasped sarcastically. "No condiments? That's a travesty. What the hell was he thinking?"

I sat next to him and whacked his arm. "Condiments are what make tuna edible. By the way, that was Tony on the phone. He quit the force."

"Garcia? In Chicago?"

I stuffed my mouth with noodles and nodded. "He said he's sick of working for the man. He's got his PI license." I squeezed my chopsticks over another bunch of noodles, dropped half, then shoved the rest into my mouth. "Maybe I should do that too. Just in case."

"Just in case what? You get suspended again?"

"Technically, I wasn't suspended, but yes, that, or fired. In case you didn't know, I've got a bit of a temper."

"You? A temper? I had no idea?" Kyle teased. He winked. "So, what's he working? Cheating spouses or insurance fraud?"

"Insurance fraud."

"Poor guy. He'll hook up with another department soon. There's only so many fraud cases a guy like him can handle before he misses the real action. Speaking of real action, I've been looking into horse ranches and the DEA a little more."

I pointed my chopsticks at him. "You're supposed to be recovering."

"I'm recovered and bored off my ass. Anyway, a while back, I'm talking five years probably, the DEA investigated the cartel smuggling drugs into the states through horses."

I put my chopsticks down. "Really? Where?"

"They were routed from Mexico to Kentucky, but I'd have to research the files to get the details."

"Can you do that while on leave?"

He pointed to the dining room table where his laptop sat. "Shouldn't be a problem."

"What about other states? Can you check for any hits on those?"

"I can try."

I scooped up more noodles, shoved them into my mouth and spoke. I had manners. They were just relaxed at home. "You think it's possible this Haverty Ranch is working as some kind of mule?"

"More like probable."

I chewed on that for a while as I finished dinner. "Racehorses wouldn't be used to smuggle drugs would they? Everything about them is probably on record?"

"I assume so, but I wasn't involved, so I can't say for sure," he said.

"Got it. Thanks. This is good information."

"That's what I'm here for. Great sex and equally great information." He winked.

"Oh, did I say great? I thought I said good." I returned his wink.

"Ouch."

I leaned over and kissed him. "Amazing. Incredible," I kissed him again, "soul screaming." I leaned my forehead against his. "Are those better word choices?"

"Only if you're talking about the sex."

"I'm definitely talking about the sex."

I MET BISHOP AT DUNKIN' at six o'clock the next morning.

He yawned as he climbed into my Jeep. "What in the God forsaken hell happened to your Jeep?" He peered down at the mail and empty Taco Bell bags piled below his feet.

"It's Kyle's trash mail. I picked it up at the post office the other day."

"Taco Bell is mailing Kyle?"

"Those are mine."

"We haven't had Taco Bell in a while."

"I didn't say they were recent."

He grimaced. "That's disgusting, Ryder." He cracked his window. "God only knows what kind of bacteria we're sucking into our lungs right now."

"It's mail and empty food bags. They're not going to infect us with some deadly bacteria."

He bent down, scooted it into a pile and picked it up. "Can I toss it?"

I held my palm up toward the garbage can outside the coffee and donut shop's door. "If you must."

A few seconds later, and with a toothy grin, he asked, "Why did you want to meet here before we're on the clock?"

"I want to get to Haverty Ranch to talk with the employees before the owner shows up."

"Got it."

"Kyle said the DEA busted a smuggling operation about five years back. The cartel was using horses to smuggle drugs."

"Looks like we're on the right track."

"He's not sure if they were racing horses, but those have documents up the hoo-ha. I can't imagine the cartel would take that big of a risk."

"I doubt they would. They're probably stealing horses and using them." He rubbed his forearm.

I hate that idea. He rubbed his arm again. I eyed him suspiciously. "What's wrong?"

"My trainer says I'm gripping the dumbbells too tight and it's causing bursitis in my elbow and tendonitis in my arm."

I had no idea how to respond to that. "Getting old's a bitch."

"Your time will come. It's getting closer every day."

"Trust me, I can tell. Anyway, the bust was in Kentucky, but he's going to see if he can dig up anything from other states."

"Kyle had mentioned drug trafficking earlier, so maybe we're wrong about what Sean thought might be happening. Maybe this isn't about performance drugs but about human ones."

"I think you're right," I said.

14

"Dang," Bishop said. "Levy was right. This place is the mac daddy of horse ranches."

An aura of wealth and snobbery enveloped me as I drove through the imposing iron gates of Haverty Ranch. The sprawling landscape stretched before us, bathed in the warm glow of the sun rising. I'd had my windows down, and the scent of freshly cut grass mingled with the earthy musk of horses. Coupled with the stature of the ranch, the scene instantly transported me into the world of privilege and power so prominent in Hamby. "This is like the beginning scene of a movie."

"It feels that way," Bishop said.

The ranch was two hundred acres of expansive land unfolding like a patchwork quilt of green meadows and rolling hills. Towering oak trees, their leaves rustling in the gentle breeze, cast dancing shadows upon the ground.

To the left of the gravel road, a magnificent red barn stood proudly, its fresh paint not even close to hinting at years of history and tradition. As I stepped out of my Jeep, the faint scent of aged wood and hay tickled my nose. Tommy would have melted like a stick of butter from the beauty of the place. We'd planned to retire to a small, Southern town where we could have land and horses, and live a quieter life than what he'd been living in

Chicago. After his murder, I did my best to honor that dream by moving to the smaller town in Georgia and learning to ride. I wasn't quite ready to retire, but someday I would, and I hoped I'd be able to honor the rest of the dream. I cleared my mind of memories and focused on the task at hand. "Let's take a look at the stable before talking to anyone," I said. "I want to check out the horses."

"If you'd have told me where we were going, I would have brought some apples," Bishop said.

"Next time."

A row of stables lined the perimeter attached to the barn. A hint of horse smells replaced the aged wood and hay scents. The horses, their sleek coats glistening, peered at us curiously from the comfort of their stalls. Their gentle nickers echoed through the air, a symphony of equine grace that tugged at my heartstrings. While I'd once been intimidated by the monstrous creatures, I'd grown to appreciate their beauty and, more so, their intelligence. Give them time to trust you, and you'll make a friend for life.

I'd been riding more but paused shortly after Kyle's incident. I had intended to keep it up, but I wanted the time with Kyle at home instead. I'd even begun to consider myself somewhat experienced, but that had probably flown out the window already. Kyle said my excitement to ride made him want to ride again as well. He'd grown up riding, but he was still in recovery, and I wasn't quite ready to share that experience with anyone other than with my memories of Tommy.

We snuck out of the barn when one of the workers walked past.

"I thought we were going to talk to them?" Bishop asked.

"We are. Just not yet. I want a lay of the land first. Look for cameras and anything that strikes you as odd."

"Already on it," he said.

Farther ahead, the training paddock dominated the landscape, an expansive arena framed by sturdy wooden fences. The dirt and sand beneath my Doc Martens shifted softly as I walked. A young girl stood against the fence watching three horses trotting in the ring. I smiled from the rhythmic thud of hooves hitting the ground. "Wow. They're stunning, aren't they?"

Bishop admired them. "They are."

"Are you here for lessons?" The girl who'd been with the horses appeared behind me. I internally chastised myself for being so focused on the horses I didn't see her walk toward us. I'd chastise Bishop for the same thing later.

"Oh," I said with a genuine smile. "No. Are you Emma Baxter?"

She studied me carefully. "Yes?"

"I'm Detective Ryder and this is my partner, Detective Bishop."

Emma Baxter was a rider. It was obvious from her strong legs and sturdy upper body. She wore her long blond hair in a ponytail and was makeup free. Before talking, she made a point of pushing her shoulders back and jutting out her chin, both signs that she was nervous. "The ranch manager isn't in yet. If you'll tell me what you're here for I'll let him know when he comes and he can call you."

"Actually," I said. "We're here to talk to the staff. Would that be possible?" I made a point of keeping my tone light and friendly. I didn't want to scare the girl.

"About what?"

Bishop jumped in. "We're just following up with the call a while back regarding the deceased horses. Just need to clean up our notes and confirm a few things to close out the case."

She furrowed her brow. "It was so sad. Daddy says the horses had some kind of heart problem."

"Where does he purchase his horses?" I asked.

"I'm not sure. I think somewhere in Texas, but I don't know where. The ranch manager would know." She checked her watch. It was a large Apple watch with a thick leather band that made her wrist look tiny. "He'll be here in about an hour."

"Would you be willing to show us around and introduce us to some of the employees so we can follow up with our questions?" Bishop asked.

"Yeah, sure. There's only a few guys here right now. The rest come in at eight."

"What about Damian Sayers? Will he be here today?" I asked.

"He's already here. I can take you to him if you'd like. I'm sure he'd be happy to show you around."

I smiled. "That would be great, thanks."

Damian Sayers was built like a horse, and that wasn't an exaggeration. He also knew exactly why we were there.

"Sean didn't do drugs," he said the minute Emma Baxter walked away. "That's why you're here, right? Because of Sean?" He was in the middle of saddling a horse, and as he adjusted the straps, his hands moved with practiced ease, the leather creaking softly under his touch. It was clear that he had spent countless hours tending to the magnificent animals.

"How well did you know him?" I asked.

He reached into a bucket of hay and scooped up a handful, extending it towards the horse. The animal eagerly nudged his palm. "Well enough. I've known him for over, I don't know twenty years. That's how I know he didn't overdose. He never even smoked pot, so I know he wouldn't shoot something into his arm. That just wasn't him." He wiped his brow with the back of his hand, leaving a smudge of dirt on his forehead.

"Had you talked to him before his death?" Bishop asked.

I couldn't help but notice the subtle nuances of his interactions with the horse he had saddled. He never stopped caring for the creature, reaching out to stroke its neck, his fingers gently caressing the sleek coat while he listened to us talk or answered our questions.

He hesitated before answering. "A few days ago," he said. His hand slid gently across the horse's coat again. He patted him on the side. "Good boy, Racer. You're a good boy." He handed him another bite of hay. "He came by to talk to me about something, but I was busy, and he couldn't get me alone. He was supposed to call me that night, but I didn't hear from him."

"Did he say what he wanted to talk to you about?" I asked.

Pausing momentarily, he walked to a nearby stall and retrieved a soft brush. Returning to the horse's side, he began grooming around the saddle. It felt like more of an afterthought, or something to keep him busy while he answered our questions. I still didn't know much about horses, but I didn't think brushing them with the saddle on was normal.

"No, but I know what it was. He was upset about the horses dying. Sean was pretty knowledgeable about horse health, and he didn't believe they died from a hereditary heart problem. He thought something else was going on."

"Did he tell you what that was?" Bishop asked.

"No, sir."

My cell phone dinged with the standard text sound which meant I didn't have the number in my contacts. I checked it quickly. It was from Roger Doyle.

Please let me take care of my family. I don't want to be involved in this.

I quickly responded with, *We just have a few more questions. It won't take long,* and waited for a reply, but it never came.

"Do you also think something else is going on?" Bishop asked.

Damian Sayers glanced at the edge of the stable wall. My eyes followed his to the security camera. Maybe he didn't want to answer the question because we were being recorded.

"Emma said you'd be willing to show us around. Would you mind? I'm a new rider and would love to see the ranch."

"Not a problem," he said. "Come on, I'll take you over to the ring. Emma's working with a few of our newer horses." He sauntered over to a bucket, grabbed a handful of carrots, and handed them to the horse. "I'll be back, buddy. We'll go for a ride."

Only, we didn't make it to the ring. Mason Baxter, the ranch owner, showed up outside the stables. Connie had been right. He looked like a snob. He was probably in his mid-forties and exuded an air of confidence and refinement that showed signs of the Northeast. His concentrated, almost practiced movements to adjust his stance said it had been meticulously cultivated to cement that impression. His impeccably tailored clothing was a perfect blend of modern sophistication and classic rich man like clothing sold at L.L. Bean and Ralph Lauren. He wore a crisp, pastel, blue-colored shirt that showed off his broad shoulders and accentuated his athletic build, while neatly pressed chinos hugged his trim waist. His polished leather loafers looked brand new. He was not at all dressed for a day at the ranch. I glanced at his fingers. Not a speckle of anything dark under his nails. Baxter never worked on the ranch himself. He'd probably never touched dirt once in his life. Me? I ate the stuff when I was a kid.

"Damian, I see we've got guests," he said with a smarmy smile aimed as Bishop and me. "You've got work to do. I'm happy to talk with them."

"Sure thing, Mr. Baxter." Damian gave us a nod, but his eyes said he wasn't happy. I made a mental note to have Bubba get his contact information.

Emma had probably let her father know we were there. His showing up immediately didn't win him any points, though he didn't have many to win in the first place. "Mr. Baxter," I said. "I'm Detective Ryder and this is Detective Bishop. We're looking for information on Sean Higgins."

Mason Baxter sighed. "Sad news. I didn't know Sean well, but I knew he'd had some struggles as of late."

Lie number one.

"What kind of struggles?" Bishop asked.

Baxter studied me, the right side of his upper lip raised a bit. Maybe he didn't like my blue jeans and long-sleeved Hamby PD shirt? Or maybe it was my Doc Martens? Either way, I didn't care. I flashed him a toothy grin while he answered.

"Well, drugs, I assume. That's what killed him, after all." He crouched down and dusted the dirt off his shoes.

Good luck with that buddy. It's a horse ranch. Should have changed before you came to check on us.

"There's been no cause of death determined at this time," I said. Barron had said it was drugs that killed Sean, and that had been made public, but an overdose hadn't, and no one had said that to Sean's family. We'd secured the crime scene well enough to keep anybody from seeing Sean, so unless an officer leaked the information, which was possible, there's no way Baxter would have known what killed him.

Damn. His buddy, the mayor. My heart rate soared into the anaerobic zone. If the mayor and this man were out trash-talking Sean around town, we'd have a problem. No, they'd have a problem. I wasn't a fan of the mayor. In my opinion he made more trouble than he was worth.

"You said you're aware of a history of drug use with Mr. Higgins?" Bishop asked. "What do you know about that?"

He exhaled. "I don't like to talk about people negatively."

There was a "but" coming.

"But there's been some talk. Perhaps that's why he's stopped buying horses? I understand he was telling people he doesn't like the quality available, but I've not had any trouble."

"Except for the ones who've died," I said.

"Those had genetic issues. It happens."

"So, you never saw him doing drugs?" Bishop asked.

"Did he ever do them around me? No, of course not, but I did see him high multiple times. In fact, he recently approached me at Rucker's. I saw the glazed over eyes and knew something was up. When he started an argument, I did my best to keep him at arm's length."

"What was the argument about?" I asked.

"Sean wasn't a fan of competition. As I said, he hadn't bought horses in some time, and I think he was upset that I've invested in quality ones. Our training business has picked up. We've got the horse racing community locked in, and our reputation is stellar. It's hard to compete with a ranch of our stature, so combine that with drugs, and you've got someone destined for suicide."

I clenched my fists. Did he think we were idiots? There was no way he could buy horses to sell for racing. Not unless he was faking the paperwork, which was complicated but possible. Stiff and regulated procedures had been created for racehorses because so many scammers had sold horses not cut out for racing.

Bishop cleared his throat, likely knowing I was about to lose it. "As my partner said, there's been no cause of death determined for Mr. Higgins at this time. We're doing our due diligence to assist the medical examiner with his final determination."

"Maybe I used the wrong term. Accidental overdose, perhaps?" He looked behind me. "Didn't he overdose on something laced with fentanyl?"

We hadn't received any information on the drug from Barron yet. "It can take weeks, even months, for blood tests to come back," I said. "Where did you hear that?"

He blinked. "One of my guys mentioned it. Ranching is a tight community. The employees are all connected. As I said, I guess it could have been an accidental overdose, which I'm assuming in your line of work is different than suicide. Either way, drugs killed him. If you're asking me if anyone here might have been the one to sell him the drugs," he shook his head. "I'd say no. I run a tight ship, and I don't have time for drugs or drug users." His eyes shifted to Bishop. He smiled, then moved his smile in my direction.

"Now, if you'll excuse me, I've got to get to a meeting in the city in an hour, and you know how traffic is around here." He pointed to my Jeep. "You can go out the same way you came in."

"Hold up," I said. "Which one of the guys told you Sean's death was fentanyl related?"

He blinked. "I can't remember, but that's the thing these days, right? Lacing everything with fentanyl?" He turned to leave.

"Mr. Baxter," I said. "One more thing. Is it possible drugs killed your horses?"

He pivoted back to us, his cocky smile replaced by a frown. "Drugs? Are you implying I drugged my horses?"

"I'm not implying anything."

"It's not possible. Not in the least, detective."

"His daughter called him," I said to Bishop in my vehicle. I squeezed the steering wheel tightly, making my knuckles turn white. "Everything he said was a lie. He knows what happened to Sean. I'll bet he talked to his buddy the mayor, found out it was a drug overdose, and spread it around like wildfire. I swear, if Sean's blood tests come back with fentanyl, we're bringing Baxter in."

Bishop connected his seatbelt, let it snap back toward him, and then pulled on it to loosen it. "Agree."

"We need to call Barron and get a rush on those tests. I think we just found our murder suspect."

15

"Xylazine," Barron said.

"What is xylazine?" I asked.

"An animal tranquilizer," Bishop responded.

"Damn," Bubba said.

"He's right," Barron said over the phone. "But that's not it." There was a slight pause, as if he was carefully choosing his words. "The blood analysis showed a combination of fentanyl and the Xylazine, commonly referred to as tranq dope, in Mr. Higgins's system."

Levy and I made eye contact. She tilted her head down and raised her eyebrows. She knew what I knew. Sean didn't inject that cocktail into his arm, at least not willingly.

"That son of a bitch," I mumbled under my breath. Baxter played the wrong card. What was he thinking? Was he so arrogant he thought he could get away with it? He would go down for Sean's murder. I'd make sure of it.

"Is this common?" Levy asked.

"More so than before," Barron said. "The government now considers it an emerging drug threat and a public health crisis."

I whispered to Bishop, "How did I not know this?"

"It's not well publicized," he said. "I'm sure Kyle knows about it."

"It's been shoved under the rug for some time," Barron said. "But given the importance of xylazine for veterinarians, it's next to impossible to list it as a controlled substance."

"Would that even matter?" I asked. "Given even a small amount of fentanyl is enough to kill someone."

"Yes, however overdosing on xylazine also leads to death."

"So, which killed him?" Bishop asked.

"He had 9.1 milliliters of fentanyl in his system. That's almost twice the lethal dose," Barron said.

I was going to end up on high blood pressure medicine if I didn't calm myself. I took a deep breath and released it slowly. "Sean wouldn't knowingly inject that crap into his system."

"I can't say one way or another. That being said, given this and other factors, I'm not comfortable marking him as an accidental overdose just yet. I think it's worth more investigation on your part," Barron said.

My shoulders relaxed. Jimmy was also in the room and heard it straight from the doctor's mouth. "What other factors?" he asked.

I knew what he wanted to say. Me. Because I believed Sean wouldn't do that, and neither did his family, but that wouldn't be enough for Jimmy.

"Nothing in his test results indicates Mr. Higgins had a history of drug use. As we discussed at the autopsy, his organs all looked healthy, and as I expected, they showed nothing life-threatening on any reports. In all aspects, he appeared to be a healthy man in his thirties."

"People die from fentanyl every day," Jimmy said. "They think they're buying painkillers on the street, but they're straight fentanyl."

"Sean didn't buy pills off the street. Someone shot them into his blood," I said.

"We can't prove Sean didn't do this himself," Jimmy said. "Accidental overdose." He rubbed his temples. "We need evidence that can, without any doubt, prove this was murder, or we'll have our asses handed to us on a platter by the district attorney's office."

"You said the assistant DA wanted to move forward," Bishop said.

"Because he thought horses were being pumped with performance drugs, and now you think that's not the case. I can't sell this to the DA's office, and you can't either. I'm sorry."

"Just a few more days," I pleaded. "Please, Jimmy. We know Baxter is rolled up in this somehow. Just give us time to figure it out."

He exhaled then said, "Thanks, Doc. We appreciate the information."

Barron said he'd send the report via email, and we ended the call. Jimmy closed his eyes. "A couple days. If you don't have something by then, we're done."

I placed my elbows on the investigation table and pressed my palms into my forehead. I needed a minute to let that all sink in, to process it and connect the dots, if that was even possible.

Bubba tapped away on his laptop. "Xylazine can cause reduced heart rate and blood pressure in horses." He jabbed his keys faster. "And respiratory depression. If given too much, the horse's heart can stop."

Bishop's fingers traced an imaginary pattern on the table. "And look like heart disease."

Levy, sitting opposite Bishop, absentmindedly fiddled with a paper clip, twisting it between her fingers.

I clenched and unclenched my fist. "What if Haverty's horses were being used to smuggle fentanyl into the states, and the tranq drug was used during surgery to remove them?"

"Damn," Michels exclaimed, his hands gripping the edges of the table. "Or somehow the fentanyl got into their system?"

"What are they doing? Forcing the horses to ingest bags of the stuff?" Bishop asked.

"We can find out," I said.

Levy, still toying with the paperclip, raised an eyebrow. "Sean expressed concern about the quality of horses of late, so Rachel's theory is valid. It's possible they were being used to smuggle fentanyl from Mexico into the states."

Michels, his hands now resting on the table, nodded in agreement. "Right. They drop off the horses in Texas, eliminate any traces of drugs, and then sell them off to unsuspecting ranchers like Baxter."

"Or," Levy said. "They're not sold off, just transported to other states where the rancher or someone on the ranch retrieves the drugs and distributes them to the cartel but doesn't care about the horses after the job's complete."

"That sounds more like Mason Baxter," Bishop said.

"And Sean figured it out," I said.

"We need to find out where they're getting the horses from, how they're being transported, who's doing the purchasing and transporting, and how often they're getting them," Bishop said.

"I'll get copies of the vet reports on them," Bubba said.

"We need someone working on that ranch," Michels said. "Someone undercover who can bond with the employees and watch what's going on."

It came to me then. "I think I have just the person."

Bishop side-eyed me. "Kyle's still recovering from his injuries, and I doubt the DEA would let him assist."

"Not Kyle. Garcia."

"Your old partner?" Levy asked. She found two additional paper clips and connected them together to create a small chain.

"Yes. He's independent now."

"We could use someone undercover from the department," Jimmy said. "Less expensive."

"Garcia's Hispanic. He's worked undercover multiple times in Chicago, and he'll come cheap," I said, my tone bordering on begging. "How many Hispanic officers with undercover experience do we have at Hamby?" The answer was none.

"You've made your point," Jimmy said. "I'll pay three hundred a day. If you get me something in the next few days, and we can move forward, I might up it. If you can't close it by shortly after that, he's done."

"We'll close it before then," Bishop said.

Jimmy nodded then left the room.

"Call him," Bishop said.

16

"He's getting on a plane in two hours," I said after hanging up with Tony. "He reminded me that he worked on a farm as a teenager, which has always amazed me, but it'll help. I stared at the growing stack of case files before me. "We need to figure this out."

Bishop leaned against the wall. "If this is cartel related, Kyle's got to have something more to say."

"Actually," I said remembering our brief conversation. "He was checking into something." I picked up the department line and called him.

"Yeah," he said. "We had a tranq drug case. I can come by and tell you what I know."

My shoulders stiffened as I kicked right into protective girlfriend mode. "You can tell us on the phone. I don't want you out and about too much."

Bishop cleared his throat. I'd been overly protective of Kyle, and rightfully so in my opinion, but no one except for Michels agreed with me, and he only did because he'd been the same with Ashley.

I gave my partner the side eye. "Fine," I said, my eyes glued on Bishop. "How long till you can get here?"

"I'm getting in my car now," he said.

"See you in a bit." I turned toward Bishop before he griped about Kyle being a big boy and all that. "I know. Don't say it."

"I wasn't going to say anything."

"You're a horrible liar," I said.

"Cathy says that as well."

"Oh, I meant to tell you Jessica's father texted me. He said he didn't know anything else, and he asked to leave him alone so he could focus on his daughter."

"Really? That's interesting. Not sure that's the route I'd take. Not that I wouldn't want to take care of my kid, but I'd want to be informed on the progress of the investigation."

"Agree," I said.

"If he knows more but he's not saying, it could be because he's worried about her safety. You want to give him a surprise visit?" Bishop said.

"Not yet. Let's see what else we can learn first. If we have more information, and he does know something, he might be more willing to tell us," I said.

Fifteen minutes later, Kyle stood in front of the white board in the investigation room giving us the 411 on the tranq drug. The team was scattered around the table, our attention fixated on him as he shared details about an investigation in Florida over a year before. He wasn't involved, so he'd had to access the DEA system, which would likely come back to bite him in the ass, but he didn't seem to care. "This was a high-stakes operation involving the Mexican cartel smuggling fentanyl from Mexico to the US."

Levy stood to stretch, then sat again, her pen poised to take notes. She gestured for Kyle to continue, her eyes focused on him.

"They had been tracking this cartel for months, gathering intel from informants and collaborating with various agencies," he explained. "The main lead came from a confidential informant who tipped off the DEA about a key figure within the cartel, a man named Ramiro Hernandez. He was responsible for overseeing the production and distribution of the tranq drug for that particular cartel."

Bubba's fingers raced across his keyboard. He pulled up a photo of Ramiro Hernandez on the screen. "Doesn't look like a drug dealer."

"They usually don't," Kyle said. "They play the role of regular citizens, typically living in wealthy neighborhoods in suburbs like Hamby, feigning executive management positions in large companies. The fronts are rarely questioned by people in the community. The companies are even real most of the time. The point is no one checks."

"Because they're Hispanic and no one wants to appear racist," Levy said.

Kyle pointed his dry erase marker at her. "Exactly. They live these wealthy lives managing billions of dollars in drug trafficking, socialize with their neighbors and kill their kids."

"Dear God, "Bishop said. "When you put it that way it's worse than people imagine."

Kyle nodded. "It's a simple process, and those are the ones that are usually brilliant. They fly under the radar for years before we figure them out."

"And they used horses to smuggle drugs into the states?" Bishop asked.

"Sometimes, yes. They set up a ranch in Davie, Florida. Fully functioning, with real business, and of course, their drug smuggling. They developed relationships with ten livestock veterinarians in Kentucky and Tennessee—"

"Relationships?" Levy asked.

"Blackmailed and bullied them into recommending their ranch to the clients. When the clients bought the horses, the vet would come to check them and remove the drugs. Usually, they'd had them in baggies in their anus."

Nikki blanched. "That's disgusting."

"But effective," Kyle said. "Who wants to check a horse's ass at border patrol?"

"They didn't?" Michels asked. "Wouldn't that be required?"

"One would think," I said.

"Did they have any of the horses swallow bags of drugs?" I asked.

"Not that I'm aware of, but I wouldn't say it doesn't happen," Kyle said.

"Did any of the horses die?"

"Three, based on the information I found. One of the ranch owners actually became suspicious, and that's how the investigation started." He stared at the screen. "The DEA believes there are several of these situations running at the same time. Different cartels, different locations, and sometimes, there's no ranch. Just a fake business."

Levy jotted down the key points, her mouth pursed and eyebrows furrowed, the look she usually had when she was processing details. "How did the DEA manage to infiltrate that operation?"

Kyle smiled with a hint of pride in his eyes. "An undercover agent named Sarah. She posed as a middleman, offering to transport and distribute the tranq drug on their behalf. It would have taken months, if not longer, of careful planning and strategizing to ensure her safety and maintain her cover."

Michels raised an eyebrow. "What about the money? How did you trace the cartel's financial transactions?"

"The DEA worked closely with financial institutions, analyzing suspicious transactions and following the money trail. It's a complex process, but the team managed to identify several key financial connections that led them to their main funding source."

"And the takedown?" Michels asked. I had a feeling he secretly wanted to be DEA.

"The report says the team coordinated a multi-agency raid, targeting their main production facility and distribution hubs simultaneously. According to the report, it said, verbatim, 'With SWAT teams, tactical units, and specialized assets in place, we executed the operation with precision.'"

"Which means, what?" Bishop asked.

"They arrested Ramiro Hernandez and his top lieutenants, seizing a significant amount of fentanyl, Xylazine, and other drug-related paraphernalia," he said. "It was a major blow to the cartel's operations, and the team managed to disrupt their supply chain significantly, but it was only one cartel. There are several cartels, and each has multiple distribution programs running at once."

"Haverty Ranch could be the one funneling the drugs," I said.

"It's fairly obvious," Levy said. She nodded toward Bubba. "We need that vet information."

"And Garcia on the inside," Michels said.

"The vet is Doctor Habersham. William Habersham," Bubba said. "From Dawsonville."

Michels angled his head to the side. "We have three livestock vets in Hamby. Why wouldn't he use one of them?"

"They chose the weakest one," Kyle said. "The one who couldn't resist the money."

"How do you know it's him?" Bishop asked Bubba.

He swirled his laptop toward the rest of us. "Facebook is like a diary of people's lives. They put everything on it."

Bishop rolled his eyes. "And that's why I'm not on social media."

"Preach, sister," I said.

He gave me the finger.

Nikki laughed. "And Emma Baxter is seventeen so she wouldn't think to keep some information private."

Bishop agreed. "We need the vet records."

"I can't access those," Bubba said. "Not without a warrant, and it would be easier to get them from the vet directly."

"I can work on that," I said.

"Because you know a guy," Bubba said with a smile.

Everyone chuckled. "I'm talking about a judge, not Joey, smartasses. Nowak won't give me a warrant for the vet unless we have something, but I can find out what he'll want for one." I made the call. Judge Nowak and I had bonded over our mutual admiration for the Chicago Cubs and the city in general. It was his hometown, though he'd moved South several years before me.

"Good afternoon, Detective," he said. "I have about three minutes until I'm due in court. What and who is the warrant for?"

He was on speaker. The team all smirked at his quick assessment of my call. "It's a livestock vet in Dawsonville, but you won't give the warrant on what we have. May I call you later this evening and give you the details?"

"The wife is with her mother, so that would be fine. Tell Bishop I said hello." He disconnected the call.

17

I sat in my car tapping my fingers impatiently on the steering wheel and staring at traffic as I waited in the cell phone lot outside of Hartsfield airport. The speed limit inside the grounds was twenty-five, but no one did it except those from out of town. Georgia drivers were something else, though they didn't quite match Chicago drivers.

I glanced at the clock on the dashboard and groaned. Tony's flight should have landed half an hour ago. I was anxious to see him, but more anxious to move forward on busting Sean's killer. Driving with idiotic drivers during rush hour traffic was stressful enough, and then I also had to deal with his fashionably late ass.

My cell phone dinged with his text tone. *I'm at the end of Delta.*

Be right there.

I eased my way into the cluster of cars and maneuvered through the chaos like a pro and caught a glimpse of him standing near the curb as I pulled up to the arrivals area. He appeared effortlessly stylish in his black t-shirt and faded blue jeans. I rolled down the window and flashed him a sly grin. "Look at you." I whistled. "Once a stud, always a stud."

He climbed into my Jeep and grinned. "It's hard being ruggedly gorgeous."

"Some things never change." I stuck my finger in my mouth and gagged.

It felt good to see him again. It had been too long. We'd been through some serious stuff back in Chicago, Tommy's death notwithstanding, and our bond was unbreakable. Once a partner, always a friend, unless that partner was dirty, which neither of us were.

He leaned back in his seat and stretched as I merged into the heavy traffic. "Before you ask, I quit because Besterfield is dirty. He gave Johnston the promotion I should have had."

He'd always thought Besterfield was dirty, but he'd never been able to prove it. I saw the fury in his eyes. "You still think he was taking bribes?"

"He promoted Johnston."

"I don't remember Johnston."

"Right, because he was a new patrol when you left. He's only been detective for a year, and he hasn't closed a single damn case. My record is eighty percent, one of the highest in the city."

Tony was an excellent detective. He and I had been the ones given the hard cases, the ones no one could clear. He should have been promoted years before. "How did Ramirez handle you leaving? You'd been partners a while now."

"He was disappointed, but he understood."

"But you're free to do as you please," I said. "Mr. Private Investigator."

"It's boring, but it pays the bills. So far. That's why I jumped on this. I needed some action."

The traffic finally started to ease up as we approached the outskirts of the Atlanta suburbs. Finally, the buildings of Hamby came into view. "Almost home sweet home," I said.

"Only Chicago is home."

KYLE HAD ORDERED BBQ for a late dinner and had it out when we arrived. After Garcia had sized Kyle up, he hit him hard with the interview process. I smiled. Garcia and Tommy were close. "Ever married?" he asked.

"Nope," Kyle said. I knew Kyle understood what Garcia was doing, and I was grateful he let it continue. "What about you?"

"Divorced," we said in unison.

"Made it two years, but cop life wasn't for her," he said.

"DEA is the same," Kyle said.

"Probably worse," I added. "He's gone for months at a time. It's similar to military families."

Neither had anything to add to that. We shared an awkward moment of silence until I babbled about the food and how BBQ was the only thing from Georgia that was better than the version in Chicago.

"She talks a lot when she's nervous in social situations," Kyle said. He smiled in my direction.

Before I had a chance to say anything, Garcia added. "Some things never change."

The two finally began to bond over my quirks and issues. We spent the rest of the evening with Garcia and Bishop came over later to work with us and map out our strategic plan.

"Are you sure you want to stick your foot in this?" Bishop asked Garcia.

He laughed. "I know enough about horses and ranches from working on the farm during the summers. It'll be easy. Once I get a contact that knows something, I'll work it and report back, but none of you will see me after tonight unless it's absolutely necessary."

Bishop flicked his head my direction. "She'll stay in touch."

"He'll stay in contact with me," I said. "Which means all of us."

Garcia held up a burner phone and I grabbed mine. "Through these."

"We can't guarantee he'll hire you," Bishop said. "We need an alternative plan in that event."

"He'll hire me," Garcia said. "I know how to make myself important."

I rolled my eyes. Garcia had an ego bigger than most actors and politicians. Thank God it worked for him. "But in the event he doesn't, he'll somehow connect with Damian and work that route," I said.

"You think Damian's involved?" Bishop asked.

I nodded. "I think it's possible. If he is, we'll get him a deal through the district attorney."

"He's going to need more than that," Kyle said. "Once the cartel knows he rolled on them, he's going to need WITSEC. The cartel doesn't play around."

"This could end up being handed over to you all anyway," Bishop said. "Which makes that easy." He smirked. "And cuts our budget."

My heart immediately beat faster. "Not if I have anything to say about it."

Kyle raised an eyebrow.

"It's our investigation," I said.

Garcia laughed. "Either way, I'll hint around to what we think is happening without being obvious. If I have to get a job at the victim's ranch, we can arrange that, right?"

"Yes," I said. "Would that be to make a connection there?"

"Yes. Word will get out if the cartel is working a ranch."

"Good idea," Bishop said. He stood in front of Louie's glass castle and dropped a few pellets inside. Louie scurried out, snatched a pellet, then swam back under his rock to eat. "The workers go back and forth between the ranches. They've all got to know what's going on." He eyed me. "We'll get a warrant to talk to the employees if we have to."

"Which reminds me," I said. "I need to call Nowak about the vet. We can tell him what's going on."

Nowak answered on the second ring. "It's after ten. I expected a call around six."

"Sorry," I said. "Investigating murders is a twenty-four-hour job."

"I can't disagree with that. Is this the ranch owner's death?"

"Yes. I've got Kyle Olsen with the DEA here. He can give you the rundown on what we suspect is happening. We're looking for vet records and a way to force a ranch owner's hand to give us access to his staff for interviews."

"He won't let you?"

"We haven't officially tried," I said. "But he showed up minutes after we started talking to the assistant ranch manager."

"Video cameras," Bishop added.

"An unfortunate necessity these days," Nowak said.

Kyle filled him in on what we thought was happening. He would know what to say to push the right buttons given his knowledge of that kind of thing.

After he finished, Nowak said. "They're selling horse tranquilizers to humans? What the hell kind of world do we live in?"

"We aren't exactly sure," I said. "The tranq drug is a possibility given how Sean died, but it could also be they're just smuggling in fentanyl."

"How many deaths related to this tranq drug have you had?" Nowak asked.

"Just Sean Higgins at this time," I said, "but we don't know where the drugs are going or if the vet is the one providing the xylazine. He could just be the one to remove the fentanyl."

"And you all believe Mr. Higgins didn't overdose," he paused. "Is that correct?"

"Yes," I said. "We believe he was given the drug because he found out what was happening." I backtracked and informed him of the rest of the investigation to date.

"I need more for the vet, but if you can't get the interviews from Mr. Baxter, let me know. I may have a talk with the mayor. They're golf buddies. In the meantime, get me something on the vet, and I'll get the warrant."

"Thanks, Judge," I said and ended the call. I had hoped for more, but I knew it was a shot in the dark anyway. "We need something on the vet."

"I'll get it," Garcia said.

GARCIA and I met Bishop at the station at seven o'clock the next morning. Jimmy had created a rolling undercover vehicle program with one of the local car dealerships where the dealership provided used and hard to sell vehicles for undercover work and received tax credits from the city and county. The program had worked so well the governor had worked with him to design a statewide program. It would be active within the year.

Garcia received one of those vehicles. "Nice," Garcia said. "A Nissan Pathfinder circa what? 2010?"

"Fourteen," Bishop said.

Garcia ran his hand along the passenger side. His fingers made lines through the dust and dirt. "I'll take it."

He had created his own background information, gave us the details, put my burner phone into his contacts with a fake name, and after giving him directions, headed out.

"Say a prayer he gets in," Bishop said.

"Garcia's Catholic. He's probably said fifty prayers by now."

18

An hour later I received a thumbs up via text message from Garcia's burner. "He's in," I said.

Michels pumped his fist in the air. "Yes!" He acted as if the losing team had hit a homer in the last inning of a baseball game.

Bubba walked into my cubby with his laptop in hand. It was getting crowded in the tight space. "Mason Baxter's out of town. He's buying three horses." He held his laptop toward us. "Emma can't wait to get them."

"Does she say where?" I asked.

He shook his head.

"Then Damian or the manager must have hired Garcia," Bishop said.

I agreed. "We couldn't have asked for a better scenario."

"Bubba," Levy said. "Can you get any information on Baxter's previous horses? There's got to be a paper trail."

"I can try."

"Thank you," Levy said.

Jimmy stepped into my cubby and motioned for both Levy and Michels to follow him. Levy eyed me with her eyebrow raised as she walked out.

"Let's go have a talk with Mr. Cooper," Bishop said. "If anyone's going to talk about Baxter and his ranch, it'll be him."

"Unless he's in on it as well," I said.

∼

BENNETT COOPER'S ranch was the opposite of Mason Baxter's. Kudzu, or as Georgians called it, the vine that ate the South, clung to the trees hiding Cooper Creek Ranch from the road like the humid air stuck to my skin right after a summer rain. Just the front entrance, with its opened, large chain-link fence, told me the Coopers weren't on the same social or economic level as the Baxter's. "This isn't Baxter's ranch. It's more of a farm, like Sean's place."

Bishop turned left into the front entrance. "It's both, but it wasn't always that way. When Julia's father owned it, it was a farm only, but since Bennett Cooper took over, he added the horses. I've run into Bennett Cooper a few times. He's not a bad guy. Comes from Texas. Be prepared. He'll probably ma'am the hell out of you."

"I'm okay with it if he's not condescending."

"Right," Bishop teased. "You read the riot act to someone on patrol calling you ma'am last week."

"He said it condescendingly."

"That's your imagination," he said.

"No," I said. "It's my perception, and perception is reality."

The ranch felt like a living, breathing entity, humming with the quiet rustle of the wind through the tall Georgia pines. They stood sentinel around the edges of the property, their dark green needles stark against the sky, their trunks gnarled and aged and rooted deep into the earth for God only knew how long. Trees didn't grow that tall in Illinois, and they were still one of my favorite things about Georgia. We pulled up to the main building and parked. Bishop cut the ignition as a man walked outside.

"That's Cooper," Bishop said.

Bennett Cooper was tall, standing a good head above most, with a powerful build that must have come from a lifetime of wrangling livestock and mending fences. Deep-set lines creasing his weather-beaten face radiated out from the corners of his blue eyes. Eyes that looked like they'd seen a lot.

I admired his worn, leather cowboy boots and his Texas shaped silver belt buckle, the sort of ostentatious thing you'd buy as a souvenir or to remember where you're from when you're a thousand miles away. He wore a red and white checkered shirt with a leather vest that looked like it had been through more than a few cattle drives.

Though cautious, my gut told me Bennett Cooper was the kind of man who shook hands on a deal and didn't go back on his word. A rare type. I stepped out of the car as Bishop climbed out.

"Mr. Cooper," Bishop said. I walked beside my partner. "Detectives Bishop and Ryder. We'd like a minute of your time."

Cooper had been carrying a large metal bucket. He set it down, wiped his hands and extended his right one to my partner. "Bishop? We've met already, right?"

"Yes. At a Hamby High School football game."

Cooper's eyes smiled. "That's right." He pivoted to me. "I don't believe we've met. Detective Ryder."

"We haven't."

He shook my hand with a firm and commanding grip. "Pleasure to meet you, ma'am." He placed his hands on his hips. "I'm assuming you're here to talk about Sean Higgins?" He bent his head down and shook it. "Sad thing. Sean was good people."

"He was," I said. "We've got a few questions about the ranches and how things work around here."

"Sure thing," he said smiling. "Let's go inside." He pointed to the right where a fenced area with several pigs charged around a kiddie pool as a young man dressed similarly to Cooper filled it with water.

I stopped to watch them bump into each other and snort then finally heave their chunky bodies into the water. "That's adorable."

"The pigs get a little rowdy when they go swimming," he said.

Sometime after we solved the case, I'd come back and watch the pigs swim.

The main office area was similar to Sean and Connie's. A small store, a large counter, and offices.

A woman sat at the counter clicking on a mouse as she stared at a laptop screen. "We've got three today hon," she said to Cooper with her head still down. When she looked up, she looked surprised to see us. "Oh, we've got guests. I didn't realize."

Cooper introduced us to his wife Julia. After a brief amount of chatter, we walked into his office. He offered us two chairs while he leaned against his desk. We chose to stand. Sitting put us in the submissive position, and as detectives, we needed to either be on level, or preferably, in the dominant position.

"So," he said. "What can I tell you?"

"How well did you know Sean?" Bishop asked.

"Well enough to respect him, but not enough to call him a friend. We were more like acquaintances." He smiled. "If you want to know where I was the day he died, I was here. I've got several employees who can confirm that."

"Good to know," I said. "You were at Rucker's with Mr. Baxter and Mr. Higgins, correct? When you were seen arguing."

He pressed his lips together and nodded. "I was there, but I wasn't part of the discussion. I stopped the fight and that was it."

"What did he get heated about?" Bishop asked.

"I'm not sure. From what I gathered, I walked in just after it started. I can't say who started the argument, but Baxter was telling Sean to back off. Sean didn't like hearing that. He leaned in toward Baxter and looked like he was going to throw a punch, so I stepped in between them."

Given his stature, I had a feeling both Sean and Baxter backed off. "What happened next?"

"Baxter told Sean it was his last warning and left."

"And Sean?"

"He said I didn't have to do that, but he thanked me, then said something about Baxter being scum."

I couldn't help but smile. Sean was right, and I'd only met the guy once.

"Did you think to tell us about this before or even after Sean died?" Bishop asked.

"What's to tell? Two men argued and almost threw fists. That's a daily thing where I'm from."

"You're from Texas, correct?" I asked.

He smiled. "I've been here too long if you can't tell by my accent. South Texas, around Corpus Christi. My dad has a horse ranch out there. My grandfather had a cattle ranch, and since neither of them decided to leave them to me, I went to college in Georgia, met Julia, and let's just say the rest is history."

"How many horses do you have?" I asked.

"Right now? Six."

"Where do you buy your horses?" Bishop asked.

"Kentucky. I only buy thoroughbreds."

"Have you ever purchased from Texas?" I asked.

He raised an eyebrow. "This about the cartel thing in Florida that happened a while back?" He squinted as if staring at something, but all that was behind me was a wall. "Hernandez, I think."

"And you know about that how?" I asked.

"Horses are my bread and butter, ma'am. It's my job to be informed."

"What about the drugs?" I purposefully didn't provide details to see what he knew.

His upper lip twitched slightly. It reminded me of what Kyle did when I'd humor him unintentionally. "What about it?"

"Know anything about it?" I asked.

"I know my horses are clean, if that's what you're asking. I would never dose them with performance drugs, nor would I ever allow them to be mules." He leaned forward, crossed his right foot over his left and then his arms over his chest and said, "What's this got to do with Sean Higgins? Was he transporting fentanyl from Mexico?" He shook his head. "I mean, I didn't know the guy that well, but I can't see it. Seems too honest to me."

"What about Baxter?" Bishop asked.

Cooper's eyes widened. "You think that windbag's working for the cartel?" He laughed. "I haven't given him enough credit if he is."

"You think it's smart working for the cartel?" Bishop asked.

He laughed again. "Hell no, but I also don't think Baxter's got the balls to do it. That's what I mean." He paused for a moment and then said, "Listen, I grew up in South Texas. As you know, the cartel is a big threat there. This kind of thing happens there all the time. You see a sicario, you turn around and walk the other way."

If Cooper knew the term sicario, he knew about the cartel. Sicarios were the muscles, the ones no one wanted knocking at their door. If they knocked. If they walked toward you, you ran. "Go on," I said.

"You know the cartel doesn't mess around. If they hooked Baxter, there's a reason. He went because they had something on him, or he needed something from them."

"What do you think that could be?" Bishop asked.

"Money." He flicked his head to the side as if to point it toward Baxter's ranch. "The cartel can see a weak man from a mile away. Weak and broke, that is." He smirked. "You think Baxter's involved in Higgins's death. Was he murdered?"

"We're investigating," I said.

"The tranq drug?" he asked. "If Sean overdosed, and it was from that, then you've got a livestock or large animal vet wrapped up in this crazy too." He shook his head and half laughed. "Damn, never thought I'd see that come up here. Poor Baxter. If he's in, he won't be around long, especially if they know he's on your radar."

"You know about the tranq drug?"

"Again, ma'am, horses are my wheelhouse. I make it a point to know everything related to them. I can tell you this. If Baxter's working for the cartel, he ought to be coming to you, not the other way around."

Cooper knew his stuff. If Baxter was involved, which I was confident he was, then he didn't have long. The trick would be getting to him and making him flip on the cartel before they got to him. And even trickier was getting to him before the feds got involved. If that happened, we'd be out, and Sean's murder would be tagged a suicide for sure. The feds didn't care about a small ranch owner in the middle of the Atlanta 'burbs. They cared about the drug bust, especially during an election year.

"Have you ever discussed the drug with a vet or anyone from the horse community?"

"Sure. It's come up. Everyone's had their concerns. Xylazine is a necessary drug for large animal vets. If the government tries to regulate it, we have a problem. The problem is, it's killing people. Even if it's not mixed with fentanyl, too much is still lethal, and something needs to be done."

He was right. The problem was what that something would be. "And you've had this discussion with Sean Higgins or Mason Baxter?"

"Like I said, it's come up. I'm as anti-drug as you'll get, but I know our vets need to use xylazine. I also see how it's a revenue generator for the cartel. But, if you're looking for quick cash, and you're stupid, aligning your-self with the cartel and a vet willing to remove the drugs from the horse, or say, provide the xylazine to the cartel, it's a no brainer."

"Let me get this straight," I said, wanting to confirm what I thought. "The cartel ships horses with fentanyl to the states where a rancher buys them, then a vet removes the drugs. Does the vet mix the drugs?"

"Yes to most of that. As for who mixes the two, I'm not sure, but if I had to guess, I'd say it's someone from the cartel located here."

"A vet couldn't get a hold of that much xylazine," Bishop said. "They've got to be getting it somewhere else."

"It wouldn't take much to get someone high," Cooper said. "It's meant to knock out a horse. I don't know about you, but I don't know anyone big enough to handle something like that."

"The trick is finding who's providing the xylazine and who's mixing them," I said.

"I can't say," Cooper said. "Is there anything else?"

"We understand the employees switch ranches," Bishop said. "We'd like to talk to yours."

"Sure thing," he said. "I've got a small room in the stables. It's closer to my guys. I'll bring you there. You want them all at once or one at a time?"

"One at a time," Bishop said. "How many are there?"

"Today? Only three. I may have some day workers tomorrow."

Neither of us cared about his day workers' immigration status, so we moved on. "We might come back," I said.

"No problem, but I can't promise the day workers will stick around to talk."

"Got it," I said.

"Y'all want some water or coffee?"

"Water would be great," we both said.

19

The ranch manager lived above the stables in a small apartment. His wife was just leaving as we walked over.

"Sarah," Cooper said. "These are detectives from Hamby PD."

She laced her fingers together and smiled at us briefly. "Hello." She turned toward Cooper. "Are you looking for Ray? He went upstairs for a second. He should be right down."

"Thanks," Cooper said. "You heading to work?"

"Yes sir."

"Have a good day then," he said. He watched her as she walked toward the parking area. "Poor girl's had it rough. Lost a baby last month. She was four months along."

"That's terrible," I said.

A tall, lanky man with lean muscles and very little fat walked out of the stables. He smiled and approached Cooper when he saw us. "Morning, Ben. You looking for me?" He gave Bishop and me a good once over. "New customers?"

"Hamby PD Detectives," I said. I extended my hand. "Rachel Ryder. This is my partner, Rob Bishop. We're here to talk with you and the other employees about something."

"Ray Davis."

He made eye contact with Cooper. "Answer their questions," Cooper said. "When you're done, send in the others one by one. Let them know I've given approval to tell them whatever they want to know."

"Yes, sir," Ray said as he tipped his head down once.

We sat in the small room inside the stables. It wasn't exactly a conference room, but it did have a table and a few chairs. I opened my bottled water and wet my throat while Bishop explained why we were there. A quick glance around the room told me there were no security cameras, but I wasn't surprised. Cooper seemed like the kind of guy that trusted his employees, though I wasn't sure that was a good idea, and it didn't take possible theft into account.

"I knew Sean," Ray said. "He was a good guy. Can't believe he's gone. Rumors say he accidentally overdosed, but I don't believe it. That wasn't Sean. Do you think that was the case?"

"We're investigating," Bishop said. "When was the last time you spoke to Mr. Higgins?"

"I saw him the other night at the fair." He tapped his finger on the table. I noticed dirt underneath his short nail. "Come to think of it, he was acting strange."

"Strange how?" I asked though I suspected I already knew.

"Worried. Maybe a little paranoid. It was strange. I hadn't seen him in a while, but I haven't seen him act like that."

"Did he appear under the influence?" Bishop asked.

He dragged his hand down his cheeks. "If he was, I didn't notice, but like I said, that wasn't him."

"Are you aware of any conflict between Mr. Higgins and any of the other ranch owners in town?"

"I mean, sure, there was competition, but mostly Mr. Baxter at Haverty Ranch was the one to compete." He shook his head briefly. "With all due respect, the man walks like he's got a stick up his ass. Thinks he's better than the rest of us."

I bit my lip. It was a perfect description of Baxter. "Is he?" I asked. "Better than the rest of you?"

"If you like entitled rich boys who get their money from their dad, then yeah. I prefer associating with men who make a name for themselves."

"Like Mr. Cooper?" Bishop asked.

He nodded. "I've worked for him for two years now. Before I was with Haverty. Ben's good people."

"Were you involved in Baxter's horse sales?" I asked.

His easy-going expression hardened. He stared at me for a moment before saying, "Initially, but I came to work for Ben after a horse died."

"How did the horse die?" I asked.

"According to the vet? Cardiac arrest."

"This was over two years ago?" I asked to confirm.

"Yes, ma'am. The whole thing seemed a little strange to me. Now he's had a few more die. Can't say for sure what's going on, but the horse that died, and a bunch of other ones he sold? They weren't race quality horses. He sold them as such, but it must have been to some stupid-ass people because if they knew horses, they'd know they weren't race quality."

"What was the difference?"

"Type of horse, age, general condition. Looked like he was buying rejects. I didn't trust him, so I left."

"William Habersham was the vet?" Bishop asked.

Through gritted teeth, he said "Yes."

"Not a fan of him either?" I asked.

"You could say that. I'm not comfortable with his work ethic."

"Tell us about it," Bishop said.

According to Davis, Habersham was locally grown, and a graduate from the University of Georgia for his bachelors and vet medicine degrees. He specialized in large animals and livestock, but saw other animals as well, and he overcharged his clients. Davis thought he was shady.

"I don't like accusing people of things when I don't have the facts, but Baxter's lost several horses to heart problems on his watch. Just confirms to me the horses Baxter buys aren't race quality."

"It confirms that how?" I asked.

"If Baxter supposedly buys race horses and resells them, common sense would say if one died from a hereditary heart condition, he wouldn't buy another from that bloodline. So, how's he getting so many horses with heart conditions?"

We couldn't ask him about the tranq drug directly without leading him that direction, so I nudged him as best I could. "What do you think's happening?"

"He's killing the horses for the insurance money, maybe? I can't say. Whatever the reason, I think Habersham is involved because when he was unavailable and we were dealing with a sick horse, Baxter used another vet. None of those horses ever died." Someone knocked on the door. "It's open," Davis said.

A younger man, maybe in his early twenties with a perfectly styled Flock of Seagulls hairdo peeked in. "We're grooming in stall six, but she's got a lot of energy right now. We've got to get her out for a run first."

Davis nodded. "Good luck."

"Thanks," the kid said and closed the door.

Davis smirked. "Lola's a little hard to handle."

"Most women are," Bishop said.

I just rolled my eyes, but Davis laughed. "She's a dam. We're hoping for a foal this year, but we'll see. If we're finished here, I'll switch out with one of the ranch hands and send him in."

"Actually," I said. "I'd love to see the dam. Can we walk out with you?"

"You ride?" he asked.

"Taking lessons, but not for a few months."

"Where?"

"In Alpharetta."

"You ever feel like coming here, Ben will cut you a deal. Unlike Baxter, he does it because he loves to ride."

"I'll keep that in mind," I said and followed him into the horse stall area. Though I did want a look at the horses, I was more interested in checking out the stables themselves. Since the small room didn't have security, I wondered if the rest of the place did. There hadn't been any horse thefts since I started at Hamby, but there was always a chance.

Lola had been cooped up in the stall all night. I was still learning about caring for horses, but I knew enough to know it wasn't smart to go straight from a night in the stall to tied and groomed for some horses. Horses could be reactive. They needed to release energy, and for some, making them feel trapped with ties after hours in a stall wasn't an effective way to start a grooming process.

"We can continue our conversation at the paddock if you're okay with that," Davis said.

"Works for me," I said. Bishop agreed.

Lola and the two hands were still in the stall. Lola wasn't happy to see them, and whatever they were trying to do, which I assumed was slip on her halter, wasn't going well. Davis jogged over to help while Bishop and I took our time.

I glanced up at the ceiling but saw no security cameras. "Look," I said quietly and pointed to the ceiling.

"There were two outside the entrance. Maybe there's an alarm. Davis lives above. It wouldn't be hard for him to get down here fast, and I'm not sure he's someone I'd want to mess with."

A ticking sound distracted me. I froze for a second and then grabbed Bishop's arm and stopped. "Do you hear that?" We shared a look. My heart quickened, my ears straining to catch the faint sound I knew indicated trouble. I swept my gaze around the stables searching for any shadows, any movement that might betray an unseen presence. Beads of sweat formed on my temples. I focused on the ticking to try to locate it.

"It's coming from over there," Bishop said. He calmly walked to a stall numbered two.

I watched the three men struggle with Lola for a moment to determine how long it would take them to get the horses out, then met Bishop at the stall. He'd gone inside and moved a pile of hay. "It's a bomb," he said. "Get them out of here, now!"

20

"There's a bomb over here," I yelled. "Get out now!" The bomb was buried under a pile of hay. The red light flashed at six minutes and fifteen seconds, each second ticking away with a deafening resonance. The tension weighed on me, suffocating my senses. I immediately got on my radio. "This is Detective Rachel Ryder. We've got an active bomb with less than six minutes on the timer. I repeat, less than six minutes." I rattled off the location. "There are at least three or four horses and four men not including Bishop and myself. I need fire out here stat."

"Ten-four," dispatch said. She contacted Hamby fire. "Detective Ryder, Hamby Fire is enroute. Contacting Fulton County bomb now."

"They're getting fire—"

Bishop cut me off. "I heard. Get them out of here!"

"Bishop, we have to get out of here! We can't defuse this thing."

"I know," he said. "But we need to know what we're dealing with. Get them out of here. I'll meet you outside."

I glanced at the men who were trying to get the horses prepped to move. I raced over to and locked eyes with Davis. "Come on! We need to get these horses out of here now. Take them as far out as you can." I yelled, "Now!"

The two younger men's eyes widened. "I've got Lola," Davis said. "Go!" They dropped the halter and rushed to the other horses.

Davis stared at me then bent down and picked up Lola's harness that one of the others had dropped on the ground. "Where is it?"

"Stall two. We can't defuse it."

"Shit." He draped the halter over Lola with an expertise that surprised me. There were three more horses. The two men had each gone to two of the stalls, but we needed to get the other horse from the last stall.

"I can get her," Davis said, pointing to the last horse.

"Get them as far away as possible." I eyed the radio on his belt. "Get Cooper and tell him to clear the area too."

"Yes, ma'am," he said and took off dragging Lola by his side.

I hollered to Bishop. "How long?"

"Coming down to five minutes."

He was checking the area around the perimeter of the small stall. "Get out of here."

I wiped the sweat from my brow and rushed back to him. "I'm not leaving you here with that thing."

"Both of us could die," he screamed.

"I don't care."

My radio burst to life. "Fulton County here. Is this Ryder or Bishop?"

"Ryder," I said. I checked the timer. "Four minutes and twenty-eight seconds left. It's seven sticks of dynamite with a timer. We can't defuse it."

"We've got men on the way. Clear the area. It's going to blow big."

"Ten-four," I said.

Bishop and I bolted out of the stall.

We made it to the edge of the pasture where Cooper and his men were hauling at least a dozen horses and several other farm animals into a small barn near the edge of the property. How they got them all that fast escaped me.

"Is that all the animals?" I asked Cooper.

"Yes, thank God. We just sold off our pigs and chickens."

Bishop checked his watch. "Two minutes."

Sirens blared nearby.

"Can they cut the wires?" Cooper asked.

"No. This isn't Hollywood," I said while catching my breath. "It's going to blow."

Cooper dragged his hand through his hair. "Are we far enough away? Shit. We're going to lose everything."

"We don't know that. It's possible it won't reach far," I said. "Where did your wife go?"

"Work. I need to call her." He dug into his pocket for his cell phone.

"Wait. It's going to get loud."

"One minute twenty seconds," Bishop said. "Keep moving!"

A wire and wood fence separated the land from a small back road. The sirens grew louder. Finally, the fire trucks and ambulances pulled to a stop near us.

A firefighter jumped off the truck and rushed to the fence. "Officers have the main road blocked for traffic." He scanned the area. "Is this everyone?"

Cooper said, "Yes."

"Good. We've got the rest of our trucks pulling through the gate now. Once it blows, we'll get in there." He ran back to the truck.

"Five seconds," Bishop said. "Get down!"

A deafening explosion followed by a loud boom erupted from the stables. We covered our heads as the sound ripped through the air with an ear-splitting roar. Seconds later, the shockwave reached me like an invisible force as the ground beneath me quivered and vibrated up through my legs.

The vibration ended as fast as it had started.

"Everyone all right?" Bishop hollered.

We got confirmation on everyone, and Cooper said, "Check the horses," to his men.

"I can't tell if anything else was hit," Bishop said.

The four of us rushed back outside to see the damage as the horses' terrified screams filled the air. Flames erupted from what was left of the stables. Heat radiated from the blaze, reaching out like a malevolent hand, scorching the grass near the paddock. The air grew thick with smoke, making it difficult to breathe. I tasted the bitterness, a mixture of ash and soot, and struggled to swallow. I covered my mouth with my hand. "I can't tell if it's contained to just the stable," I yelled.

"Neither can I," Bishop said. He coughed. "We need to get to the ambulance and get some masks."

"I'll stay with the men," Davis said. "We'll make sure the animals are okay." He tapped his radio and looked at Cooper. "Let me know what's going on." He shook his head. "I need to call my wife. The stable's gone."

21

Bennett Cooper was grateful we'd found the bomb in time to get the animals to safety. "I don't understand why someone would do this," he said.

We stood outside the remains of the stables. The fire department had left, and the smoke had cleared for the most part.

"Do you have any idea who might have planted the bomb?" Bishop asked.

Cooper stood with his hands on his hips, staring at the burned mess. "I don't have a clue. We're a small ranch. We keep to ourselves and don't cause any trouble."

"I noticed you had cameras outside the stables," I said. "Can we take a look at them?"

He nodded. "We only have them at the front. Had," he said. "There are two more entrances. Were two more entrances. I hadn't gotten around to putting those up, but I didn't think I needed to be in a rush."

We headed back to his office to watch the videos on double speed. During the first three no one other than employees and day workers had entered the stables, and those who did, had nothing directly obvious with them.

It was the fourth video I questioned. "Who's that?" I asked.

Cooper stopped the video. "I don't know. A day worker, I'm assuming."

He expanded on the frame. "I don't always know them, and I'm not sure I've seen this one before."

"Can you send me the video?" I asked.

"Sure."

I gave him my email address.

He spun his wheeled desk chair to the side. "Do you think this has something to do with Sean's death?"

I wasn't surprised he went there. It was the first place I'd gone.

Bishop answered before me. "We aren't going to rule anything out."

"Do you keep a list of your day workers?" I asked.

"No, ma'am." He pursed his lips. "Is this going to—"

"We're not concerned about who you choose to employ or how you pay them," I said. We're just looking for a reason this would happen."

"I pay them cash, but one of us usually picks them up at the same place daily. I'll get with my guys and see if they know him." He'd sent his men to the hospital for checkups just in case. The only one who refused to go was Davis, and that was only because he wanted to be with his wife. "But I'll let you know what they say."

"Appreciate it," Bishop said. "Where do you normally pick them up?"

"Off Highway Nine in Roswell, near Wills Park. Wait, that might be Alpharetta."

"It's Alpharetta," Bishop said. "Do these men work at the other ranches as well?"

"I assume so, but I can't say for sure."

"We'll be able to find out," I said.

Bishop stood. "We'll file a report and have it at the station first thing in the morning. You can let your insurance company know."

"Do you suggest I send my family back to Texas until this is resolved?"

"We can't make that decision for you, Mr. Cooper," Bishop said. "But we'll find out why it happened, and if it has anything to do with Mr. Higgins's death, we'll find the person or people who did it."

He nodded once. "I think I'll send them, but I'm staying. Regardless of why this happened, I've got a business to run. I'm not going to let it scare me."

Investigating a bombing required a lot of effort, and a team of people with various specialties neither Bishop nor I had. We did our best to assist, but if there ever was a time I'd felt inadequate and amateur, it was then. I promised myself I'd look into specialized training in the future.

Nikki and her new part timer, Max, a recent college graduate who made me feel ancient, worked with the fire department and bomb squad to find anything that could lead us to the person who planted the bomb. They weren't successful, but the head of the Fulton County Bomb Squad said that wasn't uncommon.

"Especially with these elementary homemade bombs. Anyone can find out how to make them online, so tracing them is a problem," he said.

"Understood," Bishop said. "It's illegal to buy dynamite unless you're a licensed blaster, which requires a lot of effort on someone's part, so my guess is this was stolen."

"One hundred percent," the man said. "The tape can be bought at any store, and the timer, based on your description, is easy to get online." He stuffed his hands into his jeans pockets. "I hate to say it, but your chances of finding your guy through the bomb are slim to none."

"We expected that," I said.

"If you need anything else, give me a call." He handed us each a card. I stuffed it into my back pocket knowing I'd keep it for future reference.

As he walked away, Bishop said, "You think it's related to Sean's murder?"

"I don't believe in coincidences."

"Right there with you."

Cooper and Davis continued to work the ranch while the remains settled. The burned remains would be removed in about a week because the cooling process, even though it was all drenched, required time. We'd suggested they transport their animals to a new location, but the smoke wasn't bad, and it didn't reach the back stable, so they began the process of making room for their other livestock. Davis's wife was a wreck, and we all felt for her. Apparently, they'd had personal items for the baby in their apartment over the stables. Things they'd received from family, and things that belonged to them as children. My heart broke for them.

～

"How long will they be out?" Bishop asked.

Jimmy had just explained that he'd sent Michels and Levy to assist Alpharetta on a drug case that had ties to Hamby residents. The city line divided the two towns on a busy street filled with strip malls, businesses, and hotels, and often the same criminals committed crimes on both sides of the street, so the two departments worked together.

"They're on the assist for the day," he said. "They'll be back tomorrow." He moved around his desk and sat. "Tell me about the bombing. Do you think it's related?"

"We're looking into why it happened," I said. "But if you're asking us what we think right now, yes. It's related."

"Why? How?"

We explained what Cooper had said about the tranq drug issue, his opinions on Baxter, and Sean.

"What about the employees?" he asked.

"They hop between ranches," Bishop said. "But they also hire day workers off Highway Nine near Wills Park in Alpharetta."

"Which means one or more could be part of the cartel," I said.

"Has this Cooper guy talked about the tranq drug with any staff?" he asked.

I cringed. "Didn't ask that."

He raised an eyebrow. "Why not?"

"Because we screwed up, Chief," Bishop said. We always kept it professional when we dropped the ball, which thankfully, wasn't often.

"If the bomber is cartel," I said. "Then they either knew we were going there and expected Cooper to tell us something, or they view him as some kind of threat."

"Which would mean our timing was good," Bishop said. "Or bad, depending on how you look at it."

"Right," Jimmy said. "We need Garcia heavy on these guys. When are you supposed to update him?"

"We're meeting him tonight," I said.

"Keep me posted."

We stopped at Bubba's office.

"Get anything we can use?" Bishop asked.

"I traced the horses to a ranch along the Texas border in Webb County. Evergreen Ranch. The owner, Hal Jacobs, auctions horses once a month." His fingers glided across his keyboard. "Happens tomorrow. It's strange. They don't have a website or a social media presence, but they're listed on a horse selling site with a one-star review."

"How do you know there's an auction tomorrow?" I asked.

"I did a search for the ranches selling sick horses, and they came up. I saw a post on Reddit about it. This Hal Jacobs is a ghost though. He's nowhere around when his horses get sick. I can't say he's gone there, but the puzzle pieces fit together with the horses that have died."

"So, this Hal Jacobs is part of the program," Bishop said.

"I'm assuming so," Bubba said.

"We'll look into it," I added. "Let's call Cooper."

We made a call to Bennett Cooper from the investigation room.

"Evergreen Ranch?" he asked. "Never heard of it. What county is it in?"

"Webb," I said.

"Seems right then. Webb has a lot of cartel activity. Want me to check into it? I have connections."

"We've got it," Bishop said. "How're things at your place?"

"The cleanup is going to take weeks, and the rebuild months," he said. "You have any idea why this happened?"

"We're working on it," Bishop said.

"It's not a one-off bombing. This is connected to Sean's murder," he said.

I leaned closer to the landline speaker. "You're leaning more that direction. Why?"

"Your interview questions. Davis and I talked. You think Sean's murder has something to do with Baxter and the tranq drug."

"We do," Bishop admitted.

"Then you need to get in front of Habersham. If I can help, you call. I'm there."

22

We met Garcia at a Doubletree in Roswell. It was a risky move, but we had him followed by an on-duty officer in an undercover vehicle to make sure no one was onto him. If they were, they were too good to be noticed.

Bishop and I each drove in department issued undercover vehicles, driving different routes, and arriving at different times. Better safe than sorry, Bishop had said. Just like my mother used to say when I was five.

The hotel room felt surprisingly spacious considering it was a Doubletree. Soft golden lights emanated from the lamps scattered strategically around the room, casting a warm glow on the wooden furniture and cream-colored walls. A small kitchenette with a microwave, stovetop, and refrigerator occupied one corner, while a large bed dominated the center of the room, dressed in crisp white sheets.

"Not bad," I said. "Hamby definitely rolls out the red carpet for our undercover contracts."

Garcia laughed. "I'm blessed."

I sat on the edge of the bed and flipped through a local magazine absentmindedly while Bishop lounged on a plush armchair, engrossed in a thick file. He occasionally glanced up, his piercing eyes narrowing as he analyzed the information. Garcia stood at the sink washing the remnants of his dinner off the plates.

"So," I began, breaking the silence that had enveloped the room. "You make any contacts?"

Tony wiped his hands on a dish towel and turned to face us, his dark hair still damp from his shower. "Getting there," he replied, his voice tinged with a touch of exhaustion. "I did what I was supposed to do, watched and learned, but I didn't just walk up to a guy and ask if he was part of the cartel. It's going to take some time."

I raised an eyebrow, setting the magazine aside. "We don't have a lot of time. Did anyone look like cartel?"

He tossed the dish towel onto the small counter and turned toward me. "I look like cartel. To the average person, any Hispanic person looks like cartel if you don't know what you're looking for."

Had I hit a nerve? "You know what I mean."

A smile crept across his face. "Just giving you a hard time. Cartel members are a lot like sociopaths in the sense that they look like normal people, but don't worry. If there's one working there, I'll find him."

"You might have to move up the ladder quicker than we thought," Bishop said.

"Why?" Garcia asked. He began unpacking the rest of his bag, placing his socks in the top drawer of the small dresser first. "You got a better option?"

"Not exactly," Bishop said.

Garcia placed his t-shirts in a drawer, closed it, then leaned his butt against it to face us. Smirking, he said, "Do tell."

"We had a bomb go off at another ranch. Convenient timing as we were there."

Garcia looked at me with concern covering his face. "You okay?"

"We're good," I said. "Bishop's last few hairs were singed almost off. We've started a charity jar for hair plugs." I tried hard not to laugh but failed.

"Bite me, Ryder," Bishop said with a smile.

Garcia chuckled and flicked his head. "She tease you about your accent?"

"I tease her about hers. The *youse guys* was a tough one to break."

I gave him a death stare. "I've never said that."

"Damn," Garcia said. "Bishop's rough."

"Definitely old fashioned. He doesn't even know what LOL means."

Garcia laughed.

"As we were saying," Bishop said. "The owner, Bennett Cooper, believes Baxter is involved with the cartel." He explained the connection and added, "He's purchasing horses tomorrow in Texas. We believe he'll bring them back, have this Habersham vet remove the fentanyl, and then give it to a cartel employee, who'll run with it. We need someone there for that hand off."

"I can make that happen," he said. "Just tell me when he's coming back."

"It'll be a few days," I said. "In the meantime, you can still work toward that contact. We need to know who's been there the longest, and who the day workers are. Specifically, the ones coming from Highway Nine in Alpharetta."

He walked over to his small fridge, grabbed a beer and held it up. "Anyone?"

"No thanks," Bishop said.

"I'm good," I said.

He popped the top and guzzled a good amount. "I know the drill. I'll have a contact tomorrow."

"Be careful," I said. I walked over and gave him a hug.

"Always am." He smiled. "And I got to say, I'm enjoying this a lot more than I expected. It's not bad breathing in the southern air."

"Don't go outside in this area then," Bishop said. "You'll eat exhaust."

I PAID attention to the vehicles around me. I'd been followed and run off the road too many times, and I couldn't afford an injury that could put me out during Sean's murder investigation. It was too important.

I took the most direct route back to Hamby, then detoured off Highway Nine to drive by the four horse ranches in town. Cooper's was dark, though Bennett Cooper and his family lived on the ranch. The home was on the far right side of the property, toward the back, and away from the explosion. If he was home, I wouldn't know. His home was hidden by woods his wife's family had kept dense to maintain privacy. There were no cameras anywhere around his entrance.

Moonlight lit up Sean's ranch, but other than that, the place was dark, and the gates didn't have cameras anywhere I could see. No one lived on the ranch. According to a conversation I'd once had with Connie, the previous owners had turned their home into the main office, living in a trailer while thinking they would build a new house, but a massive heart attack took the husband, and the woman sold the property.

Some would consider that an omen. For me, it was Murphy's Law.

Haverty Ranch looked like the others. I pulled over on the side of the road just ahead of the ranch and killed my lights, then climbed out of my vehicle, slid my weapon into its holster on my belt, and with my hand on it, walked toward the gate. I noted three security cameras hitting from different angles. I couldn't risk taking photos, knowing the flash would show up on the cameras, so I committed their locations to memory. I climbed back into my vehicle and headed back to the station.

Surprisingly, Bishop was there as well.

"I thought you were going home," I said outside our vehicles.

"I could say the same to you." He bent down and touched his toes. I wasn't sure he'd done that since I'd met him.

I watched him and whistled. "Look at you."

He shot up. "Admiring my backside, are you?"

I pursed my lips and quickly shook my head. "That's close to incest, not to mention nasty."

"I agree." We headed to the electronic door of the back entrance. "What brought you back?"

"I drove by the ranches. The only one with security cameras at the gate is Baxter's."

"Does that surprise you?" he asked.

"No, but it does intrigue me." Always the gentleman, he held the door open, and I walked in first. "Why'd you come back."

"Cathy's got book club tonight. She doesn't come home until around midnight, so I figured I'd come here and do a little research on the drugs and the cartel."

"Wait." I stopped in the hallway. "Home?"

He looked at me strangely. "Huh?"

"You said Cathy doesn't come home until around midnight. Are you two living together?"

"Not officially, but she's given me a few drawers and some closet space."

I laughed and walked toward the kitchen to grab a bottle of water. "She's at the dock but clearly afraid to jump."

"It's not her," he said from a few feet behind me. "I'm the one staring down at the water and scared shitless."

I stopped and turned around, surprised that he'd admitted that, but more surprised that he felt that way. "Really?"

He walked past me nodding. "We've got a good thing. I don't want to screw it up by moving in."

I angled my head down toward my left shoulder. "You think living together will screw up your relationship? It's clear you two are in love, and it seems natural you would take the next step."

He opened the refrigerator and removed two bottles of water, then handed me one. "I'm old school, Rach. The next step for me is buying a ring. My generation doesn't typically dive in without a marriage license."

Bishop had never talked about wanting to remarry, but he had hinted at believing it wasn't an option. I'd always thought that was because he hadn't met the right woman, but he had in Cathy, so maybe it was something else. "Do you have a ring?"

We walked over to a six-seat oval conference table in the middle of the pit. Bishop sat on one side while I sat on the other. He opened his laptop and plugged the charging cord into the outlet on his right. "No."

"No? I think I'm going to need a little more than that." I'd already opened my laptop and had logged in to my e-mail, but I lowered the screen and eyed my partner. He had yet to respond and appeared to be typing on his keyboard as if I hadn't said a thing. "Bishop."

He glanced up at me. Raising an eyebrow, he said, "Yes?"

I held my arms toward him with my palms up. "Well?"

He leaned back and sighed. "I did that once. It didn't work out, and things are good between us. I don't see the point in changing everything when it works good how it is."

Oh. He wasn't even on the dock. The water was at least a mile away. "Have you discussed any of this with Cathy?"

"She hasn't asked."

I closed my laptop and pushed it aside then leaned forward with my elbows on the table, looked my partner dead in the eyes, and said, "I used to think you were an idiot, and apparently, I was right."

"Thank you for being honest."

I laughed. "I understand that you're old fashioned, and maybe a little slow in the relationship thing, and God knows I am the last person who should be giving any advice on this, but of the two of us, I feel like I'm miles ahead of you. And also, contrary to popular opinion, I'm a female with emotions and expectations, like normal females. Like Cathy." I rubbed my forehead with my right palm feeling a headache building right inside my skull. "If a woman has to ask where your relationship stands, it's already teetering on the edge of over." I took a deep breath. "It doesn't matter how old she is, the natural progression of a relationship is from dating to falling in love to the next step, whatever that may be. For me and Kyle, it's living together. For you that next step is a ring. I suspect Cathy knows this about you. So, if that isn't something you think you can do, walk away now. Leaving her hanging on to something that isn't going to happen is just cruel."

He dug his readers out of his pocket and placed them on the tip of his nose. When he looked back at his computer and began typing again, my jaw dropped.

"Are you trying to tell me you don't want to talk about it?"

We made eye contact. "I understand what you're saying, and you're right. I should tell her how I feel, but I could lose her, and I don't want to. I love her."

That was the most selfish thing I'd ever heard Bishop say. "You'll lose her anyway." I pushed out my chair and walked over to the printing station, grabbed some copy paper, and tossed it onto the table next to my laptop. I grabbed a pencil as I sat and began sketching out Baxter's entrance.

23

Kyle was asleep on the couch when I got home. I came in quietly, hoping not to wake him, and before taking off my equipment, tiptoed to the couch to check on him. I wound up ogling him with both admiration and lust in my eyes. I cleared my throat, and his left eye popped open.

"Oh." I stepped back, lost my balance from hitting my legs against the trunk we used as a coffee table and fell backwards, then hit the trunk and rolled off to the side. "Damn," I whined.

Kyle laughed. "I was awake when you pulled into the garage, but this made keeping my eyes closed worth it." He flung his legs over and stood, then reached out his hand.

I gladly took it and cringed when he winced. "I'll go on a diet."

He laughed. "It's not you, it's me."

I knew that, and I hated his strength wasn't yet where it had been before being shot up. "You'll get there," I said. He pulled me into a kiss. I gave him a quick one then backed away using kissing in front of Louie for a reason. Mostly, I felt grimy and dirty from the bombing.

"You smell like fire," he said. A smile pulled at his mouth. "I was going to say dyn-o-mite like Jimmy Walker, but you wouldn't get the reference."

"Who's Jimmy Walker?" I asked.

He pressed his hand against his heart. "That hurts. He's a seventies TV star. Used to walk around saying dyn-o-mite."

I pursed my lips. "I don't get it."

He grabbed my hand and took me to our bedroom. "Get undressed, and I'll get your shower ready."

I didn't deserve to be treated so well. "Thank you." I kissed him lightly. "I do not deserve you."

"Yes, you do." He smiled and headed for the shower.

While I showered, he made me a grilled chicken sandwich. When I climbed into bed, he served it on a tray with chips and fresh fruit, and I ate it like I hadn't eaten in years.

"Tell me about your day."

I laid it all out for him.

"I can make a call to an agent in Webb County if you'd like. See if they have anything on the ranch out there."

"No," I said. "If you look into it, they'll take it away from us."

"Probably." He snuck a chip from my plate. "What're the odds the bomb was meant for you?"

"I'm thinking more than fifty percent. If Baxter is our guy, which both Bishop and I think is the case, then he's going to want to stop us from digging into this. A day worker could easily have planted that thing."

"But he'd have to be there to turn on the timer."

"The cameras only cover the front of the stables. The other entrance is blind."

"What's the distance from the road? Could someone walk to it?"

I nodded while I chewed. "We think they planted it sometime between us showing up at Baxter's and today, obviously." I stuffed the last of the sandwich into my mouth. "Which means they knew we were there."

"Or they're watching the ranch."

"Or someone there is involved." I grabbed my cell phone and called Bishop, anxious to share this theory with him. If he was mad, he was mad. The truth hurt sometimes.

"We'll get back there tomorrow," Bishop said when he answered and listened to me for a minute. "There were two younger men there. It could be one of them." He yawned. "It's late. I'm checking out for the night. I've got a personal training appointment at six."

I called Ben Cooper. "Do you have contact information for the two younger employees at your place this morning?"

"You think one of them bombed the stables? Didn't you have someone talk to them?"

"We can't rule anyone out." We had decided to have an officer interview the men, but he hadn't learned anything that made either of them seem suspicious.

I climbed out of bed to grab my notepad, but Kyle grabbed my arm. "Tomorrow," he whispered. "It's late."

"I'll give you a call in the morning. In the meantime, I'd appreciate you texting me their contact information."

"I'll do that now," Cooper said.

After disconnecting the call, Kyle said, "You move on them tonight, and they'll be gone."

He was right. Besides, I was exhausted. "Agree." I quickly planted a kiss on his lips. "Thanks for the dinner." I took the tray back to the kitchen. It took about five minutes to clean up, and when I walked into the bedroom, Kyle was sound asleep.

I stayed up a few more hours, my mind racing through scenarios and thoughts. We'd have to hit Habersham, but we couldn't do it in a way that would cause suspicion. We had to tread carefully so we didn't lose him. The cartel doesn't mess around, and even though medical professionals were smart, their street smarts didn't equate to anything close to cartel level. If Habersham ran, he'd wind up dead and useless to us. We needed him.

～

KYLE WAS GONE when I woke up. He'd left early to go to the gym. I wondered if he was meeting Bishop. The two of them working out painted a hilarious picture in my head. Kyle, still recovering, and Bishop, still learning. They could wind up a social media sensation.

Michels and Levy were in the kitchen when I walked in. I smiled. "How's the Alpharetta thing?"

"Over," Levy said.

"Thank God," Michels said. "They don't know how to run an investigation." Michels, a newer detective, was often critical of other departments.

"There is more than one way to run an investigation," I said. "We did it differently in Chicago. I thought y'all were as slow as molasses when I came here." I pressed my lips together and hit the K button on the Keurig to make my coffee.

"A woman with a Chicago accent trying to talk country is painful," Michels said.

"A Philly accent is probably worse," Levy added. She finished stirring her coffee and smiled at me, then looked back at Michels. "Well, we're off like a herd of turtles."

I laughed as Michels said, "You're right. It's worse."

"Bishop in yet?" I asked.

"Nope," they said together.

I wondered if our discussion had frustrated him more than I'd thought. It hadn't been my intention to upset him, but facts were facts, and I liked Cathy. I liked Bishop. I liked them together, and I didn't want to see either of them get hurt. I breathed a heavy sigh. Maybe I needed to work on my delivery.

"You coming?" Levy asked.

"Be right there," I said. I tapped out a quick text to my partner.

On your way?

Be there in five. Grabbed coffee after the gym.

Got it.

At least he'd responded. If he was mad, his text didn't sound like it.

I gave Levy a once over in the investigation room. She'd picked up the dry eraser and swiped it across one of the boards. "You'd look good as a redhead."

She flipped around. "What?"

"Your complexion. It would look good with red hair."

"I'm not interested in dyeing my hair."

"How about a wig?"

She placed her hands on her hips. "Where you going with this?"

"We need an in with Habersham."

"What kind of in?" She walked the few steps to the conference table and pulled out a chair, then sat. "Professional or personal?"

"I'm not sure yet. Bishop is on his way. We'll discuss it when he shows up."

That was ten minutes later.

"Send Levy in as a customer?" Bishop asked.

"Or something else," I said.

Bubba had been pounding his keyboard loud enough for us to notice when he stopped. "They're not hiring."

"Habersham's place?"

"Yeah," Bubba said.

"Then it looks like she's going in with an animal."

My cell phone rang. "Detective Ryder."

"This is Ben Cooper. The contacts I sent you last night? One of them didn't show up for work this morning. I called him but the call went straight to voicemail."

"Which guy?" I asked.

"Juan Ortiz."

"How long has he worked for you?"

"He's been with me about six months, but he came from Haverty, where he said he worked for over a year. Moved to the country two years ago."

"I haven't looked at the contacts yet. Is his address on it?"

"Yes, ma'am."

"Is he legal?"

"To the best of my knowledge, yes."

"I'll be in touch." I disconnected the call and checked the text message, then forwarded Ortiz's contact to Bubba. The room silenced when his cell phone erupted into song.

His mouth dropped open. He quickly yanked his phone from his pocket and stopped *My Way* by Frank Sinatra from continuing.

"Is that my text ringtone?" I asked, trying hard not to laugh. "I'm not sure if I'm insulted or impressed."

Michels laughed heartily. "Don't respond to that," he said to Bubba.

"It's just a song," he responded. "Bishop's is *Something Stupid*."

"Seriously," Michels said. "What is it?"

"*Something Stupid*," Bubba repeated.

No one in the room knew what that was except Bishop. "It's another Frank Sinatra song." He peered at Bubba. "Oh, hell. You did that on purpose."

"No. I just like Frank. He's my man." Bubba was of Indian descent, and I'd never expected his darker skin to redden to the degree it had. I couldn't help but laugh.

"What's mine?" Levy asked.

The red intensified. "The Lady is a Tramp." He turned his phone over and placed it on the table. "But I usually silence my phone. I guess I forgot to this morning."

"What's mine?" Michels asked.

He probably hadn't heard a full Sinatra song once in his life.

"Nothing," Bubba said. "I don't have one for you."

"I call bullshit," Levy said. "Spill it, Bubba, or we'll confiscate your phone."

"You can't do that."

Levy stood. "Bet?" Her tone was serious but the smile on her face gave her away.

"Fine," he said. "It's The Girl from Ipanema."

Bishop lost it. He'd been chuckling, but he'd gone into a full throttle laugh turned into coughing fit from too many years of smoking.

Michel's rolled his eyes. "I don't even want to know."

"Okay," I said. "Can we get back to work now?"

Bishop's coughing fit dropped to a reasonable level.

"I just texted you the contact information for Juan Ortiz. Get me what you can and let me know if he's here legally."

"On it," Bubba said, nodding as he retreated behind his laptop screen, his fingers flying across the keyboard.

I leaned forward and explained Cooper's words to the group, my gestures emphasizing certain points.

Levy raised an eyebrow and asked, "Which is first? The vet or this Ortiz guy?" She leaned back in her chair, crossing her arms.

"Officer Manny's wife is a hair stylist and makeup artist," I replied, pointing towards Levy. "Get with him and see if she can set you up with a wig and a new look. I'm thinking rich woman, moving to Alpharetta, buying land for a horse ranch. Interviewing vets." I made a sweeping motion with my hand to indicate the transformation.

"Hence the red wig," Levy remarked, smirking.

Michels chimed in, leaning closer to Levy. "You'd look good as a redhead."

Levy shot him a stern glare, her eyes narrowing.

"I'm just saying," Michels shrugged, leaning back in his chair.

Levy turned to me and nodded. "Set up the appointment but make it for the end of the day," I said.

"If he'll see me then," Levy said with a note of uncertainty.

Bubba, still engrossed in his work, chimed in, "They're already open, so you should be good to go."

"Got it," Levy acknowledged with a determined expression on her face.

Michels shook his head, smirking. "In case anyone's going to ask, I'm not putting on makeup."

I turned to him and raised an eyebrow. "You got any ranch attire?"

He blinked, caught off guard. "Uh, no, but there's a Goodwill on exit 2. I'm sure I can find something. You're her top guy," I said, nodding toward him. "You'll need to be in on the interview."

Bishop leaned forward, concern evident on his face. "Won't that be suspicious?"

I smirked and replied, "If they don't play their parts right, it will."

Levy interjected confidently, "We can do it."

"Meet us back here at six," I instructed the two detectives.

Levy and Michels exchanged quick glances and then hurried out of the room, their movements purposeful.

Bishop leaned back in his chair and sighed. "I hope they get pictures."

I raised an eyebrow. "Of Habersham?"

Bishop smirked mischievously. "Of themselves."

24

"About last night," Bishop said after everyone left the investigation room. "I want you to know I understand what you're saying."

"Okay." I wasn't sure what to say. I didn't want to create tension between us, and Bishop's life was his to live however he chose. Me offering unsolicited opinions wasn't smart, and I needed to learn to keep my mouth shut, even if my intentions were good.

"And I'll figure it out."

"Not much to figure out. Be honest with yourself, and then be honest with her. Seems easy to me." And there it was. Me offering unsolicited opinions once again, not even realizing it was happening until the words vomited from my mouth.

He dipped his head down and raised his eyebrows. "Says the woman who couldn't tell her significant other she was taking horse riding lessons again."

I hated it when he was right, and I didn't want to push further, so I changed the subject. "We need to get to Juan Ortiz's place, and then we ought to go to where Cooper gets his day workers off Highway Nine."

"By Wills Park."

"Yes."

He closed his file. "What're the odds of Ortiz being home?"

"Slim to none if he's cartel and knows we're on this. If he's just not interested in being a ranch hand and hasn't found another job, the chances are better."

"Tough call on where to go first," Bishop said. "Either way, if we go to Ortiz, then we need back up. He's off Windward. The last thing we need is to chase him around heavy traffic."

I had an option. "We can send a few patrol cars to the apartment complex. Have them keep a watch on the area, check on his building, and see what they can find. We go to the day worker pick up site first, then head over there."

"Sounds like a plan," he said.

I received a text from Savannah. I hadn't heard from her in a while, and I'd been too busy to check in.

Trying not to bother you given the circumstances, but I'm here if you need to vent. Also, I'm fat, hot, and ready to kill the next person who says I look beautiful pregnant. I feel like an elephant.

Elephant mamas are loyal and amazing, I replied. *And they can stomp someone to death.*

I'd just have to roll this big belly over someone's head, and I could suffocate them, and that someone may just be your boss.

I laughed out loud. *If you do, please have someone take a video.*

LOL. Check in when you can. Worried about you, she wrote.

Worried about you too but excited for that baby. Go pamper yourself. It'll help.

She sent a heart emoji.

"Poor Sav," I said to Bishop. "She's losing her mind."

"She looks great pregnant," he said. "But it's got to be rough."

I wouldn't know. The whole idea of babies had come and gone, that little urge beaten down by Sean's murder and the fact that his daughter would grow up without a father. I couldn't do that to a child. Couldn't risk my lifestyle with a child. Louie was already a big enough commitment.

Bishop arranged for patrol to cruise through Ortiz's apartment complex and keep watch on his building while I checked with Bubba for updates.

"Baxter is coming home this evening," he said. He rotated his laptop in my direction. "Three horses. Emma Baxter is stoked."

The horses were stunning. I hated what they were being used for. "Did she say a time?"

He shook his head. "Just that they'd be home tonight."

"So, he flies out there, *picks* the horses, for lack of a better term, then has someone drive them back? I can't see Baxter driving them back himself. Who drives them here? Did he fly someone out with him?"

"My guess is someone drove there with the horse trailer." He scrolled through the Facebook page for the ranch. "Here. I thought I saw a trailer picture the other day. Read the caption."

"Brad and Austin made it back with the new horses," I said.

"One of those is one that died."

"Last names?"

"They're tagged in the photos." He clicked Brad's name, and it brought him to his personal Facebook profile. "Brad Turner." He clicked on the about section, but Brad hadn't put anything online.

"Check his posts."

He clicked and showed me that everything on his page was things he'd been tagged in. We moved on to Austin. His last name was Carter, but like Brad, he posted nothing on social media.

"Facebook's kind of an old person's thing. I can check Snap."

"Please."

Bishop walked in. "Find something?"

"Baxter's drivers. Checking Snap now."

"Snap Chat," Bishop said as if he was hip with modern slang. At least he was getting there. "Cathy has one of those. She doesn't use it, but she does check on some of her problem kids."

"Interesting," I said.

"There are a lot of Brad Turners." He rolled his chair to another computer and tapped like he'd had too much coffee. "Over one hundred in Georgia." More tapping and then, "And weird. Over one hundred Austin Carters too. Didn't think that would be popular, but I go by Bubba, so what do I know?" He rolled back to the other laptop. "It'll take some time, but I'll go through all these and see if I can find them. I'll check the other socials too."

"Thanks," I said.

"Any warrants coming? I'd like to start digging into something other than socials."

"We're working on it," I said.

∾

THE AREA where the day workers stood wasn't as close to Wills Park as we'd thought but was closer to the recycling building on the opposite side of Highway Nine.

"Must be a slow morning," I said. I counted twelve men but didn't get them all.

"More like slow economy," Bishop said. He pulled past the group and edged his vehicle onto the side of the road. Since it was clearly a government vehicle, the men didn't budge. Normally, they'd run to any vehicle slowing near them, hoping to be the pickup car, but not Bishop's.

"You're not a popular guy."

He laughed. "Maybe they don't like the government license?" His tone was snarky.

"Nah, I think it's you."

We approached the group of men huddled together on the side of the road. The sun had risen just enough to beat down on us, but with the cool breeze, it wasn't too hot.

I noticed a man among them who seemed visibly on edge. His darting eyes and fidgeting hands set off alarms in my mind. Sensing trouble, Rob and I exchanged a quick glance. "Atlanta Braves baseball cap. He's going to run."

Bishop carefully placed his hand on his weapon. It wasn't a bold move in any way, but it did light a fire under a few of the men. Three backed up, grouped together as if we weren't there, and a few others stared at the ground. Before we made it to them, the man in the Braves hat suddenly broke into a sprint, leaving the others in a state of bewildered confusion.

"Here we go," I said.

"Damn, we did legs this morning," Bishop said as he lunged forward and into a run.

Our training and instincts kicked in. The man sprinted across Highway

Nine, nearly getting smacked by a minivan, jumped over the small ditch, and bolted toward the park with us on his tail.

"Stop! Police!" Bishop's voice rang in my ears, urging me forward.

The guy could run. I pushed my body to its limits, muscles burning with exertion as we charged toward the park. We'd notified Alpharetta of our appearance on their turf, and the blaring sirens of their approach filled the air.

He jumped over the park fence and sprinted down the hill toward the playground area. I groaned at the thought of jumping the fence, but when Bishop passed me and practically vaulted over it with an ease I couldn't comprehend, I busted my ass to do the same.

"He went right," Bishop yelled.

I caught sight of the runner near the bathrooms, his steps echoing on the playground's pavement as he dashed past a group of people, alarming children and parents alike.

"Police! Stop running! We just want to talk!" I shouted, trying to appeal to his reason, which clearly didn't work by the way he'd doubled down on his speed.

Four Alpharetta patrol vehicles pulled up to the bathrooms and blocked the guy from running past them. He froze as the officers jumped out of their vehicles with their weapons drawn. Bishop kept running and got to him first, then threw himself on top of the guy. The two of them crashed to the ground. Someone yelled something but I wasn't sure who or what.

I dropped my knees onto the man's legs while Bishop cuffed him, and two Alpharetta officers kept their weapons aimed at them.

"I'm legal! I'm legal!" The man yelled.

"You ran, dumbass," Bishop said. He stood, and watching him was rough. He'd been beaten up badly a while back. Regardless of what he said, that was the reason he'd been on a health and wellness kick, but his body was still recovering from that beating. He shouldn't have been running and dropping himself onto anyone or anything.

I watched as he clutched his side and dropped a list of cuss words that would make a Chicagoan proud. "I've got this," I said.

The Alpharetta men got the man onto his two feet. "I'm innocent," he said. His accent was thick, and it was hard to understand him.

"What's your name?" I asked.

"Lucas Javier. I'm legal. I have papers."

"Citizen?" I asked.

"No, but I have papers. I'm allowed to be here."

I advised the Alpharetta officers that we only needed one for possible transport to their jail. The others left, but the one officer stuck around, and a little too close for comfort in my opinion. "Why'd you run?" I asked Lucas.

"I don't like police."

I didn't either, most of the time, but probably for different reasons. "I'm going to need a better reason than that." Bishop had caught his breath and stood beside me. Neither of us planned to play any card related to Baxter until necessary.

His eyes shifted left then right. "My lady. She threw me out. She said she'd send the police if I tried to come back."

Dear God. "Let me get this straight. You got kicked out of your place, and to keep you away, your girlfriend said she'd call the cops if you tried to come back?"

"Sí."

"You ran from the side of the road. Try again."

"That's the truth, I swear. My lady, she don't play around. I thought she called you because I just texted her and said I wanted to come home. I didn't want to be arrested."

I held out my hand, palm up. "Show me the text."

He removed his phone from his pocket and swiped up then tapped his finger onto the screen. "Here. See? She said she'd tell you I beat her."

"Did you?" Bishop asked while I read the text thread.

Lucas Javier shook his head. "No, no. I love her."

He hadn't lied about the text messages. "Mr. Javier, we didn't show up near the park because your girlfriend sent us. We're looking for day workers who've worked the horse ranches in Hamby. Are you one of them?"

"I did not steal anything."

Bishop told the Alpharetta cop he was good to go.

"I'll wait around in my vehicle and drive you back to yours," the cop said.

"Which ranch?" I asked.

"The big one."

"Do you remember the name?"

"No, but I think it starts with an H?"

Bingo. "Haverty?"

He nodded repeatedly. "Sí. Sí. Haverty."

"What about Cooper Creek? Ever work there?"

"Sí, but not many times. They don't use us often."

"When was the last time you've been to any of the ranches?" Bishop asked.

"I go to Haverty last week. The other one, not for a while."

"Do you know of anyone who's gone to work there over the past few days?"

"No, sir. You want me to ask around because I don't want to start no trouble."

"We don't need you to ask around." Bishop handed him a business card. "If you hear anything about the ranches in Hamby, you give me a call, okay?"

"Sí. Sí. I will."

"We'll give you a lift back," Bishop said.

"No, thank you. It will look bad, me with you. I'll walk."

"Suit yourself," Bishop said.

The side of the road was empty when we returned.

"You have a knack for scaring off men," Bishop said.

I smoothed down a cuticle with the tip of my finger. "Nothing new."

25

"Yes, my name is Susan," I lied. I'd called Haverty Ranch. "Is the ranch manager in today?"

"You mean Billy White, yes, ma'am. I can get him for you."

"No, that's okay. I was going to stop by. I want to talk to him about riding lessons. Would that be okay?"

"Come on by. Billy will be happy to help."

"Thank you," I said.

"Susan?" Bishop said with a smile. "Susan's a polite woman's name."

"No, Susan's a liar."

He laughed. "You're not going to pull that off, especially with me there. One look at me and they'll know I'm the fuzz."

"I wasn't planning on trying." I rolled my eyes. "By the way, no one calls cops the fuzz. I don't think they have since the seventies."

"Po-po?"

"Please, stop."

We arrived at Haverty Ranch without another police slang term uttered from Bishop's mouth. Thankfully.

Neither Emma Baxter nor any other family member was at the ranch.

"Are you Susan?" a woman in the main office asked.

I pretended to not know what she was talking about. "I'm Detective Ryder, and this is Detective Bishop. We're here to talk to Mr. Baxter."

"Oh, he's not here," she said. "Is there something I can do for you?"

"Is Mr. White available?"

"May I ask why you're here?"

"The county has seen an increase in ranch crimes over the past few months. We'd like to discuss it with Mr. White," I said.

"Offer advice on keeping the ranch secure," Bishop said. "Especially since Cooper Creek Ranch was bombed."

"Oh, I heard about what happened to poor Mr. Higgins. Is that why?"

"Yes," Bishop said.

"Then I'll get Billy up here right quick."

"We'll wait outside," Bishop said. "Thank you."

We stood in front of the office for about five minutes. I checked around for video cameras and found them quickly. "Lots of cameras," I said as I moved a few feet from the office and out of the cameras' lines of sight.

"Can't imagine why," Bishop said. It was obviously sarcasm.

Garcia walked by but acted as if we were invisible. He stopped to talk to a man about six inches taller and fifty pounds lighter than him. When the man saw us, he walked over with Garcia at his side.

"Morning," he said. "You're here about the bomb over at Cooper Creek Ranch or the death of Sean Higgins? Think they're connected?" He dropped his head and shook it. "Terrible, what happened to him. He was a good fella."

"We're looking into both," I said. "Were you two friends?"

"More like acquaintances, but he had a solid reputation. Hard not to see that in him the few times we did talk." He checked his watch. Was he nervous or in a rush? "Is this something we should be worried about here?"

"We're talking to the ranches in the area," Bishop said. "Have you noticed any new faces? Maybe new employees or visitors? Anyone come and go quickly?"

"You think someone associated with the ranch is involved? Mr. Baxter does a good job of vetting staff. He's only had to let a few go since I've been here, about three years now. Sure, we've got people who hop from one ranch to another, but I can't see any of them doing something like this. They're all hard workers."

"What about day workers?" I asked. "How often do you have them?"

"Usually, a few times a week. We've got three new horses coming in today." He checked his watch. "Should be here in a few hours. I have two day workers to help with the load."

"What do they do?" I asked.

"It depends. I'm short a guy today, which is why I have two. Mr. Baxter likes to have the extra staff while the vet checks them out. Some horses get a little testy around vets."

"Which vet do you use?" Bishop asked. When White angled his head and gave him a questioning look, he added, "We like to rule out as many people as we can while investigating."

"Yeah, sure. Understand. Mr. Baxter and Dr. Habersham have worked together for years. Any time we get a new horse, Habersham comes by after his office closes and examines them. A few times he's run into some things that needed fixing, and then we lost three horses recently, but none of that is unusual."

"It's not unusual to lose three horses in a short period of time?" I asked. Garcia stood silent, but I noticed the smile tugging at the corners of his mouth.

"Not when you're buying them from a ranch who brings them in from Mexico. We believe the horses come from bad stock, and honestly, I think Mr. Baxter got screwed. Those people know they're selling bad horses. They just don't care."

"So how does it work?" I asked. "Your boss buys them from a Texas rancher who bought them from someone in Mexico?"

"No, ma'am, though I can see why you'd think that. He buys them at an auction held at a ranch in Texas. The ranch doesn't own the horses. The owner in Mexico brings them up and sells them there. I've tried to convince Mr. Baxter to go to Kentucky instead, but he prefers Texas. I don't know what he pays for the horses, but I suspect he's getting a deal he wouldn't get in Kentucky."

"Do you know what ranch he uses?" Bishop asked.

"I do, but I'd have to find the name. If you give me a minute, I'll do that."

He nodded to Garcia. "Go take care of the eastern stables. We'll be putting the new horses there."

Garcia responded by heading in that direction.

"Be right back," White said.

After he was out of hearing distance, I said, "So, they're direct from Mexico after all."

"That's an interesting update."

I admired a horse as a man guided it past us. "Doesn't mean this Hal Jacobs and Evergreen Ranch aren't involved."

White returned. "Evergreen Ranch. Owner's Hal Jacobs." He handed Bishop a yellow stickie note. "Wrote down his contact info. You think this has anything to do with Sean's death and the bombing?" He paused for a moment and added, "Could this be horse drugging?"

"We're not sure what it is," I said. "That's why we're asking questions." I smiled. "Thanks for the number."

"Sure, anything else I can do for you?"

"Actually," I said. "Can we take a look at the stables? We'd like to do a quick run through, you know, to make sure there's no bombs here."

"I'd appreciate that, and I'm sure Mr. Baxter will too. We've got two stables. This one here," he pointed to the closest stable, "is our west side stable. The other is the east side." He motioned for us to follow him.

We walked into the stables and ran into Damian Sayers. His focused look turned into a wide-eyed, almost paranoid one when he saw us.

"Sayers, these are Detectives—I'm sorry. I can't remember your names."

"Ryder," I said. "And Bishop. We met the other day."

"Oh, you've already been here?" White asked.

"Only briefly after Sean's death," Bishop said. "Wanted to give a heads up to the owner just in case something was going on we hadn't hit on then."

"Got it," White said.

"Nice to see you again," Damian said. He rushed away.

I watched him turn around twice and stare at me.

I counted five security cameras inside the stable. Bishop and I did our due diligence and checked the stalls for bombs. Not surprisingly, we didn't find any. "You've got yourself a nice stable here," Bishop said. "We didn't find anything here, but we'd still like to look at the next one."

White nodded. "Come on let's go do that now."

On the way out, I counted two more cameras at the back end of the stables and two more just outside that exit. That made a total of nine cameras.

The east side stables only had five cameras. Two on the outside at both entrances and one on the inside. It didn't take a genius to know what that meant. We got out of there quickly, passing Damian Sayers on the way out. He barely looked at us.

Bishop and I talked over each other in his vehicle.

"Sorry," I said. "You go first."

"How many cameras did you count in the first stables?"

"Nine."

"And the second?"

I smiled. "Only five. doesn't take much to figure out what that means. They're bringing the horses in and putting them in the back stable with limited security cameras where Habersham removes the drugs."

Bishop agreed. "Right now, all the horses are in the stable closest to the office. That could mean they made room in the other stables for the new ones, or they move them up once the drugs are out."

"What happens to the horses after the drugs are removed?" I asked. "If they don't die that is."

"You think they take them back to Texas?"

"That doesn't sound like a good business practice for the cartel," I said. "It would cost money to ship them back. I don't know much about selling horses, but I imagine there's something they do to verify if the horse is one they've sold before when it goes up to auction."

"True," Bishop said. "But if this Evergreen ranch is only working with the cartel, Baxter isn't buying the horse. He's grabbing them, and bringing them to Georgia where Habersham removes the fentanyl, then what? They wouldn't have any paperwork, so he can't sell them. At least not to anyone credible."

I stared out the window. There was an answer, but I liked the one I was thinking. "I'd like to think he's selling them to small farms where they live happily ever after or maybe giving them to horse sanctuaries. The problem is, it's very likely they're being disposed of."

"Unfortunately, that's what I think is happening," he said.

I knew he'd think that as well. "We can put a GPS tracker on one and see."

"Do you really want to know what happens to them?"

I nodded. "If they're going to good homes, great. If they're being disposed of, that's another crime we can add to Baxter's list."

"Slaughter is only a misdemeanor, and there are a lot of boxes to check to make it a crime," Bishop said.

"It shouldn't be too hard to track one," I said. "I'm sure Kyle's got someone who can implant a tracker on a horse."

He turned into the department parking lot. "Why would we plan to track a horse? Why not just plan to bust Habersham when he removes the drugs?"

"I hate it when you make sense."

He pulled into a parking space and killed the engine. "I love animals too, and busting Habersham and Baxter is a way to save horses."

"Some of them."

"We can't save everyone, Rachel."

"Maybe not, but I'm going to spend my life trying."

THE ENTIRE POLICE pit full of officers whistled when Levy walked through. I really hoped they knew it was her, or they'd all end up on suspension for it.

"Thank you," Levy said. She gave her hips a little wiggle as she strutted toward Jimmy's office. The three-inch heels she wore made my feet ache. I held my breath waiting for her to fall on her face, but she didn't. She actually rocked the model walk in those things. I was even a little jealous. I would have definitely fallen on my ass.

"Wow," I said. "You clean up good."

She sat beside me in front of Jimmy's desk. "Thank you, love." Her Southern accent was on point. "But you're not my type."

Michels laughed. He and Bishop stood behind Jimmy sitting in his chair. They all admired Levy, who I think they saw as a woman for the first time. It had to be the wig and the push-up bra. A good push-up bra worked miracles, but that wig was phenomenal on her.

"I'm impressed," Jimmy said. "Next time we need someone as an undercover hooker, you're the one."

"Hey now," I said. "I can be a hooker."

They laughed.

"Right," Michels said.

"If they want one that kicks their ass instead of screws them," Jimmy hissed.

"That hurts."

Bishop whistled an unfamiliar tune as he looked at the ceiling. Smart partner.

"Anyway," Jimmy said. "We have a change of plans."

Levy's eyes widened. "Please don't say this is off. It took me three hours to look like this."

"It's not normal for her to be a woman," Michels said.

She flipped him the bird, and he laughed.

"You better watch it," I said. "Those heels are ball poppers."

He cringed.

Levy laughed and said, "Damn straight they are." She looked back to Jimmy. "I've got an appointment at 6:30. His last appointment."

"You're still on," he said. "The only change is that you're looking to buy horses. Cheap."

"Racehorses aren't cheap," she said.

"You're not buying racehorses," I said.

Bishop and I filled them in on what we'd learned.

"Oh, hell," Levy said. "They're slaughtering them. We need to stop this."

"I agree," I said. "But Bishop had a point. We can't stop it all, but we can change things one pathetic excuse for a human at a time."

"We take out Baxter and Habersham, and the cartel loses key players in the area."

"And the tri-county area is a high profit area for the cartel," Kyle said. He'd just walked into Jimmy's office. He smiled at me. "Thanks for the invite. I do have some information for you all."

"I called Kyle about the horses," I said. "Figured he'd have some input."

"Appreciate it," Jimmy said. "What do you have?"

"If horses are being slaughtered due to felony drug trafficking, it's not a misdemeanor anymore, but as I told Rachel, it's a matter of the chicken before the egg. You'll have to find a way to trace previous horses and link them to the case. The drug bust comes first."

"We know that," I said. "It's just frustrating."

"So, what do we do?" Michels asked.

Bubba walked in. "They got your missing employee."

"Who's they?" Jimmy asked.

"Alpharetta."

"That's not good," Bishop said.

"Nope," Bubba said. "Found him behind the recycling center about an hour ago."

"He was involved," I said.

"And the cartel considered him a risk."

"I'll call Ben Cooper. He'll want to know," I said and stood to step out of the room.

An officer tapped on Jimmy's door. "Lunch is ready, Chief. I put it in the investigation room as you asked."

"Thanks," he said. He smiled at us. "I ordered Subway for us. You'll need to grab and go."

Bishop nodded. "Ortiz knew something. We'll need to coordinate with Alpharetta."

"I'll call Cooper on the way then," I said.

"Sounds good," he said. "I'll notify patrol, have them keep tabs on the area. If necessary, we'll send one to the apartment."

26

Bishop and I arrived at a crime scene smelling of a mix of burnt rubber, gasoline, and something stale and sweet intermingled with the metallic tang of fresh blood. A storm was moving in, the dark clouds hiding the sun and casting ominous shadows on the already depressing scene. Flashing red and blue lights from the police cars added further to the unsettling atmosphere. Though all to be expected, it didn't stop the heaviness of a murder from seeping into our heads.

"I hate this," I said. "We know nothing about this guy. He could have been an honest, hardworking person who didn't deserve to die."

"Or he was a drug dealing murderer," Bishop said.

"You're so compassionate."

He laughed. "Kids, animals, and the elderly. Those are where my compassion goes. If this guy turns out not to be a part of this, then he'll get it too."

"What happened to innocent before proven guilty?" I asked sarcastically. In cases like Ortiz, we reserved our compassion until we had the facts. We also reserved our judgement, but we had to work diligently at that.

The tension in the air was palpable, almost suffocating, even with so many officers on scene. Alpharetta's department was double the size of Hamby, with a department of crime scene techs, all working the scene.

A tall, lanky man wearing a pair of jeans and a blue, striped button down headed our way. He offered a slight smile. "Detectives Ryder and Bishop?"

Bishop nodded. "You must be Detective Rogers."

"Yes, sir." He smiled at me. "Let me update you on what we've got." He motioned for us to follow him toward the scene. "Looks like an execution style shooting. One shot, center of the forehead. Blood splatter against the back of the building says the shooter was only a few feet away."

I relaxed my shoulders. "And you're sure it's Ortiz?"

"Driver's license matches the victim."

"From Georgia?" I asked.

"California."

California gave driver's licenses to undocumented immigrants, so the odds of Ortiz, if that was his real name, being in the country legally were slim. "Any papers?"

"Not on his person."

"Cell phone?" Bishop asked.

"Yes. Locked. We'll have to get access to get anything from it."

Ortiz's body lay lifeless near the building with a pool of dark crimson blood stretched out like a grotesque canvas around his head.

"Any idea who did this?" Rogers asked.

I spoke first. "We're investigating the possible murder of a horse ranch owner in Hamby. It looks like there's a possible link to the cartel."

"This the place that was bombed?" he asked.

"No," Bishop said. "But Ortiz was one of the workers there when it was bombed."

"And you think he planted it," Rogers said.

"We were looking into it," Bishop said. "And if he did, we think it's because the cartel knows we're getting close to blowing up their party."

"So, they decided to blow it up first, or at least try," I added.

Rogers glanced at Ortiz's body. "And our vic here was no longer useful to them."

"Most likely," Bishop said.

Barron approached. "Evening, folks." He smiled at me. "How's Nikki holding up?"

"Seems to be fine," I said. "Thanks for letting her come. I think she's considering going to school to take your place."

"She can have it." He adjusted his belt. "It's no fun being the last one invited to the party."

I would have laughed, but it didn't seem right.

"So," he said, eyeing the victim. "Looks like we got ourselves an execution."

"Looks that way," Rogers said.

Barron looked at Bishop. "And you two are here because?"

"We think it's connected to the Higgins murder and the bombing at Cooper Creek Ranch."

"Heard about that," Barron said. "I don't know what the hell's going on in Hamby. It used to be a quiet, law-abiding place. Seems like it's overrun with criminals these days."

"Bigger town means more opportunities for crime," I said.

He exhaled. "That's too bad." He walked over to Ortiz's body. "Let me get on with this. I'd take a guess at his cause of death, but there's always something to surprise me during the autopsy, so I'll wait on that."

"Yes, sir," Rogers said. He turned toward us. "I'm guessing you'd like to assist?"

"No assist necessary," Bishop said. "But we'd like to exchange information."

"I've got Ortiz's address, but it would be great if we could deliver the notice," I said.

"Is it in Hamby?"

I nodded.

"Sounds good. Have them meet me at the morgue in say, three hours."

"Can do," I said. "May I take some photos?"

"Not a problem," he said. "Now, if you don't mind, I've got some work to do."

I took photos after he walked away. "Ortiz works for Haverty but moves to Cooper Creek. Why?"

We headed back to Bishop's vehicle. "He was either scouting other opportunities or keeping track of the other workers. Maybe they were recruiting or worrying about questionable characters."

I laughed. "That's not at all ironic."

"If Baxter's in with the cartel," Bishop said.

"He is," I said as I climbed into the vehicle.

"Then he's probably paying his men better than the other ranches."

"To keep them with him and quiet."

"Right," he said. "We promised Cooper a phone call, so let's see if he knows anything about hourly rates."

"And what though?" I asked. "If the job sucks, or Baxter's an a-hole to work for, and someone else pays around the same, wouldn't people leave?"

"Not those who are keeping an eye on Baxter and involved with the drug smuggling. They'd stick around."

"Except those who are told to work at the other ranches." I bit my bottom lip and thought that through. "After we give the notice, we need to get with Connie. Match up employee records with the other ranches, including Sweetwater. We haven't been there."

"Levy and Michels checked it out, but you're right. We should do the same."

JUAN ORTIZ WAS MARRIED to Clara Ortiz and had a three-year-old son. That didn't mean he didn't work for the cartel. In fact, I leaned closer to a yes on that question. He'd be paid better by them. Of course, there was the constant threat of no longer being useful, which is likely what happened to Ortiz. His wife spoke decent English and seeing us with our badges told her why we'd come.

She appeared angry, not devastated. "They killed him, sí? I knew it. He didn't come home last night. I knew he was dead."

"Who do you think killed him?" I asked.

"The cartel." She rattled off a bunch of Spanish too fast for me to translate.

"I'm sorry," I said. "I only got a little of that."

"I told him to stay away from them, but he promised me it would be okay. That we'd have more money. Now what am I to do? Move back to Mexico?" She shook her head. "No. I cannot do that."

"He told you he was working for the cartel?" Bishop asked.

"Sí. The pay is better, but now he's dead, and I have nothing." She bounced her son on her knee.

"Papa," the boy said.

She wrapped her hand around his head and leaned him close to her chest. "What happens now?"

"We'll need you to go to the morgue and verify it's your husband. Detective Rogers from the Alpharetta Police Department will meet you there."

"He was not at the ranch?"

"No, ma'am," Bishop said. "Was he supposed to be there?"

"He called and said he had to work late."

"Do you know the name of the ranch?" I asked.

"No," she said, shaking her head. "I do not know that, and I know nothing about his job. He tells me nothing. I only know about the cartel because I heard him on the phone last month."

"What was he saying?"

"That they have another shipment coming." She rubbed the top of her son's head. "That's how I know." Tears fell from her eyes. "He wanted a good life for us. We move here for that, but it is so hard for him, working so much and paying our bills. He sends money to his family in Mexico and supports us. He needed more."

Her son wiped a tear from her cheek. *"No llores Mamá. Te traigo una galleta. Estarás major mejor."* He climbed off her lap and ran toward the kitchen.

He offered to get her a cookie to stop her crying. My heart shattered into pieces.

"I do not know what to do. What do I do?"

"Are you in the country legally?" I asked.

She didn't say anything.

"Ma'am," Bishop said. "Staying here might not be safe, not if the cartel knows you know anything."

"Or thinks you know something," I said.

"Where do I go? What do I do?"

We ran into these situations too many times to count, and the last time I tried to help someone didn't work well. We didn't have the budget to hide or protect her. I already knew that. "Do you have family anywhere else in the country?"

"No, but my papa's close friend is in Tennessee."

"Can you go there? It would be safer than here," Bishop said.

"If I leave, they will know I know," she said. "I cannot do that. They will find me."

"We can't protect you," I said.

She walked over to a small cabinet near the apartment's front door, opened it, and removed a nine-millimeter. "I can protect myself."

"Do you know how to use that?" I asked.

"Sí. My papa, he taught me before I came to America. He said I would be safe."

There wasn't much either of us could say.

"Did your husband ever say anything else that made you think he was involved with the cartel?"

She shook her head and placed the gun on the coffee table. I glanced at the child who had hurried in with a cookie and handed it to his mother.

"You really shouldn't leave a weapon near your child," I said.

As if on cue, the boy moved to pick up the weapon. Clara yelled, "No!" She grabbed the gun and put it on top of the cabinet and out of his reach.

I handed her a card. "If you hear or remember anything, or if you need something, please call me. I'll do my best to help."

"Sí," she said.

"Clara," Bishop added. "Do not answer your door for anyone, and I strongly suggest you go to Tennessee, or anywhere else but here."

"No. I will not leave my home. Juan worked hard to give us these nice things, and I am not leaving them. If the cartel comes, I will kill them." She held the door open for us.

I wanted to say more, to offer her some kind of hope that things would be okay, but I couldn't say something I didn't believe.

~

SWEETWATER RANCH WAS on the far end of unincorporated Hamby. Rebecca and Ray Grant were nervous, which was to be expected.

"First a tragic death and now a bombing," Mrs. Grant said. "We moved from the other side of the city because we thought it was safer here."

I didn't have the heart to tell her that nowhere was safe anymore. "Had you met Sean Higgins?"

"Yes, briefly," she said. "My husband and I already told the other two detectives that came by."

"What about your employees? Have any of them come from any of the other ranches?"

"No, sir," Mr. Grant said. "We are a family-owned ranch, and we have family working here. We're not involved in buying and selling racehorses. We rent our stables for people who own horses but need them cared for elsewhere, and we're growing our own food as well as tending to our cattle, pigs, and chickens as food sources. Aside from electricity and gas, we're self-sustaining. Our goal is to become fully self-sustaining, but that won't happen for a bit."

"We have three homes on the land," Mrs. Grant said. "Ours and two for Ray's brothers and their families. We have four children. Ray's brother Thomas has three, and his brother James has three, so, we all work on the ranch, or as we like to call it, farm together."

"But you've had interactions with the other ranches?" Bishop asked.

My cell phone dinged with Garcia's burner phone text tone. I quickly checked.

"In the simplest of terms, yes," Mr. Grant said. "We are all God's children, however we choose to stay rooted with our faith and those who believe as we do. We've only spoken with others when necessary."

"What faith?" I asked. They didn't dress Amish or Mennonite, but there could have been some modernized version I didn't know about.

"We're Mormon," Mr. Grant said. His tone said he was annoyed to tell us. "Now, is there anything else we can help you with?"

Bishop gave him his card. "If you hear anything in regard to the bombing or Sean Higgin's death, please give me a call."

"We probably won't hear anything, but if we do, I'll be in touch."

As we left, I said, "Garcia's in. The horses are arriving this evening. Habersham will be there at nine p.m. to remove the fentanyl, which will then be routed to the location where it's mixed with the Xylazine for sale."

Bishop's eyes lit up with a fire I hadn't seen in them in a while. "Let's get back to the department. Time to put a stop to this."

27

Our team, plus Garcia and Kyle, met in the investigation room. We had five hours before Habersham arrived at Haverty Ranch to remove the drugs from the horses. It would be a long night, so Jimmy had ordered Dunkin' coffee and a tray of chicken wings and fries and had it delivered to the investigation room.

"Why are you here?" I asked Kyle privately. "Is the DEA officially involved?"

"No. I'm here on consult privately. Free of charge. If you need our team, they'll come, but they'll take over."

"That's why I asked. This is ours. We can do this."

"I know."

"You'll get in trouble if you're involved," I said.

"Not if they don't find out."

I wasn't thrilled about that, but I knew Kyle well enough to know he'd made up his mind. "Okay. Let's figure out what we need to do."

Jimmy started the process. "Hamby has the lowest fentanyl-related death rate in the state, but it's not low enough. We're aiming for zero. We take these bastards down, and we're on the right track." He looked at Garcia. "What do you know?"

"For starters, the drug bags are inserted into the horses' rectums in Mexico."

I winced.

"Right?" Garcia said. "Can't feel good. When they're brought to the stable, the vet will use his hand to remove them. If they're too deep, he has to surgically remove them."

"In a stable?" Levy asked. "That's not safe."

"They put them down first, then remove the drugs. They don't worry about patching them up."

"That's how those other horses died," Levy said.

"Probably," I added.

Garcia continued. "Baxter's got one full time cartel employee and four working his ranch as day workers. Anything you heard about them picking them up on the side of the road is BS. These guys come when there are horses arriving with fentanyl, and that's it."

"Prepping for the arrival?" Bishop asked.

"Likely," Garcia said. "Arturo Benito is the full-time worker. He doesn't do shit for the ranch. Best I can tell, he's there to make sure everyone keeps quiet, and that things fall in line as they're supposed to. He's also the person who brings in the other four when the horses arrive."

"Are they there all day?" I asked.

"Today yes, but I haven't figured out if that's normal."

"Which could mean no," Kyle said. "And that someone's onto the investigation."

"Because of Ortiz?" I asked Garcia.

"He's not been mentioned. My guess is he was collateral damage, but yes. Someone sent him with the bomb because they know you've been asking questions."

"So, they had to assume we were going to talk to Cooper," Bishop said.

Garcia nodded. "Watched and waited. Ortiz must have stashed the bomb there somewhere, and when you showed up, he set it off."

"A warning," Jimmy said.

"I'm not sure," Garcia said. "But I'd say they were trying to eliminate you."

Jimmy breathed loudly through his nose. "Then we'll make sure they don't see us coming."

"They've got five cameras inside the main stable, but from what I've heard, they're not bringing the horses there. They'll take them to the back stable, remove the drugs, then bring them to the main stables. Tomorrow or the next day they'll be *sold* and moved."

"By sold you mean slaughtered," Bishop said.

"I think so, but the horses aren't transported by the ranch. They're picked up."

"Any idea who's grabbing them?" I asked.

"Can't get anything on that, but my guess is it's cartel."

I shifted toward Kyle. "Can we get Baxter on slaughter charges if he's not doing the transport?"

"He's writing up fake sales paperwork and signing off on the documents. He knows where the horses are going. You can get him on it, but it might be a long haul for the DA."

"Doesn't matter," Jimmy said. "We'll hit him with every charge we can." He spoke to Garcia. "Have you checked the other stable for cameras?"

"Yes. It's only got one entrance and four stalls. One camera on the entrance, one in each stall, and one each on the front and back interior sides."

Jimmy dropped an f-bomb. "That's a lot of eyes to get around."

"Not if those cameras are taken out," Garcia said. "I can make sure they're cut off when the vet arrives as long as you all are already on the property. If I do it any earlier, they may see and be suspicious."

"What about other cameras? Are there any on the property?"

"I counted five, and one in the back area by the smaller stable. There's an entrance back there, one they use for feed deliveries, but the camera's not working. Two cameras at the front gates, two at the office, and one on the pasture to the left of the ring, on the right side of the fence."

"The ring fence?" I asked.

He nodded. "It looks like it's aimed toward the right, but I can't say how far the site is."

"What system do they use?" I asked.

"Ring."

"Okay, that's easy to work with," Kyle said. "You need a warrant to have their feed blocked. The company is pretty easy to work with if you have a warrant."

"We can get that," Jimmy said. He flicked his head toward me. "Can you make the call?"

"Yep."

"Then get on the phone with Ring once you have the warrant. They'll be able to find the account with an address and name. The only caveat is if they don't have the system set to record video, you won't have anything for court, and it's probable they don't use it for that reason."

"Then why have the cameras?" Michels asked.

"They notify when there's movement," Kyle said.

"Right," Garcia said. "The cartel is going to have men close by. They'll know if someone's there that's not supposed to be. We need to be prepared for that."

"Any idea how many cartel?" Bishop asked.

"No, but I'll make sure to get you their positions. If you've got any recording devices on hand, I'll head back and leave them in the stables. I left for a doctor's appointment, but I need to get back."

"Okay," Jimmy said. He pointed to Bubba. "Get him what he needs, will you, please?"

"Yes, sir," Bubba said. Garcia followed him out.

"Rachel," Jimmy said. "Get on the phone with the judge. Make sure he knows we need it as soon as possible."

"On it," I said and dialed Judge Nowak's cell phone. I put him on speaker phone.

"I've been waiting," he said instead of hello.

"It's taken longer than we thought." I filled him in on what was going on.

"Are you sure you're capable of handling this situation without assistance?"

Jimmy responded. "Your honor, this is Chief Abernathy. We are fully prepared to handle this situation."

"Good to hear," Nowak said. "It's time we bust the cartel's collective ass and move them out of our state."

"Yes, sir," Jimmy said. "It is."

"Give me thirty minutes. I'll have this ready then."

"Thank you, your honor," Jimmy said.

I added, "Thanks, Judge. Luck to the Cubs."

"You know it," he said and ended the call.

"Okay," Jimmy said. "I'll have another vet on standby to examine the horses. We'll need x-rays to verify the bags are inside them."

"And treat them, if necessary," I added.

"Of course." He gave me a partial smile. "Let's get this done."

The first step was to get Bubba on the phone with the security staff to disable the videos and movement sensors. An hour later we had a plan. Garcia would get us in. We'd use undercover drivers in plain vehicles to drive up and down the streets on watch to update us on the arrival and be on their tail if something went wrong. Bishop, Levy, Michels, and I would surround the stables, and once Habersham removed the first bag of fentanyl, we'd go in. We had no idea whether Baxter would be there, but if not, we'd have units near his home to arrest him.

Three hours later, everyone was set and ready to execute. We'd all changed into our dark shirts, dark jeans, and Kevlar vests. Kyle fought to come, but we couldn't allow it, no matter how much I'd wanted him there. We were required to contact the Drug Enforcement Agency to bring him in officially, and since he was still on leave, they'd block his assistance and likely reprimand him for being even slightly involved in the first place.

We gathered in the pit with our additional team members and reviewed our plan. The plain clothes drivers had already hit the road but hadn't reported anything. We'd brought in off-duty officers to handle the drive-bys as well as maintain a watch of the perimeter of the area.

Judge Nowak had also given us a warrant to acquire Mason Baxter's flight information, but it was too late. He'd already returned an hour before we received the warrant. Garcia had notified us with the locations of our recording devices and Jimmy strongly suggested we keep them intact if the situation turned intense. As if saving the department's expensive recording devices would be the first thing on our minds if things went wrong.

"I'm so bummed," Levy said. She pointed to the wig she'd put back on the wig head and left on a conference table in the pit. "I looked hot."

"You did," I said. "I was jealous."

Kyle laughed. "You should bring that wig home. Wear it later tonight." He winked at me.

Levy smirked. "Maybe I should take it home with me then?"

"And what?" Michels asked. "Stare at yourself in the mirror?"

She punched him in the arm.

He grimaced. "Ouch. Why're you always hitting me?"

"Because you're always an ass," she said.

"Time for us to go," I said. "Unless you two need a minute?"

"It would take a lot more than a minute to fix what's wrong with Michels," Levy said.

Bishop cleared his throat. "Let's roll."

28

"Three men," Garcia whispered into his mic. "One at the front gate, one outside the small stable about midway into the pasture. He could see you come through, so be quick and quiet." He paused. "The other one is waiting with Baxter."

"Copy that," I said. I motioned for our team to move. "Let's go."

Levy, Michels, Bishop, and I moved toward our positions surrounding the small stable. I saw the guy in the pasture, but he wasn't facing our direction. I couldn't believe there wasn't one behind the stable, but since it backed up to a dirt road, someone hanging out there might look suspicious.

I crouched low, my heart pounding like a jackhammer in my chest. Walking into an intense environment without preparation was rough, but having a plan and knowing it could go wrong was worse. We knew what could happen and though we were prepared, we still had time to think about the worst, and that always made things more tense. I whispered into my mic. "Ryder in position."

"Copy that," Michels said.

"Levy in position," Levy said.

"Bishop in position," Bishop said.

We'd each taken a side of the stable, doing our best to stay out of any spotlights.

Moonlight filtered through the gaps in the stable's wooden boards, casting eerie shadows that danced like specters on the ground. I stood silent and stoic, my eyes focused, alert to every sound around me. Each of us needed to scope the area from our designated position to understand our surroundings.

"Trailer's pulling in now," Garcia whispered.

"Habersham just arrived," an officer said. "He's parking next to a black Mercedes. A man just walked out of the office." He described the man.

"Baxter," Bishop whispered.

"They're heading toward the trailer," Garcia said. "I'm going in."

Another officer stationed nearby with a powerful set of binoculars said, "Garcia's with Habersham and Baxter."

At first their voices were too muffled to understand, but Garcia did something to adjust his mic and the voices were clear as day.

"Get the horses to the back stables," Baxter said. "We need them checked by Dr. Habersham there instead of the big stables. If they're sick, we don't want them getting our other horses sick as well."

"Sí," Garcia said.

I smiled to myself. Garcia was born and raised in Chicago, but his family was from Mexico, and he was fluent in both languages. He had a Chicago accent but could pull off a Hispanic one with ease.

A few minutes later, Garcia said, "*El Sr. Baxter quiere los caballos aquí para sus exámenes.*"

"Sí," someone replied.

"What'd he say?" Levy asked.

"Baxter wants the horses there for the exams," Bishop said.

"Got it."

"Suspects one and two are getting in a four-wheeler. Garcia is driving the trailer to the stables," an officer said.

Michels pointed to the lights coming through the pasture. "There's the trailer."

"Okay," I said. "Bishop and I are moving to the back with you two. We'll take our positions again as soon as they're inside the building. No one goes in until Bishop or I give the okay."

"Got it," Levy said.

I eyed Michels.

"I heard you," he said.

Baxter parked the four-wheeler near the entrance on Bishop's side of the small stable. I glanced at my partner. He nodded, then removed a Swiss Army Pocketknife from his pocket. "All ready."

Habersham heaved a large medical bag off the back of the four-wheeler and lugged it inside behind Baxter. Neither of them said a word. I counted down thirty seconds quietly. "Now," I said. I watched as Bishop snuck out to the four-wheeler and pushed the knife into the right back tire. He jiggled it around, removed it, then checked for air leakage, and moved onto the next tire. He hurried back to his spot on the front side of the stable.

We needed to wait until Habersham had moved to action with at least one horse. Knowing he might have to kill one infuriated me. Garcia would give us the go-ahead with a cough.

Garcia's mic hummed with voices.

"Only three?" Habersham asked. "I thought we had six coming?"

"I don't make the decisions," Baxter said. "Just hurry up. I don't like doing this."

"But you like the pay off," Habersham said. "This one doesn't look good."

I caught a glimpse of three officers running toward the man in the pasture. "Shit! He spotted us!"

Shots rang out in the near distance, a deafening eruption that sent my heart racing even faster. The acrid smell of gunpowder filled the air as I instinctively dropped to the ground, seeking cover behind a stack of hay bales next to the stable. The gunshots continued, popping like firecrackers as half the department rushed into the pasture, guns drawn and firing in response.

Through a haze of smoke and adrenaline, I locked eyes with Bishop. He nodded, and we made a beeline toward the stable's entrance. My pulse thundered in my ears as the sound of my own breath mingled with the chaos outside. "They must have seen us," I yelled.

"Or expected us."

The stable door was shut. I tried to pull it open, but it wouldn't budge. "I need to kick off the handle," I said.

"Shoot the damn thing," Bishop hollered.

I aimed my weapon down at the handle, then pulled the trigger. The handle disconnected from the door and hung uselessly from it. I yanked on the door, but it was stuck.

"Kick it open," Bishop yelled. He positioned himself beside me, providing cover as I kicked the door hard enough to bust the wood. I grabbed it and yanked it open.

We burst inside. The horses inside the stable, startled by the commotion, let out deep, throaty roars, drowning out the sound of the firefight. The shouts of officers trying to coordinate over their microphones blended with the sound of gunfire, creating a confusing symphony of noise.

"Freeze!" I bellowed as I caught sight of Garcia, the only visible figure in the stable. His eyes flicked toward an empty stall, the absence of a horse telling me that's where the men had hidden. "On the ground!" I commanded, my voice tense and authoritative.

Outside the stable, the firefight raged on, the echoes of shots reverberating within the confined space. Bishop and I pushed forward, charging into the fourth stall. Baxter and Habersham were lying on the ground, partially obscured by a layer of hay. We couldn't see their hands and couldn't tell if they were armed.

"Hands where we can see them. Now!" I demanded. The pungent smell of hay mixed with sweat filled my nostrils as I cautiously stepped toward the pile. I nodded to Bishop and pointed to the second body. I placed my foot on the man's hands, ensuring he couldn't reach for a weapon.

Bishop swiftly dragged the other man out of the hay. He began to roll over, and Bishop's stern warning kept him in place. "Don't move, Habersham," he barked, his gun steady and aimed at Habersham's head.

Baxter's voice rose above the chaos, protesting the pressure on his hands. I crouched down to get a better look, still cautious of potential threats. "Stay down. Don't even think about moving," I said firmly, determined to maintain control of the situation. I released one hand, then quickly tugged it behind him. "Move, and I swear to God, I'll shoot you!" I steadied myself, stood up with my left hand wrapped around Baxter's arm, I leaned forward, grabbed the same arm with my right hand, kept my left foot on his right hand, then pushed his left arm against his back. "Bend your damn arm."

I crouched back down, released my foot from his right hand, pivoted slightly, then yanked it behind him and cuffed him. My eyes darted between Bishop and the two men we had apprehended. "Keep them down. I'm getting the other guy." I kicked open the stall door, my heart pounding in my chest as I aimed my weapon at him.

"Stand up with your hands in the air," I commanded, my voice resolute. Garcia avoided my gaze, his lips twitching with the effort not to laugh. I seized his arm and shoved him into the stall with the other two suspects. "On the ground!" I repeated, making sure he knew we meant business.

"You're all under arrest," Bishop said.

The shots outside finally stopped. Levy and Michels rushed in, breathless and red-faced.

Michels cussed like a sailor. "They had men hidden somewhere," he said. "Those bastards were all over us."

"Any of ours hurt?" I asked as Bishop kept his weapon focused on the three men, and I cuffed Habersham and Garcia.

"Ouch," Garcia said. He dropped a few f-bombs and muttered in Spanish for effect.

"Two shot," Levy said. "Unknown injuries."

"And the shooters?"

"Three down," Michels said. "I counted six outside, but I can't be sure there weren't more."

I whispered into Baxter's ear. "You're going down, just like you do to those poor horses."

I yanked him up and shoved him into the side of the stall. The horse across the stable roared and reared upward, striking his feet toward the stall door.

Five officers rushed in, making the horses even more nervous. One of them said, "I've got them."

The other officers escorted the men outside and, at our direction, stuffed them into squads to transport to the station. I needed a minute. I bent forward and caught my breath.

"You okay," Levy asked.

I nodded. As I straightened, I watched the officer calm the three horses. Habersham had been right. One of them didn't look well. "That one needs the vet," I said.

"Jimmy's got a trailer ready to take them," Levy said.

"Once they're calm enough, I'll walk them out," the officer with the horse said.

I smiled. "Thanks, but you'll need help."

"I'm good," he said. "I've been around horses my whole life."

"Good."

"What the hell happened out there?" Bishop asked.

"We don't know," Levy said. "They literally came out of the grass. One minute they're not there, and the next, we're being shot at."

Bishop dragged his fingers down the sides of his face. "Who tipped them off?"

"No idea," she said.

I moved for them to follow me out. I needed air. Granted, it was air filled with gun smoke, but it was still air.

29

Michels and Levy went back to the station to process Baxter and Habersham while Bishop and I followed the horse trailer to the vet in Alpharetta.

Levy sent a group text. *Both lawyered up, and we let Garcia go.*

I responded. *Expected that.*

Michels replied. *It's Martin Lansing.*

"Great," Bishop said in the waiting room of the vet. "Lansing is a badass. They'll get out."

"If they can make bond," I said. "You know how it is here. Traffickers get bond, but they can rarely pay it."

"Lansing wouldn't have taken them on if they couldn't afford it."

"You're probably right."

The vet walked out. "The x-rays are ready. Come have a look."

"How's the one?" I asked.

"He'll be fine. He's a little weak, but I suspect it's from the trip. We're giving him fluids, and we'll keep him overnight to make sure he's okay. I did draw blood, though I doubt it'll come back with anything urgent." He walked us into a small treatment room with a computer, large display screen, and an animal table. He clicked the mouse and an x-ray appeared on the screen. "Now, I hate to be the bearer of bad news, but these horses are clean."

Bishop leaned in and studied the image. "What?" He stepped back. "You can't be serious."

I took a closer look. "What about the intestines or stomach?"

The vet clicked through to another image. "This is the stomach. It's empty." Another click, and he said the same about the intestines. "All three horses have nothing in their bodies. I drew blood from the other two as well. It's possible they were used before and there are remnants of drugs in their system, but I don't expect that to be the case."

"They planned this," Bishop said.

I agreed. They'd set us up.

"I'M sorry I can't help you any further," the vet said. "We'll arrange to return the horses with Chief Abernathy first thing in the morning. These guys are tired, and they could use a good night's sleep."

"Thank you," Bishop and I said.

The weight of the failed bust was suffocating. My heart pounded in my chest. We'd been had, and I wasn't sure we could recoup from it.

"How're our men?" Bishop asked Levy, worry etched on his face.

Her response was grim. "Already home. Both were just grazed. The three men in the pasture didn't make it."

A heavy silence settled in the room as we absorbed the news. Bubba, peering intently at his laptop screen, added, "I'm trying to find out if they were cartel, but no luck yet."

Thoughts of the fallen men's families haunted me. Regardless of their criminal status, someone loved them. Someone would mourn them. "Any family in the area?"

"They didn't have ID on them," Michels replied, his voice carrying a hint of helplessness.

"Great," Bishop muttered under his breath, frustration clear in his tone.

Levy, trying to find a glimmer of hope, mentioned, "Dr. Barron's got them. He'll keep them on ice for ninety days, and then they'll be handled accordingly."

Michels, always blunt and often without tact, couldn't resist expressing his darker thoughts. "That's a nice way to say dumped in a mass grave."

Levy retorted, "I have more compassion than you."

Just then, the door swung open with a bang, and Jimmy stormed into the room, his eyes ablaze with fury and distress. Deep furrows marred his forehead, and his lips formed a thin, straight line, revealing the intensity of his emotions. It was evident that something else had gone wrong. "We have to let them go. No drugs, no charges," his voice trembled with a rare intensity, directed at everyone in the room.

I stepped forward to explain the unfolding events, "Baxter has to know we're onto him. He set us up. We bust him and don't find anything, he's off the suspect list."

Bishop chimed in, reassuringly, "But he's not off it."

"Of course not," I agreed, "but he's not smart enough to realize we're smarter than him." I turned my attention to Jimmy, a determined glint in my eyes, "Can we try to talk to him?"

"Not here," Jimmy said. "They're already on their way out. Lansing has me by the balls."

Undeterred, I persisted. "It's worth a shot to drop by Baxter's place."

"I can get all dolled up again and visit Habersham. Rescheduling my appointment is easy."

"Do that," Jimmy said. "We'll need a wire on you."

"Got it," she said.

Kyle, who had been silently observing, finally shared some crucial information, "Martin Lansing knows his stuff. He moved from Texas to Georgia in 2010. His client list in Austin featured several well-known, high-level cartel members. The DEA made multiple arrests on several investigations in the Austin area, and every time, Lansing got them off."

Bishop probed further, "In federal court? How? Are the judges dirty?"

"Some are owned by the cartel," Kyle revealed, painting a disturbing picture we all knew as truth.

Eager to understand the extent of Lansing's involvement, I asked, "What's his client list here?"

Kyle responded, "No known cartel on it, but that doesn't mean he's not still working with them in some capacity."

Michels connected the dots. "Like coming to Baxter and Habersham's rescue."

Kyle nodded, confirming, "You got it."

Levy acknowledged the gravity of the situation. "That means Lansing could be involved, but you'll never get him on any charges." The resignation in her tone was obvious.

As the reality of our adversary's power sank in, a heavy sense of unease settled over the room. We were up against an opponent held in the cartels' hand, and the prospect of escaping justice seemed all too real.

Kyle looked me in the eyes. "Lansing knows you'll go to Baxter. He's already told him to keep his mouth shut, but if what you've said about him is true, his ego will get the best of him. He'll want to let you know he got one over on you. Push his buttons. He'll give you something."

He was right. Baxter had an inflated ego, and it would make my day to poke at it.

Kyle added, "It's good Levy's going back to the vet. Since she already had an appointment, she'll be off his radar. My suggestion would be to get in there early in the morning. I'd call first thing."

Levy nodded. "That means I'll be up early getting made up by Manny's wife. I'll need to call her."

Bubba's laptop dinged with an unfamiliar sound. "They're here." His fingers attacked the keyboard like a maestro conducting a symphony.

"What's here?" Michels asked.

"Baxter's phone records." His fingers pounded the keys. "Awesome, and his financial records."

"Great," I said. "There's got to be something in them."

"Michels, you stay with Bubba. Review everything," Jimmy said. He turned his attention to Levy. "Get with Manny's wife then help them." He looked at Bishop and then me. "Get out to Baxter and make a stop at Habersham's home as well. He should be expecting you, and that'll make Levy's appointment more realistic."

"We need someone on the Texas ranch," Bubba said. "I couldn't find anything."

"I'll handle that," Kyle said. "I have some connections."

Bubba scribbled the ranch's information on a sticky note and handed it to Kyle.

Jimmy cracked his knuckles. Their popping sound reverberated through the room. "All right. I know it's late, but we're losing time. Let's move on this." He pivoted on his heels and left.

Bishop flicked his head toward the door. "Chief ain't happy."

"Nope," Michels said.

I stood. "Then let's make him happy."

Michels eyed me with a raised brow, then smiled at Kyle. "You going to let her do that?"

The corner of Kyle's mouth twitched. "If it gets the job done, sure."

I rolled my eyes. "Y'all are disgusting." I exhaled. "You all, not y'all."

"She's turning into a southern belle," Bishop said.

"Not even close," Kyle replied.

GARCIA CALLED. I put him on speaker. "You had fun, didn't you?"

"A little, but I was distracted by the whole bomb thing. Did you talk with Lansing?"

"That's why I'm calling. He informed me he represents Habersham and Baxter."

"That's it?" Bishop asked.

"Nope. He told me he knew I wasn't involved, but for my own safety, it was best I leave the ranch and better yet, town."

"He's worried you know something," Bishop said.

"And that the cartel will come after you. You need to go back to Chicago."

"Hell no, I'm not going back to Chicago. I'm staying until this is finished."

"We can't risk your safety," I said. "You're not in the budget for hospital bills."

He laughed. "I explained to Mr. Lansing that I had just moved to town, and I needed the job. I told him I have a sick mother in Mexico, and I'm sending her most of my pay. Then I asked him if he could help me keep my job at the ranch."

"What'd he say?"

"He went and talked to Baxter. A few minutes later he told me to get my ass back to work."

"They must have contacted the cartel," Bishop said.

"Not from our phone, and Lansing can't have his in the room," I said.

"I think he called his guy after the fact," Garcia said. "Maybe they plan to hook me up?"

The last thing I wanted was for Garcia to go dark with the cartel. "That's not happening."

"We'll see," he said, and disconnected the call.

"Jimmy won't allow it," Bishop said. He knew what I was thinking.

"Garcia might do it anyway."

"That's idiotic."

"I said he was a good cop. I didn't say he was smart."

"How do you want to play this?" Bishop asked. He pulled out of the department's parking lot and turned toward state route 400.

"He knows we know what he's doing. No need to pretend otherwise. He's going to deny it either way, but we can make him uncomfortable."

"He also knows he's on thin ice with the cartel. He's more afraid of them than us."

"He should be. Maybe we try to swing a deal? He gives up his bosses, we promise to talk to the district attorney on his behalf."

Route 400 was backed up. Bishop merged slowly into the crawling traffic. "You really want to make a deal with this guy?"

"Not even a little," I said. "But he doesn't need to know that."

"If the cartel is watching him—"

I interrupted. "They are."

"Then they'll know we're there."

"Right, but they won't make a move. It's too dangerous," I said.

He agreed. He tapped his finger on the steering wheel. "How do you think Sean figured it out?"

"I was thinking about that earlier. I don't know, but I have a feeling someone else might."

"His father-in-law."

30

Bishop and I cruised down the dead-end road where Baxter lived.

"Why doesn't he live on the ranch?" I asked and then added in a snarky tone, "Like the regular people?"

"He did. The ranch office was the home. He gutted it and redid it about twelve years ago."

"And didn't build on the ranch property?"

"Maybe he didn't want to be too available?"

"Or maybe he didn't want to be that close to the cartel," I said.

"He could live in Alaska and still be too close to the cartel."

Baxter's home was at the end of the dead-end street. "Dang," I said. "We're in the wrong profession."

The mansion stood imposingly, boasting an exquisite blend of traditional Southern charm and modern opulence. The exterior walls were adorned with cream-colored bricks, oozing sophistication and snobbery. Massive white columns flanked the entrance, supporting a majestic portico that screamed *look at how much money we have.*

Like most homes in Hamby, the immaculate lawn with meticulously trimmed hedges and vibrant flowerbeds created a picturesque landscape that seemed right out of a luxury magazine.

"Go big or go home," Bishop said.

I smirked. "He really likes to show off his money, doesn't he?"

He pulled into the driveway. "It appears so."

He shook his head as we walked up the sidewalk to the front door. "That chandelier cost a pretty penny."

I had to admit, I liked its intricate wrought iron design.

The digital doorbell's echoing chime broke the silence surrounding the property. Baxter's voice crackled through the microphone, tinged with anxiety. "I've been advised not to speak to you without my attorney present."

Ignoring the warning, I gazed up at the camera. "Then don't speak. Just come out and listen. I think you'll find what we have to say interesting."

We waited patiently knowing Baxter wouldn't be able to resist the urge to know what we knew. A minute later, the front door creaked open and he emerged, his features obscured in the dim light. "Five minutes. That's all you have."

"We have a lot more than that," Bishop asserted, his voice carrying an edge of authority.

Baxter led us toward Bishop's vehicle as if he wanted to hurry us off his property. His fidgety movements betrayed his fake confidence. He stuffed his hands into his khaki pants pockets and scanned his surroundings, his eyes darting from side to side. The fear was palpable; he thought he was being watched, and I suspected he was right.

We stopped near the vehicle, making the point that we weren't going anywhere until we were finished.

"Four minutes," he announced, trying to regain some semblance of control.

Bishop confronted him, his words sharp and accusing. "We know you're working with the cartel."

Baxter's face remained expressionless, but the subtle beads of sweat forming at his temples once again showed how he truly felt. His face struggled to conceal his anxiety.

"We know they're smuggling fentanyl through the horses," I revealed, my voice low but charged with intensity. "You get them in Texas then transport them to your stable. Habersham extracts the drugs, and one of your ranch workers takes them from there."

"And then you sell the horses for slaughter," Bishop added, the accusation ringing in the night air.

Baxter's eyes darted nervously between us and the shadows that enveloped his house. "You don't know what you're talking about."

"Yes, we do," Bishop said. "And Sean found out, didn't he? He knew what you were doing."

Baxter blinked rapidly, the fear bubbling just beneath the surface of his facade.

"So you killed him," I said through gritted teeth as my emotions threatened to spill over.

"I didn't kill Sean," his voice quivered.

"Yet miraculously, you knew how he died." My fists involuntarily clenched and relaxed, mirroring the tension that hung in the air.

"It was obvious," he stammered. "He had a drug problem."

"That's bullshit, and you know it," Bishop said. His face had reddened. He was emotional about Sean. I understood. "He knew what you were doing, and you had to stop him from reporting it."

"I didn't kill him," Baxter insisted, shifting nervously from side to side. "I'm done now. Leave me alone." He retreated toward his porch.

Before he stepped onto it, I said, "We've got you for this, Baxter. That is, if the cartel doesn't get you first."

∼

I SLAMMED my hand against Bishop's dashboard. "That S-O-B. He thinks he's going to get away with this."

"He's nervous. He knows he's going down whether it's from us or the cartel."

"It sure as hell better be from us."

Dispatch came over the radio. "9L49, 9L24, we've got shots fired with a possible 10-43 at 3928 Sanders Lane. Repeat Shots fired at 3928 Sanders Lane. Sending backup."

The two officers she'd contacted responded.

"10–4. Officer 9L49 Approximately two minutes out."

"Officer 9L24 one street over."

"That's the townhomes across from mine," I said. I checked my watch. We were a short distance away. "If there's a body, they'll call us," I said.

He flicked his head toward the mic. "Go ahead."

"Dispatch, this is Detective Ryder with Detective Bishop. 10-76 and 10-77 of twelve minutes. Ten-four."

Moments later the closest officer had arrived on scene and notified dispatch. "Officer 9L24 10-23."

The other officer arrived a minute or two later.

"Officer's 9L24 and 9L49 status?" Dispatch asked.

Officer 9L24 said, "Ten-zero. Front door. Looks kicked open."

"Ten-four," Dispatch said. "Stand-by."

"Officers' Bishop and Ryder 10-77 three minutes. Stand-by 9L24 and 9L49. Do not enter."

"Copy that," both officers said.

We arrived just before the fire department.

Like mine, the townhome was an end unit. I stepped out of the vehicle and noticed the pickup parked in the driveway. "I've seen that truck before," I said.

"So have I," Bishop said.

I followed Bishop toward the kicked-in front door of the townhome.

One of the officers rushed out to the ambulance. As he passed us, he said, "One DOA, house clear."

"Wait," I yelled. "Dispatch told you not to enter."

"We thought we heard someone inside, so we had to."

"Got it," Bishop said.

We slipped on our booties and gloves and stepped inside.

My eyes locked onto the lifeless body sprawled across the living room floor. The victim lay motionless in a pool of crimson.

"Damn," Bishop said.

I crouched down in front of Damian Sayers's body. "He's the one who told them we were onto them, and they got rid of him for it."

Bishop squatted beside me, groaning as his knees lowered to the ground. "Because they didn't need him anymore."

"He's been shot multiple times," I said. "Why not just one to the head like other executions?" The dark, ominous splatters of blood painted a gruesome tapestry across the walls and furniture, each droplet a silent witness to the brutality of Sayers's last moments.

Bishop shook his head. "No clue."

I smelled a trace of burnt gunpowder lingering in the air. "It just happened." I contacted Dispatch and asked who reported the crime. She responded with a name and address.

I didn't need it. The woman was standing behind the yellow tape when I walked outside, already being interviewed by an officer. I politely interrupted and introduced myself. "I'm sorry to make you repeat," I said. "But can you tell me what happened?"

She scrutinized my face. "You're the officer from Chicago."

"That's me," I said as cheerily as I could. "Did you hear the gunshots?"

"I heard the fight first. These walls are terribly thin. I was going to pound on mine and scream at Damian to stop yelling, but I thought that would defeat the purpose. Then I heard the gunshots, so I ran into my bedroom and called 911."

"Did you get a look at the person inside Damian's home?"

"No. I was too afraid they would see me."

"They? Was it more than one person?"

"Yes, I believe it was two," she said. "But I can't be sure. I think they had accents."

"Hispanic?"

"Maybe? It was hard to tell. I can hear the yelling, but I can't quite make out the words. The gunshots though, I could make out those." A tear slid down her cheek. "Is Damian really dead?"

"Yes, ma'am. I'm sorry to say he is. Do you happen to have a video doorbell or security camera?"

"No. We're in a gated community. I didn't think we'd need it."

"Better safe than sorry."

"Yes. I believe I'll get one now."

I asked her a few more questions and then got her number just in case I needed more information. I walked back into Damian Sayers 's place while texting Mr. Doyle. "Damian Sayers was murdered tonight. We need to talk. I'll be there in an hour. What's the address?"

He responded with just the address.

Mike Barron showed up looking as though he'd just crawled out of bed. "You okay?" Bishop asked.

Barron coughed. "Damn spring allergies are killing me." He glanced around the room and saw the blood splatter and Damian Sayers's body lying on the floor. "Excuse the poor choice of words." He heaved his bag over to our victim and did a quick examination. When he finished, he said, "Looks like a murder to me, but you know how this works."

I nodded. "Sure do." I turned toward Bishop. "I got in touch with Doyle. I can get a ride over there and you can finish up here?"

"Sounds good," he said. "I'll meet you back at the department."

31

Roger Doyle had been waiting outside when we arrived. He sat on the front porch with a bottle of scotch on the small table beside him and a glassful in his hand. He walked off the porch and stood in front of me on the sidewalk. "What do you want to know?"

"So, you do know something. Why didn't you tell us before?"

"I don't want to put my family in any more danger than they're already in."

"Have you received any threats?"

"No, but I assume they think we know something."

"I don't think so, but it's good to watch your back." I scanned the yard. "Are we doing this here?"

"Inside," he said. "Follow me."

The Doyles had a modest home for Hamby. I guessed it to be around 4200 square feet, which was 2000 less than the typical home in town. Some people in the area would have considered his community lower income. In Chicago, it was upper middle class if not higher.

We sat in the front room, the room most Southerners called the living room. He didn't offer me anything to drink, which was fine, and he completely skipped the pleasantries. I appreciated his desire to get to the point.

"Sean knew Mason Baxter was working for the cartel."

"How?" I asked.

"Damian."

"And he told you?"

"Not at first. He came to me for advice a few weeks ago. He wanted to know what he should do."

"Tell me what he said to you. As much as you can remember."

"He said Damian had come by the ranch looking for a job. Sean was surprised. Damian had said he really liked working at Haverty Ranch. I'm not sure why. Mason's always seemed like an asshole to me. Sean said they didn't have any openings, but he said he could tell Damian was upset about something, so he asked him what it was." He stared down at the beige carpet. "Damian told him he'd seen Habersham in the back stable with the new horses a while back. He didn't think much of it at first, but when a black SUV pulled up behind the stable and one of the day workers went out with a bag, he got curious. The next time Baxter bought new horses, he waited around and watched. He saw Habersham remove small bags from the horses' rectums. Sean said he put them in a black bag, and one of the day workers took it to another black SUV. He wasn't sure what was going on, but he knew it involved drugs. A few days later he set up a few video cameras and figured it out. He went to Sean with the videos. They agreed Damian would stick it out at the ranch to see what he could find out, and once they had enough evidence, they'd report it."

"What did Sean do?"

"Research. He found a few cases of drug smuggling through horses on the internet and looked into it. He found the ranch he believed Baxter pretended to get his horses from but told me it's a fake listing. The guy that's supposedly running it, some Hal Jacob or Jacobson, maybe, doesn't exist. He wasn't sure, but he thought that was how the horses were being smuggled into the country. Under the claim they were being taken to be sold."

"Did he confront Baxter?"

"He ran into him at Rucker's. He told me he didn't outright say what he knew, but that he didn't have to. He made some crass comment and Baxter got the message."

"And what did Baxter do?"

"Threatened him and the girls. Told him to mind his own business if he wanted to see his daughter turn one."

"Did he tell you anything else?"

"He mentioned Baxter's former business partner. Riley Jefferson, I think. Said he thought he was involved, but he wasn't sure."

"Was this man a partner with the ranch?"

"Not that I know of. I've never heard of the guy, but Baxter came from Montana, so he could have been someone from there."

I exhaled. "Why didn't Sean go to the police?"

"I don't know," Roger Doyle said. "I told him to let it go. He had my daughter and granddaughter to worry about."

"Except he did contact me, and then he was murdered."

"He'd been acting more and more paranoid. He thought they were watching him. I think that's why he contacted you." He paused for a moment, then said, "I've hired a security group to keep my daughter and granddaughter safe. I had to refinance the house to do it, but I'll spend every dime I have to keep those girls alive."

Roger Doyle was a family man. Any man who put his family first, at the risk of God knew what, was a good man in my book. "And that's why you didn't tell us. You didn't want the cartel to know."

He nodded. "But now Damian's dead too, and I'm worried they'll come for Jessica and the baby. Security or not."

"Did Sean document any of this?"

He stood and opened the drawer of a small cabinet on the back wall of the room, then removed a file folder. "These are the names of the day workers he thinks are connected to the cartel. He told me to give them to you if anything happened to him."

It infuriated me that he'd waited so long. I should have had those names the day Sean was murdered.

He must have sensed my frustration, because he said, "I chose to obstruct justice to keep my family safe. Sean was already dead. Finding his killer wouldn't bring him back."

~

I HANDED Savannah a glass of ice water. She had been sitting on their couch fanning herself with a hand fan. It was only early spring, but she was dressed in a pair of shorts and a halter top that showed her baby bump. Though it was more like a volcano ready to erupt. Or maybe that was her temper. Jimmy was dressed in a pair of jeans and a sweater. The house was freezing.

"Is the air on?" I asked.

Bishop rubbed his hands together.

"It better still be," Savannah said. "Sweet baby Jesus, it's hotter than blazes in here. This baby's going to melt and come out like soup."

Bishop began to laugh, caught himself, then took two steps back, out of Savannah's reach.

Savannah narrowed her eyes at him. "You'd better take a few more steps back Rob. I might be a hot mess, but I'm still fast on my feet."

I bit my bottom lip. She wasn't fast on her feet without a baby in her belly, but Bishop wasn't about to test her. "How about an ice pack on the back of your neck? Will that help?"

"I'd rather have a triple shot of tequila."

I laughed.

She threw her hand fan at me. "If I could, I'd get out of this chair and give you a whoopin'."

I spun around and escaped to the kitchen to get her a bag of ice. I felt for her. She was as big as a house, though incredibly beautiful, but I knew she'd hit the miserable part of pregnancy, and the baby wasn't quite ready to arrive.

I overheard Bishop filling Jimmy in on Damian's murder. I returned with the ice bag and gently placed it behind Savannah's head.

"Rachel talked to Roger Doyle, Sean's wife Jessica's father. I'll let her tell you what she learned."

"He knew what was going on," I said.

"How'd he find out?" Jimmy asked.

"Sean told him."

Jimmy dragged his hand down the sides of his face. I knew he was angry, but he did his best to keep calm. I finished reiterating my conversation with Roger Doyle and waited for a response. The room was quiet except for the humming of the air conditioner.

Savannah groaned. "I'm going to bed." She attempted to push herself off the couch but couldn't. She held out her hands. "A little help would be great."

I pulled her up. "Hope you get some sleep."

"It's unlikely," she said. She grumbled something unladylike and not at all normal for her and padded off toward her bedroom without another word.

Bishop and I made eye contact. He raised his eyebrows.

"But Sean had no proof," Jimmy said. "Not that I'm aware of."

"This Riley Jefferson. I've never heard of him."

"Doyle thinks he's from Montana and they were partners there. I'll have Bubba look into him in the morning."

He nodded. "Okay. At least we're moving forward."

"We still have no idea who killed Sean," Bishop said.

"It was either Baxter covering his ass or the cartel because they found out what Sean knew," I said.

"Right. We'll get there," Jimmy said. "Baxter's nervous. He knows his time is running out on both ends. I'll get men on him. He'll lead us to his contacts. In the meantime, you two find out about Jefferson, and keep pushing. We need this arrest ASAP."

"IT's NOT the first time that's happened," Kyle said. He offered to make me dinner, but I declined.

I'd showered and tossed on a pair of sweats and a Chicago Bulls t-shirt, had a brief, one-sided chat with Louie, and then curled up next to Kyle on the couch. "The fake ranch and auctions? Why didn't you mention that?"

"I honestly didn't know. I did some research tonight and found out."

"Anything on Hal Jacobs?"

"Nothing. Called a few contacts and left messages but haven't heard back yet." He rubbed his chest and winced.

I pushed myself off his side and placed my hand on his chest. "Are you okay?"

"I'm fine," he said smiling. "Just a little sore."

"From the shooting? Is it your lung? See, I told you to stop pushing yourself so hard. You still have a lot of healing to do."

He pushed my hair behind my ear and stared into my eyes. "I'm fine, Rach. It's not my lung. I did a chest workout at the gym today."

I pressed my lips together. "Oh. Well, you should be careful. It hasn't been that long since you almost died."

"You don't have to worry about me."

I adjusted my position and leaned my head onto his shoulder again, then wrapped my arm around his abdomen. "Do you worry about me?"

"Every single day."

"Then when you stop worrying about me every single day, I'll stop worrying about you every single day."

"That's never going to happen."

"I think I've made my point."

I felt his smile on the side of my head. "I'd like to go to bed and make a point or two."

I jumped up from the couch. "Oh, I like that idea."

32

"If he's talking to anyone outside of his regular contacts and getting paid by the cartel, he's not doing it with his own phone or bank account," Michels said.

"But he's had some larger deposits recently," Levy said. "We tried to match them with the dates he's had new horses, but Emma doesn't update their Facebook page with the horse purchases consistently. What we did find didn't match the deposits."

"Where are those deposits coming from?" Jimmy asked.

"They're checks," Michels said. "They've got boarding fees written on the notes section. So far, it all matches up."

"He's hiding the money," I said.

"Or he's not getting any," Bishop added.

"That's possible," Jimmy said. "But unlikely. The cartel pays local mules well. It's how they bring them in."

I finished my third cup of coffee while finishing up Levy's disguise.

"Late night?" she asked.

"Yes."

"Hope it was worth it because you look rough."

"It was, and gee, thanks."

She smiled. "Someone else would have said it anyway."

I laughed because she was right.

Manny's wife had done another amazing job on Levy's makeover. The guys offered a few one-liners about prostitutes and undercover work, and Levy agreed. "I'd make a great hooker, but we were going for stuck up woman from the east."

I kept her back facing the men. "I think it's the wig," I said. "It's kind of got a hooker vibe." I adjusted the wire on her chest and secured it with surgical tape. "Okay." I backed away as she buttoned her shirt.

"Can you see it?"

"Not at all," I said. "Damn, I do good work."

She turned toward the men. "Look at my chest."

Michels laughed. "Dang woman, I'm engaged, and you don't have to be so aggressive."

"Shut up, Michels," I said smiling.

"He's just mad he can't play dress up this time," Levy said.

Michels agreed. "I bought the clothes and everything."

"We don't want to be too obvious," Jimmy said. "Best she goes in on her own."

"About the wire?" Levy asked.

"Can't see it," Bishop said.

"Thank you," Levy eyed Michels. "At least one of you is mature."

"I wouldn't go that far," I said under my breath.

"I heard that," Bishop said with a smile.

"Remember," Jimmy said to Levy. "You found out from someone, and you want in. That's it. Don't say anything about what happened at Haverty, or about Sean. Got it?"

"Got it," she said.

"You get the list of day workers to Bubba?" Jimmy asked.

"I did. He's looking into them, but we both know most of the names are probably fakes."

"Still worth a shot. Can you get the names to Garcia? See if he knows any of them?"

"Already did that too."

"Good. Keep me updated," Jimmy said.

~

LEVY AND MICHELS DROVE SEPARATELY. Levy in her personal vehicle, Michels in his department one, and Bishop, Bubba, and I together in a van. Bubba was responsible for handling the technical aspect of the situation while we handled the physical aspect. We'd arranged back up with the Dawsonville PD in the event things went south, so while Levy went her way, we set up down the street and let them know where we were.

"We're close by. If you need us, just let us know," their officer said.

"Ten-four," Bishop replied.

Michels's climbed into the van. "Should be any minute now."

Shortly after, Levy notified us that she was going in.

"Hi. I'm Evelyn Stafford. I'm here for a consultation with Dr. Habersham." She thickened her Philly accent.

"One moment," a woman responded.

Michels leg bounced. "I should be in there with her."

"She'll be fine," Bishop said.

"Habersham's not going to do anything at his place of business," I added.

Bubba pressed buttons and turned knobs.

"He'll be with you in a minute," the woman said.

"Thank you," Levy said.

It was almost two minutes before Habersham spoke. "Ms. Stafford?"

"Yes," Levy said.

"Come on back."

"Thank you." Her heels clicked on the floor.

A door closed. "Have a seat," Habersham said. "So, you're new in town and looking for a vet for your horses?"

"For my personal horse, yes, but I'm also looking for mares I can breed, preferably retired racehorses or ones with a healthy bloodline. I understand you're the best vet to work with in the area, and that you have connections for breeding."

"Have you been in the business long?" he asked.

"No. I recently came into a large sum of money and am moving to Alpharetta. I'm closing on the ranch later this week, but it's a private transaction at this moment, and it's costing me most of the money I've got. I have my own horse, but that's it. I used most of that money to purchase my ranch, so I'm looking for ones I can breed, but aren't too costly."

"Where in Alpharetta?"

"I can't say until the closing is complete."

"How did you hear about me?"

"You came recommended from Rucker's."

"She needs to speed this up," I said.

Bishop nodded.

"I can help you with your horse, but I'm not that involved in the racing business anymore. I'm not sure I can connect you with the right people. And I'm sure you're aware of this, but if you're looking for quality horses, they cost a lot of money."

Levy cleared her throat. "May I be frank?"

"Of course," he said.

"I spoke with a ranch hand at Rucker's. He works somewhere in Hamby, I believe. He suggested I come to you because of an arrangement you're involved in with Evergreen Ranch. He thought I might be interested in participating."

"Who told you this?" His tone had changed from friendly to guarded.

"I didn't get his name," Levy said. "But I am very interested. I could use the money and then breed the horses."

"I'm not sure I understand what you're saying," Habersham said.

In a semi-seductive voice, Levy said, "Now doctor, I'm quite sure you understand exactly what I'm saying. I want in, and I want you to help me with that."

"I'll have to discuss this with my associates," he said. "But I believe they're looking for a new ranch to work with."

"So, they already have a relationship in the area? How is it going?"

"I'm not able to discuss the details, but it appears that relationship is ending."

Bishop looked at me. "They're getting rid of Baxter."

"Sounds like it."

"Please let them know I'm ready to begin," Levy said.

"I will. Ms. Stafford, have you told anyone else about this?"

"Of course not."

"Great. I'd like you to keep it that way. I can't make any promises, but I can talk to my associates and put them in touch with you. May I have your number?"

"Here," Levy said. "I've already written down my contact information."

"I'll contact them today, and they'll be in touch."

"Thank you," she said. When her car door closed, she said, "That was a lot easier than I expected."

Bishop contacted the Dawsonville PD and gave them the all-clear.

"That's too bad," Bubba said.

"What's too bad?" I asked.

"I was hoping for a little action. It's rare for me to leave the station. I thought it would be better than this."

"We'll do our best to make the next one better," I said smiling.

He blushed. "I didn't want anything bad to happen. Maybe a chase or a take down. Nothing dangerous."

"Hate to break it to you, Bubba, but if any of that had happened, you'd have been stuck in here."

"I figured," he said.

Bishop drove the van back to the department.

LEVY STRUTTED through the pit to whistles and applause. "This is the last you'll see of Evelyn Stafford, so soak it all in, boys."

I laughed, then leaned into her and said, "Way to prep them for a sexual harassment claim."

"No need. They all know I'll kick their ass if they try anything."

"That they do."

We all gathered in the investigation room, Jimmy and Kyle included.

"We've already got eyes on Baxter," Jimmy said. He directed his attention to Levy and Michels. "I'd like the two of you on that as well."

Both nodded.

"I'd like to change and wash my face first." She patted her cheek with her fingers. "This stuff is caked on so thick my face is about to crack."

"Not a problem," Jimmy said. "We've got that burner number ready to record, so keep it close."

"What if they want to come to my ranch?" she asked.

"Put them off until the closing," Jimmy said. "The goal is to have them shoot themselves in the foot on the call."

"Got it."

"Alpharetta's chief updated me on the Ortiz murder," he said. "It's already cold, so let's try to connect it to our investigation."

"It's already connected," I said.

"I mean a connection the district attorney can use in court."

"Understood," I said.

"I looked into Riley Jefferson," Bubba said. "He and Baxter owned a ranch in Montana. He was murdered six years ago."

"He's correct," Kyle said. "Jefferson was tied in with the cartel, but they found nothing on Baxter."

"Smuggling drugs?" Bishop asked.

He nodded. "Jefferson was also a vet, so he removed the drugs on his own. He got cocky and stole a few bags, the cartel did the math and killed him."

"Who handled the investigation, DEA or the local department?"

"Both," Kyle said. "Once local figured out it was connected to the cartel, they called us in."

"Can you get more details? Was Baxter involved?" I asked.

Kyle shrugged. "Baxter kept himself clean."

"No way," I said.

"There's more to the story, but I don't have all the details," he said. "And I don't think I can get them."

"What happened to the Montana ranch?" I asked Bubba.

"Jefferson owned sixty percent. His wife bought out Baxter."

"He was running," Michels said. "They wanted him, and he was trying to get away from them."

"You can't get away from the cartel," Kyle said. "Not without professional help."

Bishop eyed me. "You think he's doing this involuntarily?"

"Does it matter?"

"No," Jimmy said. "And it gives him an even bigger motive to kill Sean."

"Right," Michels said. "He needed to keep Sean quiet. He knew what happened to Jefferson when he screwed up, and he didn't want the same thing to happen to him."

"You think he killed Sean himself?" Levy asked me.

"Baxter doesn't like to get his hands dirty."

"Never underestimate a desperate man," Bishop said.

"All right," Jimmy said. "Let's move on what we've got. Levy, Michels, keep close to Baxter. If you see anything out of the ordinary, get your backup. They're out there."

"Will do, chief," Levy said. "Off to wash my face and change." She walked out of the investigation room with Michels and Jimmy behind her.

"Bubba, can you get me a number for Riley Jefferson's wife?

"Sure." He closed his laptop, gathered his things on top of it, and left the room.

Only Kyle, Bishop, and I were left. "Thanks for the information," I said to Kyle. "But please tell me we're not going to wind up assisting the DEA on this."

"My contact in Montana used to be a state trooper. He won't say anything."

"Thank you." I turned toward Bishop. "I think we need to give Connie an update. We should check on her anyway."

"Agree. We'll get Dunkin' on the way there."

33

Bishop and I grabbed coffees in the Dunkin' drive thru. I stretched my arms and yawned as they handed him the drinks. He pulled away from the window and turned toward me. "Levy was right. You're looking pretty rough. Did you get any sleep?"

"A little," I said. I tried to stop smiling, but it was impossible.

"Hmm," Bishop said. "Good for Kyle." He exited the Dunkin' parking lot. "But I don't want the details."

"I wasn't going to give them." He looked tired as well. "Did you work out this morning?"

"No. I'm still sore from before. These early morning workouts are tough."

"Maybe it's time to cut back a little? You've been pushing pretty hard. That can't be good considering what happened."

"Trust me, my body doesn't let me forget what happened."

Seeing Bishop battered and almost beaten to death during an earlier investigation had brought me to my knees. Was it part of the job? Yes, it was always a possibility, but it shouldn't have been him. The crime rate in town had grown along with the population and his once cushy job busting kids for misdemeanors had morphed into something more intense. He hadn't been prepared, and to see him getting in shape was good. He wouldn't let that happen again. He'd made that perfectly clear.

Bubba texted with Riley Jefferson's wife's information. I thanked him and asked Bishop, "Should we call Jefferson's wife on the way?"

"Sure," he said.

I dialed her number on my phone and put it on speaker. It rang twice before she picked up. "Hello?"

"Is this Sophia Jefferson?"

"Who's calling?"

"This is Detective Rachel Ryder from the Hamby Georgia Police Department. I'd like to talk with you about your husband and Mason Baxter." I'd learned to get the first question out without waiting for a response.

The phone went silent for a moment before she said, "I'm not interested in talking to you," and ended the call.

"That went well," Bishop said.

"She lives in Billings. Let me try their department." I searched the internet for the non-emergency phone number and made the call. After jumping through a few hoops, I was connected to the detective who handled Riley Jefferson's murder along with the DEA, but of course, got his voicemail. I left him a message and asked him to return my call.

"Slower life out there," Bishop said. "He's probably not even in yet."

"He's probably digging his car out of the snow. It's still cold there."

The gate to Connie's ranch was open. Bishop drove up the drive toward the main office.

"Hold on," I said. I pointed to Connie's vehicle. "Why is her door open?"

He rolled down his window. "Her car's still running."

The rest of the parking area was empty. "Where are the ranch hands? Did they all walk to work?"

He tapped the gas and crawled closer to the building. A woman screamed. "Holy hell." He slammed on the brakes. I jumped out of the vehicle and ran inside, gun drawn. My heart pounded in my chest as adrenaline pumped through my veins. Bishop followed a second behind.

Music played through the office speakers, but Connie's desperate cries for help cut through it. "No! Please!"

Bishop and I stood outside the door. I carefully peeked in to assess the situation. One man held Connie upright while the other two mercilessly threw punches at her face and stomach with one hand while holding guns in their other. They stood in front of the counter which put us on their right. If any of them angled even just an inch our way, they'd see us. I nodded to Bishop, our sign I would go in first, and he would cover me. I raced in. "Police!" My voice was low and feral as I aimed my gun at the man closest to me. "Drop your weapons!"

"Now—" Bishop didn't have time to finish his sentence. The man holding Connie threw her to the side and pulled a gun from his waist while the other two men turned toward us and fired.

Sweat trickled down my temple as I tightened my grip on my own weapon, the metal warm in my hand. I pulled off two shots, then quickly glanced at Connie. Her eyes met mine for a fleeting moment, then she rolled onto her back. The men dodged my shots, taking cover behind over-turned furniture. My breath came in ragged gasps.

Bishop dropped and rolled behind a small, glass display case. The glass shattered as bullets hit it. As I dove in the opposite direction behind another display, I fired off two more rounds, leaving me with twelve. When Bishop signaled he was going to stand, I quickly shot another three rounds. He stood and pulled the trigger, one, two, three times. One of the attackers rushed toward him. He stumbled backward and aimed his weapon. "Stop!"

The man lunged toward Bishop, his gun momentarily forgotten. Bishop fired, the deafening sound echoing in the confined space. The bullet ripped through the man's chest, and he fell to the ground. For a split second, the room fell into a tense silence until the two men aimed their weapons at us, popping off a few more rounds, then running toward the side entrance.

Bishop and I dodged the bullets and continued to shoot as they ran out. One screamed. "Call for backup and check on Connie," I said.

Without a second thought, I took off running.

I'd run out the front. The side entrance was on the left toward the stables. I slowed at the corner of the building and carefully checked, seeing them run into the stables. I fired what I'd counted as my last bullet, quickly reloaded, and ran to the stables. I could hear the thud of hooves inside as the horses grew restless. I slowed my pace and stopped at the closed stable doors, my senses on high alert. My heart pounded in my chest, the adrenaline pumping through my veins, making my every breath feel electric.

I kicked the door open. I caught glimpses of horses rearing as I entered, but I didn't see the men. Suddenly, a large wooden barrel tipped onto its side. My heart leaped. Thinking I had found my target, I raised my gun to fire. But before I could, a searing pain erupted in the back of my head. My gun flew from my hand and slid across the dirt. The world spun, and my vision blurred as I fell to my knees. Through the haze, I saw one of the attackers standing over me, his cold eyes narrowed down at me, and a gun aimed at my head.

34

A shot fired. I flinched and instinctively covered my head. The man in front of me fell to the ground. His body hit with a hollow thud.

"Drop your weapon and on the ground, now," Bishop yelled.

I dove forward and grabbed my weapon, spun onto my back, and held it aimed at the man who'd hit me over the head. "Now!" I screamed.

The gun dropped from the man's hand as he fell to his knees.

"Hands behind your head," Bishop yelled. Sirens rang in the distance, growing louder each second. He flicked his eyes at me. "You okay?"

I nodded. My head still spinning, I stood and checked on the man Bishop had shot while Bishop cuffed the other one. "He's breathing," I said. "But he's bleeding from his back.

I rolled him over. "Oh, God." Blood poured out of the man's abdomen. "He's bleeding in front too. He's going to bleed out!" I surveyed the area and found a blanket lying over one of the stall gates. I grabbed it, then quickly folded it, and pressed it against the wound. "I need help here!"

The sirens blared outside and seconds later two officers rushed in.

Bishop pointed to the man who had hit me over the head. "Take him. And let the EMTs know we've got two injured in the office and one bleeding out here." He dropped beside me and took over holding the bloodied blanket against the man's wound. "We need that damn ambulance!"

One of the officers ran out of the stables while the other said, "It's here." He yanked the cuffed man up and escorted him out.

The paramedics rushed in.

"He took a shot to the side of his abdomen," I said. "Bleeding from both sides." My breaths came so quickly it was hard to speak. "It's been a few minutes now. He's lost a lot of blood."

One of the paramedics took over from Bishop. The other said to me, "Your head is bleeding."

I touched my hair and felt the sticky, wetness of blood. "I'm fine. I need to check on the woman in the office."

Bishop and I raced out of the stables.

A paramedic was already with Connie. Her eyes were barely open. I crouched down and spoke close to her ear. "They're going to take care of you. You're going to be fine."

Bishop filled the paramedics in on what had happened to her. I glanced over at the other man who had been shot, but he wasn't moving, and there wasn't anyone with him.

"Ma'am," a female paramedic said. "I need you to come to the ambulance with me."

Bishop said, "Go."

I followed the paramedic and leaned against the back of the ambulance.

"Turn to your side, please," she said. She poured something onto a cloth and wiped the back of my hair. "This is a nice cut. Are you dizzy?"

"A little. Not as much as before."

She pressed the cloth into my head. I jerked away. "That stings."

"I bet it does."

Jimmy pulled up and hurried over. "You okay?"

"Got hit in the head, but I'm fine."

"Where's Bishop?"

"In the office. Connie's pretty bad. One dead. One injured. I don't think he'll make it. Bishop cuffed the other."

His eyes widened. "There were three of them?"

"Two beating on Connie while the other held her."

He ran his hand over the top of his head. "Dear God." He looked at the paramedic. "Is she okay?"

"I think so. Might have a slight concussion, but nothing major. We may take her in and have her checked, but I need to finish my examination to decide."

He peered at me. "You'll go if she says so." It wasn't a question.

"Yes, sir."

He rushed off toward the office.

"Detective," the paramedic said. "Who's the president?"

"Biden."

"And what year is it?"

"Twenty-twenty-three."

"Can you stand without leaning against the ambulance for me?"

I did as she asked.

"Are you dizzy now?"

"Not really," I said. "I don't feel nauseous either, and I didn't right after it happened."

She examined my eyes. "Your pupils aren't dilated. What about a headache?"

"In the back, yes. Otherwise, no. Do I need stitches?"

"It's not too deep, but you're going to have a killer bruise." She checked the cut once more. "It's not bleeding anymore."

"So, hospital?"

She shook her head. "I think you'll be okay, but if any of those symptoms do appear, you'll need to go."

"I will," I said.

She smirked. "I know your reputation."

I made a cross over my heart. "I promise."

THE AMBULANCES LEFT with Connie and the man shot in the abdomen while Bishop and I explained to Jimmy what had happened.

"Any idea why they were here?" he asked.

"None," Bishop said.

I rubbed dried blood off my hair. "Sean must have had something after all," I said. "Something that proved what Baxter was doing and for who."

"We checked the office," Bishop said. "We didn't find anything."

"Hold on," I said. I walked back into the office and went to the drawer where Sean had left the gun safe key for Connie.

"We already checked the safe," Bishop said.

"I know." They followed me to the breakroom where I unlocked the safe and removed the guns.

"Sean was prepared," Jimmy said.

"Not well enough," Bishop said.

The back of the safe was lined with soft, spongy padding. I checked along the sides, tugging slightly until the material pulled up. "Bingo!" I removed the material. Behind it was a large business-sized envelope.

"Why didn't you check there before?" Bishop asked.

"I didn't think of it until now. I've seen safes with padding before, and I know they make safes with hidden pockets, so I thought it was worth checking." I opened the envelope and removed a handful of photos and a small jump drive.

Bishop eyed the items. "He knew he was in danger."

I licked my lips. "I think so."

"He should have come to us," Jimmy said. His tone bordered on anger.

We looked through the photos.

"Did he put a camera in Baxter's stables?" Bishop asked.

"How could he do that without being caught?" I asked.

"Damian Sayers."

"He wanted to take them down," I said. "Damian had to have brought Sean into it. The cartel found out Sean had something on them, so they killed him."

"But they didn't know about Damian," Bishop said.

"That's an option. If that's the case, it's why he told Baxter we talked to him about the drug smuggling. He wanted to look like he wasn't a part of Sean's deal," I said.

"Except they figured it out," Jimmy said. "And killed him too."

"But how did they know?" Bishop asked.

Neither Jimmy nor I had an answer for that.

"They hadn't looked for anything when they killed Sean," I said. "They just wanted him gone. But Damian must have told them they had pictures. That's why they came back."

"And when Connie couldn't help, they beat the shit out of her," Bishop said.

"We need to call Roger Doyle. He needs to get his family out of town," I said.

"Do it on the way back to the station," Jimmy said. He held his hand out to Bishop. "I'm going to need your weapon."

Bishop removed it from his holster and handed it to Jimmy.

"Don't worry," Jimmy said. "We'll clear this up quickly."

35

The locker room shower wasn't as good as my own, but I wasn't about to complain. The warm water running through my hair and against the cut felt like a soft massage. I rubbed shampoo into my hair, carefully avoiding the injured part of my scalp. The burn from the soap seeped into the cut anyway and stung.

I changed into a clean shirt I kept in my locker, and finished dressing, then pulled my hair into a ponytail because the thought of clipping it into a bun near the cut made me cringe. Most of the team was in the investigation room when I returned.

"Bishop's with Jimmy," Levy said. "You okay?"

"I am." I rubbed the back of my head.

She raised one eyebrow.

"I'm fine. I promise."

"I'll believe you then." She smirked. "What happened out there? Is Bishop going on desk duty?"

I sighed. One shooting death, though never okay, was easier to handle if the situation warranted, which it had. Two, however, required a review and possible investigation. In that time, the officer involved was given desk duty or suspended with pay. It wasn't a punishment, but every cop who experienced it thought it was. I filled them in on the details.

"Where are the photos and the jump drive now?" Michels asked.

"I gave them to Bishop. I didn't think he'd be with Jimmy this long."

Nikki walked in. "Hey." She looked at me. "Sorry to interrupt, but I wanted to let you know you were hit with a gun." She held up an evidence bag with a gun in it. "At least I think you were. I'll have the blood tested and see if it's a match to you and Connie Higgins. Oh, and the attackers."

"Appreciate it," I said. "I need to check on Connie."

"I did," Levy said. "She's out of surgery, but they expect she'll be in ICU for a few days."

"We need to know who put these guys on her," I said.

"When she's out of intensive care, we can find out."

"What about Sean's wife and daughter?" Michels asked. "Have you called them?"

"I spoke to her father," I said. "He has security on them, but he's taking them out of the state indefinitely."

"That's a good idea," Levy said.

Jimmy and Bishop walked in. Everyone was silent, until I opened my big mouth. "You can't put him on desk duty or suspend him. We need him to finish this with us."

"The second victim is alive," Bishop said. I could tell he was shaken. I should have seen it earlier. "Thank God."

"Are you okay?" Levy said.

He sat beside me and slid the jump drive to Bubba. "I've been better."

I knew Bishop better than anyone. He wasn't okay, but he was doing his best to pretend. Emotions run high during intense situations, and when the adrenaline wears off, those emotions hit us like bricks. He'd survive, but not without scars. I placed my hand on his shoulder. "You did what you had to do, and you saved my life. I should have thanked you before."

He cleared his throat. "No need for that."

"You did the right thing," Michels said. "I would have done the same."

"I would have too," I said.

"I'd have done it for all of you, even Michels," Levy said.

The thick air lightened with laughter.

"What about the deceased?" Michels asked. "Has anyone notified next of kin?"

"None of them had IDs. The man we arrested is sitting in a cell and hasn't said a word since he got here," Bishop said.

Bubba connected his laptop to the large screen on the back wall of the room, ready to project what he found on Sean's flash drive. "Here we go." He hit play. The video was from a security camera.

We watched as two men with horses walked into Baxter's small stables. They placed one in the first stall, then brought the other to Baxter and Habersham who were waiting at the last stall. It was hard to see what Habersham was doing, but the horse was the same as the one in the photos, and the photos were from a camera hidden above the stall. They clearly showed Habersham removing the small bags of drugs from the horse's rectum.

Habersham handed bag after bag to Baxter. The horse suddenly reared. Baxter jumped back. Habersham moved to the side and was out of view for a moment but returned with a large syringe in hand. He stuck it into the side of the horse and moved away. The horse stopped rearing. Its body swayed and then collapsed.

"Oh my God," Levy said. "Did that horse just die?"

"I think so," I said.

Nikki sniffled. "That's horrible."

"That bastard needs to rot in hell," Michels said.

"Which one?" I asked.

He responded through gritted teeth. "Both."

"We've got them," I said. I stood. "Let's go get them."

"Not yet," Jimmy said. "We want whatever cartel members they're working with too."

"How?" Michels asked. "We already set a trap. It didn't work."

"They knew we were going to do something," I said. "Sayers's got spooked and said something, so they put eyes on the ranch. I'm sure those eyes are still there."

"Let me get the district attorney here. That will help us decide how to handle it."

~

JIMMY SENT Bishop to the department therapist and gave him the rest of the day off. I was under strict instructions to stand down from moving forward with the investigation until we met with the DA. I couldn't stand doing nothing, but Detective Dick Miller with the Billing Police Department had returned my call, so I called him back.

After introductions, he said, "May I ask why you're inquiring about the Jefferson investigation?"

"Mason Baxter is a suspect in a murder investigation, and we believe he's working with the cartel to smuggle fentanyl into Georgia from Mexico."

"Sounds about right. Baxter was a slimeball here, and I've learned people don't change. What do you need to know?"

"My contact with the DEA said there was nothing linking Baxter to the cartel in your investigation. Was it because he wasn't involved, or his involvement was well hidden?"

"He was involved all right. Hence the slimeball reference. The problem was pinpointing him as the guy."

"Can you explain a little further for me, please?"

"Ma'am, with all due respect, are you aware of how the cartel works?"

"No disrespect assumed. I am well aware."

"All right then. Baxter and Jefferson co-owned one of the largest ranches in town. They bought and sold horses primarily for racing. If you're not sure how that works, think middleman with a twist. They would go to auctions and breeders around the country, purchase younger horses or foals, work with them to determine if they were racing material, then sell them. Made them a pretty penny because it saved others from doing the initial work."

"That seems like an extra step," I said. "And don't most people who own racehorses purchase them according to their lineage?"

"Jefferson and Baxter preyed on people new to the industry. They offered a service that allowed people to purchase horses with potential at a lower cost."

"Got it." I scribbled down the information. "Were they working with the cartel the whole time?"

"Not that we could tell. About six months before Jefferson's murder, they ran into some financial trouble. Jefferson liked to gamble, and when he bankrupted his personal accounts, he dipped into the ranch's. When he lost it all, the cartel came knocking. He was in too deep with his bookie to say no."

"You said you tried to pinpoint Baxter as the guy though?"

"Baxter wanted to disassociate himself with Jefferson. We believe he knew about Jefferson's problem and contacted the cartel himself."

"How would he even know how to do that?"

"Baxter was having an affair with a Hispanic woman. A girl, if you ask me because she was twenty-one at the time. Her father was one of the local top lieutenants in Montana. When he found out about Baxter, he arranged to take him out, but his daughter begged him not to, and he agreed. As long as Baxter came to work for him."

"But you couldn't prove it?"

"Nope, but we know it's the case. So, he brings Jefferson in without Jefferson's knowledge of Baxter's involvement already. Tells him it's his only option to save the ranch. The cartel will pay his debt and then some for transporting the horses from Mexico to Montana and then removing the drugs."

"They went out of the country for the horses? Baxter's getting them in Texas right now."

"Let me guess. Evergreen Ranch in Webb County?"

"Yes."

"Doesn't exist. Texas resident Hal Jacobs died about twenty years ago and never owned a ranch. Not sure how that's still making the rounds. DEA was supposed to take care of that. Can't trust the federal government to do much of anything these days."

"Can't argue that," I said with a chuckle knowing Kyle would roll his eyes. "I'm still not sure how Baxter doesn't look involved."

"It wasn't his mess to clean up. He made Jefferson do the runs. Made him the mule. Problem was, Jefferson got greedy. He was a vet himself. When he removed the bags from the horses, he dropped a few of them in the stall. Word got out he was selling them, and they killed him."

He'd reiterated most of what Kyle had told us. "Baxter then sold his portion of the ranch to Jefferson's wife and moved to Georgia." He laughed. "Thought he could escape the cartel, but we know that never happens."

"Did his wife know about the affair?"

"Can't say. They still together?"

"I assume so. His daughter is local," I said. "I understand the DEA came in and made several arrests. What about Jefferson's shooter?"

"Jefferson wasn't shot. Someone shot him up with fentanyl."

"How do you know he didn't do it himself?" I asked.

"We don't. He was in a hole he couldn't get out of. Could he have killed himself? Sure. He was a vet. He had access to medical equipment, and anyone can walk into a clinic and get a syringe these days."

"But you don't think he killed himself," I said.

"Too convenient if you ask me."

"I can make you question it even more."

"I figured you could."

"That's how our victim died. Did you continue to investigate?"

"Nope. DEA came in and took over once we made the drug connection. If I was you, I'd keep your cartel connection on the downlow. The DEA likes to pretend they're working with you, but they just run right over you and take it all."

"Understood. Did they ever arrest anyone for the murder?"

"No, ma'am. It's my understanding they couldn't get any confirmation on which cartel member did it. Poor Sophie. She's never dealt with any of this. Bought out Baxter then closed down the ranch and left it. Hasn't touched it since."

36

Assistant District Attorney Zach Christopher walked into Jimmy's office. He smiled at me. "Where's your partner? Everything okay?"

I eyed Jimmy. "We're good. He had to take care of some things. He'll be back."

He sat in the chair beside mine. We skipped the small talk and got right to it. Jimmy had me detail what we knew and what charges we wanted to bring against Baxter. "I don't have proof yet, but Baxter murdered Sean, and I'm pretty sure he murdered his former partner in Montana as well."

"Hold up," Christopher said. "What about the cartel?"

"What about them?" I asked.

"You don't think they did it?"

The more I thought things through, the more I realized I'd missed something. We'd all missed something. "Why would the cartel take the time to shoot someone up with drugs? It's not their MO. When we first talked to Baxter, he immediately went to Sean overdosing. No one knew that. When we told him that, he said he'd heard it, but couldn't remember from who. He showed his hand there."

"How many can you bring in?" Christopher asked.

"How many what?"

"Cartel members," he said, completely passing over what I'd just told him.

"Other than the guy in the hospital, we don't have eyes on any members, but we can get Baxter on this. We just need to know what you can do for him. He won't talk without a deal."

"What about the cartel member in the hospital? Can you get him to talk?"

"He's in rough shape," Jimmy said. "I talked to his nurse. She said he's not getting out of ICU any time soon."

"If the cartel even lets him," I said.

"Is anyone on him?" Christopher asked.

"He's at North Fulton. The Sheriff's Office put deputies on watch. I can't say whether that's enough to stop the cartel or not, but it's the best we could do," Jimmy added.

"Our biggest problem is Baxter's attorney. Martin Lansing." He had to know the name. I waited for his reaction.

"Lansing's your guy's attorney?" Christopher asked. "Then he's definitely in with the cartel."

Didn't I just explain that? Where was he? I wanted to poke him in the forehead and tell him to get the hell with it. "Which is why we haven't been able to get anything from Baxter," I said.

"We can get with the feds. They'll offer him a deal."

I dragged my hand down the side of my face. "This is exactly what I didn't want to happen. I want Sean's killer first. After that, the feds can ride our wave."

"You don't know if he murdered Sean," Christopher said. "Get me evidence that'll prove he did, and you've got a deal." He pushed his chair back, walked to the door, then flipped around and said, "I can't sit on this for long. I'll give you twenty-four hours and then I'm going to the feds."

I let loose a barrage of expletives after he left. "We need Baxter. I don't care about the cartel. We need Baxter."

"I care about the cartel," Jimmy said. "And I want Baxter too, but we have to find something to prove he killed Sean." He took a breath, ran his hand over the top of his cropped haircut, and added, "Sayers was murdered by the cartel. We already know that. We know he told Sean his suspicions, and then Sean ends up dead. But you're right. They would have executed him, not made a point of shooting him up with drugs they could make a profit on. So why not?"

"Why not what?" I asked.

"Why didn't the cartel shoot Sean? Think about it. Sayers figured out what was going on at Haverty, and tells Sean, but Sean is murdered first."

I processed what he said. "Because Sean didn't want Sayers involved." I closed my eyes and held my breath as the realization hit me. "Sean was protecting his friend. Sayers got the videos on his own, then showed them to Sean, and Sean told him he'd handle it." I drummed my fingers on the chair arm. "Except Sayers is a lot bigger than Sean. Why would he acquiesce and not be involved? Sean has a family. Wouldn't he want him to stay out of it?"

"Maybe Sayers wasn't out of it," he said. "Maybe they kept him from going to Baxter with the proof so he could stay on the inside?"

"But if Sean had the proof, why didn't he go straight to Baxter with it?" I asked. "And why did Baxter kill him if he didn't know what Sean knew?"

"He had to know," he said. "Sean must have alluded to it. You said he was paranoid at the festival, then he texts you to meet with him. He must have told Baxter he had proof to bring him down around that time. What other reason would he have to be paranoid?"

"He knew it was cartel. Isn't that reason enough?" I asked.

"Possibly, but would you be more paranoid knowing the cartel was involved or knowing you'd played your card to the man working for the cartel?"

"Good point," I said. "Go on."

"He runs into us and decides to involve you, but it's too late. Baxter needs to get rid of him, and makes it look like an overdose, then goes to the cartel and tells them he thinks Sayers is getting suspicious, because he knows they'll take him out. He doesn't want them to know there's video," he said. "It'll screw up the game, and if that happens, he's done."

"No," I said. "Baxter couldn't risk going to the cartel about Sayers. They'd just kill them all. The woman next door to Sayers said she heard men with Hispanic accents. Baxter hired men to murder Sayers and Sean." I nodded more to myself than to Jimmy. "That's it. Sean told Baxter he had something on him, so Baxter had him killed. He wouldn't get his hands dirty like that. He's too good to do the dirty work." I leaned to the side and dug my cell phone out of my pocket' "I bet it's one of the day workers on the list I gave Garcia." I dialed his cell, and he picked up, so I gave him the information.

"Not one with any of the names we know, but we know that doesn't mean much." Garcia said when I explained. "Baxter's had a lot of day workers coming and going. He's having some work done on the stables. My guess is he's paid a dayworker or two to do the jobs, but I doubt they're cartel. He wouldn't risk using his own employees or ones he thought were connected to the cartel. I have something in the works, so give me a couple of hours, maybe a day, and I should have it for you. If we get lucky, we'll know who murdered Sayers and your friend."

"You think someone's going to give them up?"

"We'll see. I'll get back to you."

Levy knocked and cracked open Jimmy's door. "Habersham called. He said his friends are ready to meet with me."

"Shit." My heart nearly beat out of my chest. "They're going to kill Baxter."

Michels walked in behind Levy. "What's the plan?"

"The plan is to close this damn case," Jimmy said.

"We need to know what we're dealing with," I said.

"I'll get on the phone with Habersham and set up a meeting," Levy said.

"Hold off on that," Jimmy said. "Let's see if Roger Doyle can give us anything more."

I dialed Roger Doyle's number again and got his voicemail. "He's got to know more than he's saying. Maybe can help."

"I'll send patrol to pick him up and get his family to a safe house for the time being," Jimmy said as he grabbed the landline. "You're always killing my budget. You're lucky Sean's family is worth it. What's the address?"

"Any family would be worth it."

"I know," he said. "Address?"

I gave him the address. "Send two. One to his place and one to Sean's. I'm not sure where he is."

"Levy," Jimmy said. "Make the call. Tell him you can meet tomorrow."

"They'll want to see the ranch," I said.

"Shit." He dragged his hand down his chin. "All right. Tell him you haven't taken physical ownership yet, but you'll have it day after tomorrow."

"I DON'T KNOW any more than I've already told you," Doyle said. He paced back and forth in the investigation room.

"Did Sean say anything about the cartel or members of it specifically?" I asked.

"No."

"Did he tell you he was worried something was going to happen to him?"

"No, but he didn't need to. It was obvious from the way he acted. I told him he needed to let it go, take Jess and the baby away for a while. He seemed like he was going to do that, but never had the chance."

Jimmy walked in. He introduced himself to Mr. Doyle.

"Is my family safe?" Doyle asked.

"We're doing everything to make sure they are," Jimmy said.

"Do you know anything about Connie?" I asked.

"She's in intensive care. They had to remove a kidney. These bastards broke four ribs and punctured a lung. She could have died."

My heart sank. I needed to see her. I needed to know if she recognized the men who attacked her.

The investigation room door opened before he continued.

Kyle walked in with a man I recognized immediately. My jaw tensed. They were there to take over the investigation, and Kyle had made it happen. I was pissed.

Kyle and I made eye contact briefly. I hoped my anger radiated from my pupils and seared his skin. Agent Tanner nodded his head in my direction. I just shook mine. I couldn't believe it had come to this. What was Kyle thinking?

"Mr. Doyle," Jimmy said. He pointed to Kyle and Agent Tanner. "This is Agent Kyle Olsen and Agent Scott Tanner with the Drug Enforcement Agency. They're going to be assisting us from here on."

Levy, Michels, and Bishop walked in. Bishop saw Kyle and Tanner and looked at me.

Levy mouthed, "What the hell?"

Bishop sat on my left, Levy on my right, and Michels next to her. Kyle and Tanner sat on either side of Jimmy. I refused to look at Kyle. I was worried I'd lose it there, and I didn't want that to happen.

"The DEA?" Mr. Doyle asked. "It's that serious?"

"Drug trafficking is a federal crime," Tanner said.

"It's also a state crime," I added.

"You are correct, Detective Ryder." Tanner looked at Doyle. "However, when drugs are moved across state lines, it's most often prosecuted as a federal crime." His eyes shifted to me. "We are here to assist the department in bringing in Mason Baxter and capturing the cartel members involved. From this point forward, your family will be under our care. We have arranged for safe housing in an undisclosed location. We have agents with your family now. They will be transporting them to the safe house, and once we're done here, an agent will do the same with you."

Doyle glanced at me and then back to Tanner. "Safe house? I can't go to a safe house. I've got a job. I have to work. I've already taken too many days off because of this. My family? Yes, of course they should go. I'm fine here. No one knows I know anything."

"I'm afraid that's not how this works," Tanner said.

"Where is the house? Can I work remotely?"

"We are taking you to an undisclosed location as a matter of safety. You will not be allowed to bring any electronics with you including your cell phone and computer."

Doyle stared down at the tabletop. "I can't believe this is happening."

"We'll do everything within our power to make sure your family is safe," Tanner said. "Excuse me for a moment." He stood and walked out the door.

I glared at Jimmy. He exhaled. I still refused to make eye contact with Kyle, though I was confident he could sense my anger from my tensed expression, tight jaw, and flaring nostrils every time I breathed.

"Detective Ryder," Doyle said. "Are you going to be able to catch these men?"

I finally made eye contact with Kyle, peering at him intensely as I responded to Doyle. "I will do everything I can to personally bring them down."

"We need to get Garcia here. He needs to know what's going on," Jimmy said. He looked at me. "Can you call him?"

"Of course," I said through gritted teeth.

37

Tanner returned with another agent who escorted Doyle into a different room where Tanner would question him privately and then release him to be transported to the safe house.

"Un-freaking-believable," I said, my eyes glued on Kyle's. "What happened to keeping this on the downlow?"

"Rachel," Jimmy said.

I whipped my head toward him. "This is ours, Jimmy. We've busted our asses on this thing. Now that we're close, the DEA dances in and takes it from us so they can get all the credit? Are you serious right now?"

"This is BS," Bishop said.

I crossed my arms and twirled my chair away from Kyle. I didn't want to see him looking at me. "Complete BS."

"What does this mean for us?" Levy asked. "I know Agent Tanner said they're going to assist us, but we all know it doesn't work that way."

"We understand our knowledge is limited, and that you've worked hard on this," Kyle said. My heart raced faster each time he spoke.

"As much as the department has grown, we don't have the people power to handle this," Jimmy said. "Nor do we have the budget for over-time. We're still lead." He looked at me. "We'll still do the work and take the win."

"With the DEA assisting," Michels said. He laughed. "Levy said it. It doesn't work that way."

"It will," Jimmy promised. "And Kyle is here to make sure it does."

"As I said before, our knowledge is limited. You know most of the players, and we have the ability to identify those you can't," Kyle said.

"The cartel Garcia's been trying to identify," I said.

Kyle nodded. "We have already identified Juan Ortiz as Jorge Ruíz. Alpharetta PD has handed the investigation to you through us. We're dropping it into this one since we know it's attached."

"Gee," I said. "Thanks."

"I will be the liaison between the two units," Kyle said. "I'll make sure we stay on our turf."

"All right," Jimmy said. "Bishop, I'd like you to observe the rest of Agent Tanner's interview with Mr. Doyle."

"So much for assisting," I mumbled.

"Levy and Michels, get with Alpharetta and find out what else they dug up during their investigation."

"Wouldn't Tanner or Kyle have that?" Levy asked.

"We don't," Kyle said. "We can get it, but since we're the assist on this, I thought you'd want to."

"Garcia will be here in under an hour. We'll check back then." He stood. "Let's get a move on, people."

"Jimmy," I said.

His eyes shifted from me to Kyle. "Work it out. I don't want it screwing up this investigation."

～

I STARED AT THE DOOR. "UN-FREAKING-BELIEVABLE."

"Rachel," Kyle said. "It's not what it looks like."

"It's not what it looks like?" I leaned forward and snickered. "Right. So, you're saying you didn't screw us—screw me over and go to your boss with this case?" I leaned back in the chair again and crossed my arms. "Because that's exactly what it looks like." A few seconds passed. I needed to move, to do something to release the energy built up inside of me, so I twirled a pen between my fingers. "I knew you were bored. I knew you wanted to get back to work, but was this really your only option?" I laughed. "A liaison? What a load of BS."

He didn't offer any explanation, didn't even so much as grunt. He just sat there looking at me. That was how he wanted to do it? Fine. Two could play that game. I kept my eyes glued to his and didn't say a word. I wasn't sure how much time passed, but it felt like hours.

Finally, he said, "Are you calm enough to talk about this now?"

"Do I not look calm?"

The sides of his mouth twitched. "You look like you want to beat the shit out of me."

He wasn't wrong. I wanted to keep my emotions in check. What Kyle did was personal and professional, but I couldn't let it crowd my brain. I needed clarity to close the investigation. "We can deal with this after the case is closed." I moved to stand.

"No. We're doing this now."

I cringed. "Excuse me?"

"You want this thing closed. Do you really think that can happen if we can't work together?"

"Then step down, and while you're at it, take Tanner and your other DEA buddies along with you."

"That's not going to happen." He paused for a moment, then said, "For the record, I didn't set this up. I didn't talk to Tanner about the case. He came to me."

"Why? How would he even know this was a cartel case without talking to you?"

"I'm on leave. Technically, I'm supposed to stay clear of work, including my laptop."

"Tanner was watching your logins?"

"Not Tanner. Apparently, our log ins are connected to an internal team that tracks them. They saw I'd logged on and reported it to Tanner."

There was nothing I could say. Kyle couldn't tell his boss to stand down, and he couldn't lie to him. He'd done the research for me. Tanner knows my job. He probably did a little digging, then went to Kyle and told him how things were going to be. I adjusted the band around my hair. "You convinced him to assist instead of take lead, and you pushed him to let you be the liaison to make sure it stayed that way."

"And so I could get back to work. You're right. I'm bored as hell sitting around doing nothing."

I exhaled, then wiped the figurative egg from my face. "I'm sorry. I should have realized—I should have trusted you."

He raised an eyebrow. "You don't trust me?" He smiled. "I knew you'd react the way you did. No. That's not true. I thought you'd climb over the table and choke me."

I laughed. "Am I that bad?"

"I wouldn't call it bad. I'd call it scary. Especially when you're mad." He stood and walked over to my side of the table, propped a butt cheek on it, and smiled again. "I know how important it is for you to get justice for Sean."

"I know you do." I rubbed my hand up his thigh. "Are you in trouble for getting on your laptop while you're supposed to be recovering?"

"Not enough to be a problem, and I'm no longer on leave."

"But you're the liaison. Does that mean you won't be involved in anything physical?"

"Oh, trust me. I'm all about the physical."

THE INVESTIGATION ROOM was standing room only. Five other DEA agents, our team, and Kyle and Tanner began tossing out ideas on how to bust the cartel while we waited for Garcia to arrive.

Bishop tapped me on my shoulder. "Got a minute?"

"Sure," I said. I studied him carefully. "You okay?"

"I'm fine."

I followed him out of the investigation room and into a small conference room. "What's wrong?" I asked.

"Did you clear things up with Kyle?"

"Yes. They were notified when he logged in to his laptop. When they saw what he was looking at, they told Tanner. Kyle worked his magic, and we got lead."

"Do you think we really have it?"

"I think Kyle will make sure we do."

"Okay," Bishop said.

"I thought you were done for the day. What happened?"

"Psych doc cleared me."

"Are you okay?"

"Better," he said. "This one hit different. I don't really want to talk about it, but the therapist and I talked it through. I explained how important this case is, that we all knew Sean, and she said she'd clear me as long as I met with her once a week for the next four weeks."

"Wow. That's a lot of talking."

"I'm hoping she'll cut me loose after the next session."

I laughed. "Good luck with that."

"We'd better head back. Garcia should be here soon, right?"

"He was five minutes out, so he's probably walking in now."

38

"You're right. Baxter knew about the cameras," Garcia said. He nodded to Bubba who opened up a photo from his laptop onto the large display. "This is Hernando Ruíz."

"Ruíz?" Bishop asked. "Any relation to Jorge Ruíz?"

Garcia raised his eyebrows and nodded. "Yep. Brothers."

"Cartel?" Michels asked.

"Yes. Hernando's only been in the country a few months."

"How did you find this out?" Tanner asked.

"He told me," Garcia said.

"He told you he's cartel?" Tanner's mouth dropped slightly. "How'd that happen?"

Garcia's superpower was drawing people into his grip and extracting information from them. Often, the person didn't know what was happening.

"I have a way with people," was Garcia's only response. "The important part is he said there's something big going down at the ranch tonight, and he strongly suggested I stay away."

"Tonight?" Bishop asked. "It's going down tonight?"

"Did he say what the job is?" Tanner asked.

"He didn't need to. When I explained that I'm always looking for big jobs, he cut me off. Said it was out of my league, and the experts needed to handle it, and then he made a gun with his finger and thumb and pulled the trigger."

"When tonight?" I asked.

"I didn't get that far. Brad Turner and Austin Carter showed up with three additional horses."

"That's impossible," I said. "It's too far to make it there and back since they returned."

"They didn't go to Texas. They picked the horses up in Alabama."

"It was pre-arranged," Tanner said. "They could be ramping up their supply."

"Or they're stocking up while they secure an additional ranch to take in the horses," I said.

"That would be why Habersham was upset on the phone when I called him, and why he wanted me to meet with his contacts tonight," Levy said.

"Upset how?" Tanner asked.

"Upset's not the right word," she said. "He was frustrated, maybe a little anxious. He wanted to know how quickly I could take possession."

"What did you tell him?"

"I told him I'd talk to my attorney and get back to him."

"They're moving tonight," Garcia said. "That's why they brought the horses. Baxter has to be there with Habersham. They'll take him out there."

"And probably Habersham as well," Kyle said. "They won't leave any witnesses."

"But they need a vet," Bishop said.

"The cartel won't eliminate their associates until they have new ones."

"Habersham is worried they're going to kill him," Levy said. "He thinks bringing me into the fold will save him."

"Then let's bring you into the fold," I said.

"What if I went to Habersham now? Told him what we know, then get him to flip on them? He's got the connections, and he's afraid he's going to die tonight."

"You think he's actually going to show up?" Michels asked.

"Either way he's a dead man," I said. "He's not stupid. He's got to know that."

I referred to Kyle. "Thoughts?"

"I think this is the right path. You flip Habersham. The risk is Baxter. If he's talked to Habersham, he could know he's on thin ice," he said.

"How is that a risk?" Bishop asked.

"He may have told his contacts within the cartel that Habersham is planning something."

"Shit," Bishop said. "To save his own ass."

"Then we need to flip Baxter too," I said. "It's the only way this can go down." I made eye contact with Tanner. "Since you're assisting, what's your recommendation?" There might have been a touch of obnoxiousness in my tone.

"I think you're right. Let's discuss how we do this."

"Our options are limited," Garcia said. "Baxter rarely spends more than an hour a day at the ranch, and he's already come and gone today. Besides, the cartel's got eyes on the place and I assume on Baxter and Habersham as well."

"And probably on his house, too," I said. "We need a way to get to him without drawing attention to ourselves."

"What about an interior design company?" Levy asked. "We did it in Philly for an investigation. We rented a U-Haul and borrowed a truck from a local interior designer, who was paid nicely, by the way. We were able to get five of our men into the house and me, the interior designer. Four guys on the truck and one with me. He was the architect."

I eyed Jimmy. "Can we get a truck from someone in town?"

"Let me make some calls."

"I can get a vehicle for Detective Levy," Tanner said. "We have one with an interior design company logo on it already. It's a Subaru," I think." He looked at Kyle, who nodded.

"What about Habersham?" Levy asked. "I can suit up and head out to his office, but I'm not sure I can get him to leave with me."

"We can get some men in there with animals to make it look busy," Tanner said. "Someone will call with a large animal emergency that will require him to leave."

"Sean and Connie's ranch," I said.

"Can't," Kyle said. "We arranged to move the animals for the time being. It's the only way to keep them safe. They're already gone."

"Even Bertha the pig?" I asked. "She weighs a ton."

"She's safe," he said.

"Bennett Cooper will probably do it," Bishop said. "He offered to help."

"Okay," Jimmy said. "We won't hold Habersham at the ranch. He'll go there, get inside, and we'll get him out through the back."

"They could be watching back there," Michels said.

"They're not watching Cooper," I said. "And there's no reason for them to suspect anything if he goes into a stable. That's his job."

"She's right," Tanner said.

"Okay," Jimmy added. "Levy, you get ready." He checked his watch. "See if Manny's wife can—"

She stopped him before he finished. "I know what to do. It's not that hard to slap on some makeup, stuff my bra with tissue, and slip on a wig."

"You had tissue in your bra?" Michels asked.

"Did you think they grew a cup size on their own?"

"I guess I didn't really think anything," he said blushing. "I'm engaged to Ashley, remember? I don't look at other women anymore."

Again with the reminder of his engagement. The man was completely whipped over Ashley. It was fun to watch.

"Right," Levy said. "And I'm a virgin."

I laughed.

"All right," Jimmy said. "We've got a plan." He turned toward me and waved his hands in small circles at me "Can you do something with this?"

"By this I'm assuming you mean me?"

"Yes," he said, "and I apologize for the way I said it."

I smiled. "It's okay. I don't think I can, but I know someone who can."

Jimmy nodded. "My wife."

I pointed my finger at him. "Bingo."

"Bishop," he said. "You can't go to the house. We don't have time to alter your appearance, and you've been seen. Can you get Christopher on the phone? Tell him what's going on and let him know to be available. Then I want you and Michels with Tanner's men. One of you at the vet and the other at Cooper's ranch. Got it?"

"Got it," they both said.

Garcia pulled me aside. "This is the Carillo Felix organization. They're top-level shit. Dangerous. You heard of them?"

"Basic stuff," I said. "How do you know it's them?"

"I overheard two guys talking about where the horses are coming from. The Carillo's are Gulf Coast. These guys are smuggling drugs into the country for one of the most dangerous cartels in Mexico." He stood closer and whispered, "Tanner knows this. Keep your eye on him."

SAVANNAH'S MOOD had lightened since Demon Sav, her pregnant alter ego, had shown up the other night. "You have no idea how excited I am to do this." She rolled two large suitcases on the bench in the women's locker room and attempted to heave one onto it, but I took it from her.

"Seriously? Do you want to go into labor right now?" I asked.

"Honestly, yes. This baby is killing my sciatic nerve. I don't know what he's doing, but every time he moves it stands up and preaches to the congregation like a Southern Baptist minister."

I smiled. "That sounds awful."

"You have no idea. Those preachers talk so loud, the churches shake." She popped open the suitcase. "Can you get the other one up here too, please?"

I was frozen in shock. The suitcase was stuffed full of clothes I'd never seen before. The woman must have had a closet under her basement. Her home was a good size, but there couldn't have been enough closet space for the amount of clothes she had.

"Snap, snap, woman," she said. "Making you look like an interior designer isn't going to be easy. Mama needs time to perform miracles."

Levy laughed. I glared at her, picked up a box of tissue on the counter and threw it at her. "Here. You need this for your bra."

Savannah laughed and so did Levy.

The second suitcase was also stuffed, but not with clothes. I removed three pairs of stilettos, all which hurt my feet just looking at them, a steam iron, and four large designer travel bags. I peeked in one and saw hair styling products and accessories I hadn't used since my wedding, and I did that under duress.

"Don't worry," Savannah said. "It won't hurt."

Levy examined the hair accessories. "Oh, may I use the curling iron? My wig needs a touch up."

"Absolutely," Savannah said. She pivoted to me, her left hand gripping her waist. "Woohoo, this kid is on fire today. I think he just dislodged my left kidney."

Levy's eyes widened. Savannah saw her in the mirror. "You don't want to know what he's done to my bladder."

"No," Levy said. "I don't."

"Okay," Savannah said. "Let's get this party started."

We finished an hour later after much complaining and whining by yours truly. Levy had finished about fifteen minutes before us and sat watching Sav work her magic.

"Yes," Savannah said. "Perfection."

I had to admit, she'd done a great job. She'd pulled my hair into something she said would poof out the hair on the top of my head, then twisted the rest into a high ponytail, added some curls, then tugged small strands out around my face and curled them into little ringlets.

"Ouch," I said with the last tug. "Careful. Some loser whacked me in the head with a gun."

She rubbed my scalp. "Oh, I can feel the bump." She pressed on it. "Does it hurt?"

"When you press on it, yes."

"How'd Kyle handle you being roughed up again?"

"I wasn't exactly roughed up, and we haven't really talked about it. I think he's finally realized injuries come with his significant other's job."

"Hmm," she said. "I wonder if you've realized this about his job?"

"I know it, but that doesn't mean I like it," I said.

"That's a little hypocritical, don't you think?"

"Absolutely, but I don't care."

She laughed. "I didn't think you did."

She finished fixing me up using cream makeup on my face, and though it made me feel like a piece of cake with too much icing, it looked amazing.

"What do you think of the contouring?" she asked. "Do you like it?"

"I probably do, but I don't know what it is."

Levy laughed.

Savannah sighed. "You have so much to learn. I'm not sure we can hit it all before I die." She traced lines on my cheeks. "See the shadowing there?" She traced a few other places. "And there? That's contouring. I should have taken a before picture because your nose looks tiny compared to reality."

"Hey now," I said. "I don't have a big nose."

"Of course, you don't, but it's going to feel like it when you wash this stuff off." She handed me the pair of nude heels she decided went best with my outfit. One she'd also picked. "Here. Put these on."

Levy rubbed her naked foot. "Five minutes in those things, and your feet will be screaming."

"I'm aware."

Savannah studied Levy, then grabbed a tube of something in her bag, and brushed it onto Levy's face like she was an artist working on a painting. "There." She smiled. "Perfect." You two all ready for your big reveal?" She tilted her head to the side and sighed at me. "Kyle is going to drop to his knees and worship the queen when he sees you."

"He won't worship me. He's not like that."

"Honey, I didn't say you were the queen."

39

He didn't drop to his knees, but he was pretty darn close. "Wow." He studied me very closely for a moment. His mouth was slightly parted. He blinked repeatedly. "Wow."

"You said that already," I said.

"You're welcome," Savannah said. She eyed her husband. "Can you please have someone bring my suitcases to the car? I need to sit. Your child is physically abusing me." Jimmy rushed to her side and helped her sit. "I swear to God this kid is going to be a football player, and he sure as heck isn't playing for Bama."

I laughed.

"Here," Kyle said. "Let me put on your wire." His eyes sparkled.

"Uh," I said, taking it from him. "Levy can do it. I don't want you embarrassing yourself." I glanced down at his zipper.

He glanced down and smirked. "I'm well aware of what's going on." He leaned forward and whispered in my ear. "You're keeping those heels for later tonight."

"Get a room," Michels yelled.

Garcia laughed. "This reminds me of the time you went undercover as a hooker. Half the department walked out with woodies after seeing you."

I cringed. "That's the most disgusting thing I've ever heard." I handed Levy the wire. She taped it to my chest, and then I taped one on hers.

"All right people," Jimmy said. "We've got the truck and the Subaru set. Tanner has men stationed around the vet, Cooper's ranch, Baxter's ranch, and his home. Rachel, I don't want you calling Baxter until you're on his street. We don't want him to run."

"Got it," I said.

"Everyone is on the radio," Jimmy said. He gave us the frequency which was different than our standard. "If anything goes wrong, we'll be there." He made eye contact with everyone in the room. "Let's roll."

"I'M GOING to drive by the place and then back up," I said to Agent Karey. He'd been assigned as my architect because he looked the part. I wouldn't have called him nerdy initially, but when he put on his glasses, it was the first thing I thought.

"Yes, ma'am." His southern accent reminded me of Savannah.

I dialed Baxter's number from a burner phone. He wouldn't recognize the number, but I expected him to answer anyway. When he didn't, I called again.

Two times later, he picked up. "I'm not interested in an auto warranty."

"Baxter, I want you to listen closely."

He cleared his voice. "Who is this?"

"Just listen and do as I say, do you understand?"

"Who is this?"

"I'll be at your house in two minutes. You're going to answer the door and let me in. Do you understand?"

"I'm not going to let—"

"If you want to live, you'll do as I say." I hit the end call button on my phone.

Two minutes later, Baxter answered the door. "Who are—oh, hell."

"This is my associate and architect, Alex Karey. It's nice to finally meet you, Mr. Baxter." I whispered, "Let us in."

He moved to the side and opened the door wide enough for us to enter.

He laid into me after he closed the door. "What the hell is this about? And why are you dressed like that? You can't just come in here and—" his eyes widened. He scrubbed his hand over his mouth. "Jesus."

"Mr. Baxter, as I'm sure you're aware, you're under arrest for a long list of felonies."

He opened his mouth to speak, but I stopped him. "In an effort to move this forward, I'll keep this brief." I rattled off a list of felonies including drug trafficking and first-degree murder, twice, then read him his rights. Doing so felt like I'd just put the cherry on top of a hot fudge sundae.

He had what Garcia called crazy eyes. Mostly he used the term when a meth user was coming off a high, but it worked for Baxter as well. "I want a lawyer."

"Right," I said. "And you can call whatever lawyer you want once we're at the department. Until then, how about you let us save your ass?" I didn't give him time to answer. "Where's your daughter?"

"She and my wife left for a riding competition today. They won't be back for a week."

"Where is it?"

"In Kentucky."

"We'll handle that later then."

"We're on his street," the officer driving the U-Haul said in my ear.

"Here's how this is going to go," I said to Baxter. "You're going to open your garage door, move whatever vehicles you have inside onto the road, and let our truck pull partially in. Four men will exit the truck and stand in the driveway with the three of us. We will discuss what items we are removing from," I examined the space, "the main living space, and the men will begin removing those items. You will climb inside the truck when I tell you. The men will then back the truck out of the garage and load up this couch." I pointed to his couch.

His face heated to bright red. "You can't take my furniture!"

"Your furniture will be returned." Probably to his wife, but I left that part out for the time being. "When the couch is loaded, the men will lock up the truck with you in it and drive away. Agent Karey and I will wait fifteen minutes and then leave. While you're in the truck, you will stay completely silent, up against the wall just behind the cab. We have moving blankets and boxes back there. You will go behind the boxes and place a blanket over you. Do you understand?"

"Yes."

"Good." I looked out the window and saw the U-Haul. "They're here. Let them come to the door."

WE ARRIVED at the department thirty minutes before Levy returned with Habersham. Baxter was already being processed and would be placed in a holding cell until we could speak with him.

Bishop and I waited in his cubicle.

"He didn't give you anything?" he asked.

"He didn't have the chance, and he wanted an attorney right away, so we couldn't ask any questions anyway."

"Levy said Habersham did the same. They won't call Lansing."

"I'm guessing Lansing is no longer representing them," I said.

Bishop grinned. "Life's a bitch." His landline rang. "Bishop." He waited a moment and said, "Which interrogation room is open?" After another few seconds, he said, "Great. Send him there. We're on our way."

"Baxter's done?" I asked.

"Assistant District Attorney Christopher is here."

"Let's go," I said.

"Detectives," he said. He removed his jacket. "Did we dial up the heat already?"

"A little," Bishop said.

The key to making a suspect confess, or at least provide information, was to make them uncomfortable. Bright lights, no air circulation, a hot room, a small glass of water, and the constant reminder of a clock ticking on the wall were all used to create an atmosphere that made the suspect desperate to leave. That and their probable guilt worked wonders during interrogations.

An officer escorted Baxter into the room. His cocky snobbishness had completely disappeared. Wearing the orange jumpsuit with his feet shackled together and his hands cuffed at his groin didn't promote confidence.

"Love the outfit," I said.

"Where's my attorney?"

The officer guided him into a chair and took position behind him.

"You mean Lansing?" Bishop asked. "Is that who you called?"

"I spoke to his secretary." His voice trembled with each word. "He's on his way."

"No," Christopher said. "He's not. I spoke with Mr. Lansing. He has informed me he is no longer representing you or Dr. Habersham. Do you have another attorney you can contact?"

Baxter's face tightened like a taut wire, every muscle drawn and strained. "What do you mean he's no longer representing me? You're lying. You're trying to stop me from having proper representation. I demand you get him on the phone right now."

Christopher dialed his cell phone and placed it on speaker. It was obvious from Lansing's tone when he answered that he expected the call.

"Is he with you?" Lansing asked.

"Lansing," Baxter said. "What the hell is going on? Why aren't you here?"

"Mr. Baxter, I'm afraid my secretary misinformed you. I am no longer your attorney."

Baxter leaned back in his chair and rubbed his hands up his face, pulling so tight his eyebrows almost reached his crown.

"Thank you, Mr. Lansing," Christopher said and disconnected the call. "Mr. Baxter, do you have another attorney?"

He shook his head. He was visibly nervous. Tiny beads of sweat formed on his face. His eyes darted around the room, hitting the clock, the door, even the corners, but never once any of us. His Adam's apple bobbed up and down, and when he finally spoke, his voice trembled. "No."

"We can set you up with a public defender for the time being. I suggest you contact your wife and have her find you representation."

"Jesus," he said. "A public defender? What the hell can a public defender do for me?" He shook his head. "Now can I call my wife?"

40

We had the same conversation with Dr. Habersham. He was equally surprised to learn Lansing would no longer defend him, however, he did have another attorney to call.

"John Bryant is general law," Christopher said. "He'll handle the initial interviews and pass Habersham off to a defense attorney. He's agreed to provide the same service to Baxter, but I'll bet they end up with different defense attorneys."

"Because one of them is going to flip on the other," Bishop said.

"Bingo," I said. "I feel bad for this Bryant. He has no clue what he's getting into."

"He does now," Christopher said. "And I'm sure he's reeling from it."

We didn't have a chance to speak to either suspect when Bryant asked to speak with us. "My clients would like to make a deal."

"A deal?" Christopher said. "We haven't even interviewed them."

We could still do that, but doing so with a deal on the table already made it less fun.

"That will still happen. Listen," Bryant said. "They're scared. Is a deal even an option or am I shooting blanks here?"

"We need information from them before the district attorney's office can make that decision, Bryant. It's basic law 101."

"I know that, but I had to make the effort."

Ten minutes later we were in front of Baxter who had reluctantly chosen to talk. The three of us sat across from Baxter and Bryant. Agent Tanner leaned against the wall behind us.

"Let me tell you what we know," I said. Baxter tried to show no emotion, but the sweat pouring down his face gave away his fear. "You owned a ranch in Billings, Montana, with Riley Jefferson and worked together selling racehorses. Jefferson liked to gamble. When he depleted his own accounts, he dipped into your business accounts. He dug himself into a pretty big hole and dragged you into it." I smirked. "How am I doing so far?"

Baxter didn't respond.

"I'd be mad as hell if my business partner gambled away our money. But you had a way out. You think you're smarter than most people, don't you?"

He still didn't respond.

"Smart enough that you let Jefferson think he could pay off his debt and replace the money he'd taken from you by working for the cartel. You probably played it like it was the only way to save the ranch, but you left something out. You didn't tell him you were already in with them because you got busted screwing a high-level boss's young daughter." I paused for an acknowledgement, but Baxter stayed tight-lipped. "He made you work for him. Any questions?"

Bryant looked at Baxter who softly shook his head. "No," Bryant said.

I knew something was up when Tanner quietly left the room. I just wasn't sure what.

"Good. That means I'm on the right track. You're the kind of guy whose status is important. I noticed that about you the first time we met. You wouldn't want to be associated with something messy like the cartel, so you made your partner do it. He made the runs to pick up the horses, then since he was a vet, it was obvious he'd remove the drugs and give them to the cartel. But Jefferson thought he was smart too. He got greedy. Started putting aside a few bags to sell himself." I tapped my pen on the table and angled my head to the side. "Here's where I get stuck. Did you tell the cartel so they would kill him, or did you kill him yourself?"

"Don't answer that," Bryant said. He looked at me. "What does this have to do with an investigation here?"

"Jefferson and our victim died the same way," Bishop said. He looked straight into Baxter's eyes. "We have the photos and videos. The ones you killed Sean for. See, you can't run from the cartel. But out here, you don't have a Riley Jefferson to take the fall for you. You've got to do it yourself, and Damian Sayers figured out your game. He went to Sean with the videos and photos. Maybe he asked him to hold onto them, or maybe he asked for help. Either way, Sean's murder spooked him, and he told you to watch for us. You thought Sean's murder would go down as an accidental overdose just like Jefferson's. You even planted that seed in the community. But there we were, asking questions. That worried you. You didn't want this coming back to you from law enforcement or the cartel.

You had Ortiz plant that bomb in Bennett Cooper's stable. You either wanted us dead, or you did it as a distraction." He kept his eyes focused on Baxter.

"Don't say a thing," Bryant said.

"How'd the cartel find out about Damian Sayers?" Bishop asked.

"I don't know what you're talking about," Baxter said.

"Sayers and Ortiz were shot execution style. Sayers took multiple bullets, but that's not uncommon. They wouldn't pay someone to shoot a lethal drug into a man's arm. It's a waste of product."

"What do you want from him?" Bryant asked.

"The truth," Bishop said. "For starters, we want to know who killed Sean Higgins, Damian Sayers, and Jorge Ruíz."

"Who is Jorge Ruíz?" Bryant asked. "This is the first time we're hearing that name."

"It's Juan Ortiz's real name," I said. "We want names, Baxter. Names of the killers, and the people you work with in the cartel organization."

Baxter wiped the sweat on the side of his face with his cuffed hands. "They'll—"

Byrant held up his hand. "We're done for now. No more questions until we meet with his defense attorney."

～

BRYANT TRIED the same tactic with Habersham, but the doctor rolled anyway. "Baxter pulled me in. Offered me all kinds of money. I've got kids in college, two mortgages, five cars. My car insurance alone is over one thousand dollars a month. I was barely making it. The money sounded too good to pass up." He dropped his head. "I don't care about me, but I don't want the cartel to hurt my family. They don't know anything about this."

"Who killed Sean Higgins?" I asked.

"Baxter hired some Mexican day workers. Gave them each a thousand bucks to make it look like an overdose."

"He told you this?" Bishop asked.

He nodded. "I kept my phone in my pocket every time new horses arrived. Had it recording a video. You can't see anything, but you can hear us talking."

"The phone we took?" Bishop asked.

"No. I got a new one the other day. I knew something was going to happen. I put the one with the videos in my safety deposit box at Bank of America."

Habersham told us everything he knew. Baxter was afraid. Habersham worried if they took Baxter out, they'd take him as well. His only recourse, he'd said, was to bring on another ranch owner. He thought the cartel would keep him around if he had more to offer.

"I'll get a warrant for that safety deposit box," Christopher said.

I relayed Garcia's concerns to Bishop before we met with the rest of the team. "Garcia said the Carillo Felix organization is in play here. Said they're top-level and very dangerous. He said he overheard a few guys talking about where they're getting the horses. The Carillos are Gulf Coast, and one of the most dangerous cartels in Mexico."

"Damn," Bishop said.

"It gets worse. He said Tanner knows all this."

"Why didn't he tell us?"

"Because he's probably going to screw us," I said.

"Why didn't you tell me sooner?" he asked.

"I've been a little busy."

He ran his hand through his thinning hair. "We need to tell Jimmy."

Jimmy already knew, and he was pissed.

41

My heart hammered like a war drum. A bead of sweat trickled down my temple. I'd dealt with the cartel before, but if Habersham was right, and the higher echelon showed up, our risk increased exponentially. The potential domino effect of the bust could take months to wrap.

Garcia was right. Tanner had switched positions. Instead of the DEA assisting us, we'd been knocked to the assist. I'd expected it to happen, but Kyle was surprised. "Scott," Kyle said. "You agreed to the terms of this arrangement. You can't change it now." His face reddened, and his veins pulsed as his jaw clenched and his neck cords stood taut like coiled springs. "That's not how it works."

"Stand down, Agent Olsen." Tanner's voice sliced through the room, the authoritative tone tightening the knot of tension that was ready to break. "We want El León, and this is how we'll get him."

"El León?" Kyle's nostrils flared. "How long have you known?"

"We've been working on dismantling the Carillo Felix organization for two years. Our agent has risked everything to expose the organization. He informed me of Hamby's investigation the day you did your research."

"Who's the agent?" I asked.

"You know I can't answer that."

"Has he verified the hit is scheduled for tonight?"

"Yes." He looked at Jimmy who was ready to spit nails at the guy. "As I told Chief Abernathy, your team has done an excellent job, but this is bigger than a dead ranch owner. This is our chance to dismantle the Carillo Felix organization and put Juan 'El León' Duran away for life."

Michels leaped out of his chair and slammed his hands on the table. "This is bullshit. We've busted our asses on this investigation. It's taken us less than a week to be in the position to take down 'El León' but you've been trying for two years, and still couldn't do it if we weren't where we are. This is ours."

"This is well above your pay grade, Detective," Tanner said.

"Agent Tanner," Jimmy said. I'd never heard that tone before. "This is my city, and my team. When you're here, you'll treat us with respect, or I'll drag your ass well above your pay grade." His words spit out like flames.

Tanner's lips pressed together in a firm, straight line. "We're sitting on billions of dollars and the possibility of losing thousands of American lives. Kids, grandparents. No one is immune. We know what we're doing. You can do it our way, or we can do it without you. You choose."

The Carillo Felix organization ran trafficking on Mexico's northeast coast bordering the southwest side of Texas. I didn't know a lot about the cartel, but I knew enough to be effective.

"El León is believed to be a former Mexican special forces soldier wanted for something like seventy-five murders in the US not to mention drug trafficking. The organization is similar to the Zetas. They employ military tactics and are known to use large caliber weapons," I said.

Kyle raised an eyebrow. I'd impressed him, but that wasn't my point.

Tanner smiled. "You're well informed, Detective, but your team will still assist."

"Agent Tanner, please give us a minute," Jimmy said. His voice was calm again, the only thread of control left in the room.

"Make it quick," he said. He walked to the door, but Kyle stayed with us. "Agent Olsen."

Kyle and I made eye contact, then he followed Tanner. He had no choice.

The room erupted into a fire of voices. Everyone spoke so loudly Jimmy had to whistle to shut us up. "Listen, we've been played. I'm as angry as all of you, but my hands are tied. The feds are the feds. We all want this, but does it matter who gets credit? We already got Baxter to confess to murdering Sean and Damian Sayers."

"I'll work with federal prosecutors to allow us to keep those charges and have a separate trial," Christopher said. "They don't care about Baxter. They care about El León."

"He's right," Jimmy said. "We'll assist, and we'll make sure the cartel is dismantled."

Damn right we would.

THE PLAN HAD BEEN basic but would be effective. The team would enter Haverty Ranch in multiple places. Several would scatter while others took spots in the stables and strategically planned places along the other buildings and the land. Agents with similar builds to Baxter and Habersham would arrive separately and enter the stables.

Habersham's double was expected to remove the drugs from the horses, then El León would arrive, and the party would begin. Since the agent posing as Habersham wasn't a vet, he would play the role with bags of placebos nearby. Tanner had assured us the two cartel members monitoring the situation wouldn't notice.

Garcia pulled me aside. "The undercover DEA agent is Ruíz." He didn't wait for me to ask. "He was playing me. I should have known."

"We were all played."

"Kyle too," he said. "You know that, right?"

"Yes. How do you know it's him?"

"I just do." He wrapped his hand around my wrist. "You've got a good group here. Small, but good."

"I know."

"And you know I've still got your back," Garcia said. "Whatever you do, I'm right behind you."

We had set up our base behind an elementary school close to Haverty Ranch.

"All right," Tanner said. "The stalls have been emptied, we've boarded up the stall where the horse should be, and our men are in position. This should be swift and easy. Olsen's agent in charge here." He peered at Jimmy. "All decisions come from me through him."

Michels suggested Tanner do something along the lines of making love to himself, under his breath. Jimmy must have heard it too because he looked down and smiled.

"Assisting isn't sticking us out here holding our dicks in our hands," Michels said. He looked at Jimmy. "Come on Chief. We should be out there."

Tanner had been walking away, but he turned around when Jimmy said his name. Tanner smirked. "You got your interviews. You got the killers' names. We're here to handle the big job."

As he turned to leave, Jimmy positioned himself in front of us, his back to Tanner, and said, "We'll go in from the southeast and northwest sides of the ranch. State your position clearly. You know the plan. Follow it."

"Yes," Michels said. He added a fist pump to stress his excitement.

Tanner whipped around and charged back to us. "Hell no. This isn't happening. I won't authorize it."

"You don't have to," Jimmy said. "You've already said we're on assist, and that's what we're going to do."

Tanner studied us with a condescending look that morphed into anger when he made eye contact with Jimmy. "I'll have your job for this."

Jimmy dropped the clip from his weapon, counted the bullets in it, and inserted it back into his gun. "Then I'll go out with a bang."

42

"Doubles have entered the stables," an agent said.

"Black limo pulling through the gates," another said.

"That's El Leon," Garcia whispered.

He, Bishop, and I had stationed ourselves behind the stables in a wooded area just over the fence. Levy, Jimmy, and Michels were a few feet away though we couldn't see them.

"Two men from the limo are entering the stables now," an agent said.

"It's El León," another one said.

"Like we discussed on the way here," Jimmy said, "We don't move unless shit hits the fan."

"It'll hit it," Garcia said. He smiled at me and mouthed, "I like this guy."

A Hispanic man spoke in Spanish, but he spoke too fast for me to get it all.

"It's Ruíz," Garcia said. "He's telling them the doctor is removing the bags now. He said they shouldn't go near the horses because it's dangerous and they could kick them."

Ruíz spoke again.

I translated it. "They're going in anyway."

Garcia smiled. "You know that fan you were talking about?" he asked Jimmy. "It just got hit."

An angry voice inside the stable said, "Qué demonios?"

A sudden disturbance pierced the radio waves—an abrupt, muffled thud followed by a jarring, sharp crack that cut through the air like lightning. The audio momentarily distorted but all of us recognized the deafening sound. Time stopped as the chaotic eruption of gunfire shattered our radios.

Tanner's voice boomed over it. "Now!"

We hurdled the fence and sprinted to the stables dodging bullets from all sides. It was a short distance, but I still fired my weapon three times. Garcia and Levy got to the stable entrance first. They raced through the open door and ducked behind barrels and open stall doors. The rest of us split up and followed.

The chaotic eruption of gunfire pierced my ears. Muzzle flashes illuminated the structure in blinding bursts, giving me enough time to assess the situation. I counted seven cartel members racing through the door, and I knew they weren't the last.

Agents and cartel members sought cover behind crates and barrels. Shots exchanged in frenetic bursts made it impossible to hear anything on the radios.

I caught sight of Garcia and headed toward him. A bullet whizzed past me, barely missing my shoulder. I dropped and rolled, bumping into Garcia behind a stall door.

He looked at me. When I nodded, he held up three fingers and counted down. We moved around the stall, our backs only inches apart as we rushed to the next open spot. I knew Garcia well enough to know where he was headed. "On your left," I yelled.

We dropped low. I peeled off two more shots. My magazine held fifteen rounds. I had ten left and another weapon tucked under my waist band with fifteen more. Shouts and commands merged into a disorienting haze. I couldn't understand a thing coming from the radio, nor did I care. We had one goal. To survive.

I spotted Bishop and Levy across the stable behind an opened stall door. A man running from the entrance must have seen them. He aimed his gun, but I pulled the trigger before he had a chance to shoot. He went down screaming as blood squirted from his leg.

Cartel members dropped like flies. A rhythmic rapid firing of bullets pierced the air.

Garcia screamed into my ear. "Machine gun. Two o'clock." He stood, fired off a shot, then squatted back behind the stall door.

I smelled the smoke before I saw it. I moved into the stall and quickly stood. A fire ignited in the corner of the stable, opposite where El León had been before the first shot was fired. I moved back to Garcia, shook his shoulder, and pointed to it. "We have to get out of here."

The fire latched onto the hay and spread quickly. A shot pierced a cartel member's back as he passed us. He fell to the ground. His weapon dropped as he fell, and Garcia grabbed it.

The fire grew, spreading in every direction and climbing up the wood walls. It would take over the stable in minutes, but that didn't stop the gunfire.

Garcia pointed across the stable. "That way." We dodged bodies as we bolted away from the fire and back to the main entrance of the stables. Bullets ripped through the air as everyone headed for the door to escape the fire.

Every breath I took seared my throat. The smoke burned my eyes. I searched for my team but couldn't find them.

Garcia's voice cut through the noise. "Let's get out of here."

"I can't find my people," I yelled. I tried to swallow but my throat was too dry. A piercing pain filled my chest, making it almost impossible to breathe. I covered my mouth and nose with my free hand. A blurred figure ran toward me, collided with my shoulder, and sent me crashing to the ground to get past.

Garcia pulled me up. "I'll go find them," he said. "You check outside."

"No!" Smoke burned my eyes and throat.

He didn't argue.

We made it five feet before a deafening roar shook the ground. "There," he said. He pointed to the roof at the opposite end of the stable as it collapsed. He grabbed my arm and dragged me into his sprint out the stable doors.

Tanner's men surrounded the area. I caught glimpses of them cuffing cartel members and tossing them into vehicles. The firefighters had been waiting at the elementary school and were already preparing to spray the building.

I couldn't run anymore. I couldn't breathe. My throat felt like it was closing.

"Come on," Garcia said. He coughed. "You need oxygen." He wrapped his arm around my waist, lifted me off the ground and tried to run.

"I can do it," I said through a major coughing fit.

Someone grabbed my other side. "We've got you," Bishop said. His face was red, but he latched onto me and the two of them carried me to the ambulance while I nearly coughed up my lungs.

Two paramedics met us near the ambulance and carried me the rest of the way. They gave us all oxygen and water. When I was finally able to speak, I asked about the others.

Bishop coughed so hard the paramedic wouldn't let him talk.

"Are they okay?" I asked.

He nodded.

Breathing finally became easier, but not because of the oxygen, because I knew my team was safe.

43

Garcia looked at my reflection in the women's locker room mirror. "Ruíz is dead."

I pressed a dry towel against my wet hair to soak up the water. I'd washed it three times, but it still smelled like smoke. "El León shot him."

"They're not sure, but it was probably the first shot fired. El León walked into the stall, saw there was no horse, then realized the men weren't Baxter and Habersham. Common sense says he knew Ruíz was in on the bust, so he shot him."

"He's dead too," I said. "El León."

He nodded.

I ran a brush through my hair. "How many?"

He knew what I was asking. "Twenty-one injured. Sixteen of them cartel. Nine dead. None were ours, but two agents are critical."

I exhaled and pulled my hair into a ponytail, then wrapped a band around it. Levy walked past in a towel. She looked at us in the mirror and kept walking.

I carried my things to my locker.

"We're in the big conference room," he said.

"Be there in five."

Levy stepped out of the dressing area after Garcia left. His being there didn't seem to faze her. She ran a hand through her short hair and tucked a few strands behind her ears as I put on my boots. We walked to the conference room after she finished dressing.

"I like him," she said.

"Who?"

"Garcia. He's good people."

"The best."

"Not bad to look at either."

"He's single, but I'm not sure he's into long distance relationships."

"Who says it has to be a relationship?"

I cringed. "Okay, that's just wrong on so many levels."

She laughed. "Not for me."

Men in suits packed the large conference room. It was standing room only, and since most male law enforcement didn't view female law enforcement as women, no one offered us their seat. We pushed through the suits and stood behind Jimmy who sat at the end of the oblong table.

Several conversations happened at once, but I heard bits and pieces of many of them. Bad plan. Poor execution. Things that made me smile. Kyle caught my eye across the room. He winked at me. We'd only spent a few minutes talking after all hell broke loose, but I'd assured him I was okay.

The door opened. A tall man in a black suit walked in and said, "Okay, people. We'll make this quick."

Tanner appeared behind him and closed the door. He didn't look happy. I glanced over at Kyle and smirked at the big smile on his face.

"For those who don't know me, I'm Sam Lawson, a representative with the DEA. As most of you here know, we've been after the Carillo Felix organization and El León long enough to have prepared a better strategy than the debacle that happened tonight."

Tanner didn't even twitch.

"El León got off easy, as did several of his people."

Zach Christopher stepped into the room and closed the door behind him. The heat in the place immediately rose.

"Thanks to the Hamby Police Department," Lawson said. "We've got two suspects with enough information to bring down the organization completely. These detectives didn't know what they were getting into, but they made the connection quickly, and without them, we'd still be picking our noses."

Bishop leaned close to my ear and whispered, "Tanner's getting a serious butt-whoopin' tonight."

I'd be lying if I said that didn't bring me joy.

The man continued. "The Fulton County district attorney will work hand in hand with the US attorney's office on this case. They can't prosecute in a federal trial, but their contribution will be greatly appreciated."

I stared at Christopher and then the chief. Jimmy noticed and nodded once.

"Habersham and Baxter will face both state and federal charges. While the state charges are not the ones Hamby would like, we have promised to do everything within our power to get justice for the victim's families."

"What about Sean Higgins' wife and child?" I asked. I didn't care if I interrupted the guy. "She and her family are in hiding. Are you keeping them safe as well?"

He glanced down at Jimmy. "Chief, would you like to answer that?"

Jimmy looked at me as he spoke. "The Higgins and Doyle families are being handled by the federal government."

I didn't have to guess what that meant.

"Great," Lawson said. "It's late, and most of you are exhausted and recovering from smoke inhalation. We will assist the federal and district attorneys in any way possible, but for now, let's get some rest."

The room cleared except for Hamby staff and Kyle.

Lawson returned. "Agent Olsen, a moment."

Kyle and I shared a look as he left the room.

Jimmy scrubbed his forehead but didn't say anything. It was Zach Christopher who spoke. "My sources tell me Agent Tanner will be switching divisions and taking a demotion."

"Good," Bishop said.

Our lack of excitement must have surprised him. "We will be actively involved in preparing for trial. The DA has already called the governor. We can't play the what if game. We don't know what would have happened if the DEA hadn't intervened, but I will personally make sure the Governor knows what a solid, excellent team Hamby PD has."

"Thank you," Jimmy said. He smiled at us. "Great work tonight. I'm proud of you all."

"We're proud of you," Levy said. "The way you ran over Tanner and put us in the thick of things? Golden."

"No regrets," Jimmy said. "However, had it turned out differently, I could have been getting my PI license like Garcia here. Go home," he said. "We'll recoup tomorrow."

"Jimmy," I asked. "Is Sean's family going into witness protection?"

He exhaled. "No one's told me, but I suspect the answer is yes." His eyes softened. "I'm trying to get you some time with Connie. That's the best I can do."

"I appreciate it."

I stuck around and waited for Kyle. Garcia and Levy hung out too. I knew what was coming, and I really didn't want to be there for it, but I didn't have a choice. "Tony, you want to stay at my place tonight? My guest bed has got to be more comfortable than the hotel bed."

His eyes shifted to Levy's and then back to me. "Actually, I was thinking of grabbing something to eat." He smiled at Levy. "You hungry?"

Her eyes lit up. "Starving, and Waffle House is open twenty-four hours."

"I love waffles," he said.

"Oh, my God," I said. "Just go before I throw up and scar my throat more."

They both laughed and hurried out, bumping into Kyle on their way.

"Where are they going?" he asked.

"To do something I'd rather not talk about, let alone think about."

A smile tugged at the corners of his mouth. "Nice."

I cringed. "Let's go home."

"Right behind you."

~

KYLE and I lay on the bed facing each other. The sun would be up in two hours. We were both exhausted, but I still had questions that needed answers, and I didn't think I could wait.

"I'm sorry about Ruíz. Did you know him?"

"No. He came from Texas. I knew we had a team watching Carillo, but out of Texas. I didn't know Tanner had a team here as well."

"Do you not communicate between the groups?"

"Only if it's necessary. Agents are safer not knowing about other investigations."

"That makes sense. Do you think they'll demote and move Tanner?"

He smiled. "Yes."

"That's good. I hope your next boss isn't such an ass."

The corners of his mouth twitched. "He won't be."

I sat up. "Oh, my God. You got his job, didn't you?"

"You're looking at the new division head of the Atlanta DEA division."

"That's incredible! Congratulations." I kissed him. "I'm so happy for you."

He pulled me close. "How about you put on those heels and show me just how happy you are?"

44

Connie lay on the hospital bed, her left eye swollen shut and the right one almost as bad. They'd beaten her face so badly she was barely recognizable. Everything was a swollen mix of purple, blue, and red. "Hey," I said. "We got them."

"Thank you," she whispered. "What happened?" Her whispers came out groggy and rough.

A tear slipped down my cheek. "Let's talk about it when you're feeling better."

She blinked.

"Ben Cooper is going to care for your animals until you're well. He's a good guy." I smiled. "He'll take good care of them."

The nurse walked in. "She needs some rest."

I placed my hand on Connie's. "She's right. I'll come back in a few days and check on you, okay?"

She slowly grabbed my hand and squeezed it.

~

KYLE PULLED his truck into the parking lot across from the Forsyth County Fairgrounds.

I gripped the side of the seat. "Why did you bring me here?"

He turned toward me, and with a straight face, said, "You're going on that Ferris wheel."

My eyes widened. "Oh, no. Nope." I shook my head. "You said we were going to dinner, and that's what we're doing." I pointed to the button to start his vehicle. "Press it."

His lip twitched. "It's a Ferris wheel, Rachel. Five-year-olds go on that thing."

"Because they're too young to understand the danger."

"Remember the first time you shot a gun?" he asked.

"Yes."

"You were scared, but it wasn't nearly as bad as you thought, right?"

"Nope. I wasn't scared, and this is different. I wasn't putting my life in jeopardy with a gun."

"Just the lives of others," he said smiling.

"Still wasn't my life."

He opened his door. "I'll be right beside you."

I took a breath.

"Just come with me. We can watch it go around a few times, and then if you're still too scared, we won't do it."

"I'm not scared."

"Yes, you are."

"Okay, I'm scared, but come on. Those things are accidents waiting to happen."

"They're like airplanes. There are hundreds maybe even thousands of them across the world, and you rarely hear of people dying on them." He closed his door, walked around the truck to mine, and opened it. He extended his hand. "Come on. I'll protect you."

I climbed out of the truck. "Protect me?" I laughed. "I don't need to be protected."

"Then let's do this."

I grabbed hold of his hand and let him guide me to the park's entrance. My fear was ridiculous, and it was time to overcome it.

EPILOGUE

James Andrew Abernathy was born on October 30th, a month early. The baby was fine, and massive, topping the scale at nearly fifteen pounds.

I would have been a raging psycho carrying that future football player around.

Mason Baxter was convicted of thirteen felonies six months after Sean's murder. The federal judge showed no mercy, and in fact, made an example out of him. Baxter received three life sentences for murdering Riley Jefferson, Damian Sayers, and Sean, and over seventy-five years for his other crimes.

We had hoped for the death penalty, but federal judges rarely pull that card.

William Habersham would serve forty-two years without parole. He would be over one hundred years old, if he lived that long, before he was free.

Sean's house sat empty for over a year. Eventually, a family with two young boys moved in. The city had approved the building of a rental community on Sean and Connie's land. Ben Cooper had kept their animals, and I would often stop by to visit Bertha. It took a while, but I finally got the nerve to feed her from my hand. She'd weighed six hundred pounds when

I first saw her, but Cooper put her on a diet, and she'd dropped two hundred. She looked like a totally different pig.

Garcia went back to Chicago. I wasn't sure, but I suspected Levy had been out multiple times to visit. If that was the case, they'd tell me when they were ready.

DARK INTENT
Rachel Ryder Book 9

The past comes back to haunt a small town when one murder leads to the discovery of another.

When a troubled young woman, Jenn Berman, goes missing at the summer fair in Hamby, her uncaring family fails to notice. That is, until a loose dog returns home with a bloodied hand. Investigators are led to a developing subdivision where they find the unthinkable: Jenn's body in a shallow grave.

The town is shocked by the murder, and Detectives Rachel Ryder and Rob Bishop are assigned the case to deliver justice for Jenn. But upon further inspection of the crime scene, a jaw-dropping discovery is made: another body is found buried deeper in the same grave. The remains belong to Caroline Turner, a young woman who also went missing from the summer fair...almost four decades ago.

The connection between the murders is undeniable. As Rachel and Rob race to narrow down their suspect list and inch closer to the truth, a dangerous threat emerges, putting those they love at risk. Can they expose the killer and uncover the secrets of the past before it's too late?

Prepare to be captivated by USA Today bestselling author Carolyn Ridder Apenson's newest gripping crime thriller.

Get your copy today at
severnriverbooks.com

ACKNOWLEDGMENTS

I'd like to take a moment to express my heartfelt gratitude to a remarkable group of individuals who've played an indispensable role in the creation of this crime thriller. First and foremost, Randall Klein, my exceptional editor, has been a guiding light throughout this journey. His meticulous attention to detail and unwavering support have been invaluable.

Julia Hastings, my associate publisher, who has been on top of literally everything, along with the rest of the dedicated team at Severn River Publishing. I'm deeply thankful for their contributions.

To my dear friend Ara, your expert knowledge of police procedures has added an authentic layer to the narrative that I couldn't have achieved without you. And, of course, to my husband, my unwavering supporter and biggest fan. Your belief in me has been my driving force.

But above all, I want to extend my heartfelt thanks to my readers. Your love for the Rachel Ryder series has been truly inspiring. Without your enthusiasm, none of this would be possible. Here's to more thrilling adventures together!

ABOUT CAROLYN RIDDER ASPENSON

USA Today Bestselling author Carolyn Ridder Aspenson writes cozy mysteries, thrillers, and paranormal women's fiction featuring strong female leads. Her stories shine through her dialogue, which readers have praised for being realistic and compelling.

Her first novel, *Unfinished Business,* was a Reader's Favorite and reached the top 100 books sold on Amazon.

In 2021 she introduced readers to detective Rachel Ryder in *Damaging Secrets*. *Overkill,* the third book in the Rachel Ryder series was one of Thrillerfix's best thrillers of 2021.

Prior to publishing, she worked as a journalist in the suburbs of Atlanta where her work appeared in multiple newspapers and magazines.

Writing is only one of Carolyn's passions. She is an avid dog lover and currently babies two pit bull boxer mixes. She lives in the mountains of North Georgia as an empty nester with her husband, a cantankerous cat, and those two spoiled dogs.

You can chat with Carolyn on Facebook at Carolyn Ridder Aspenson Books.

Sign up for Carolyn's reader list at
severnriverbooks.com

Printed in the United States
by Baker & Taylor Publisher Services